THE DEAD OF NIGHT

A DS JACK TOWNSEND NOVEL

ROBERT ENRIGHT

For DC, BE, MH, NL & SM,
You guys never stopped listening.

CHAPTER ONE

The walk home in the early morning was always Lauren Grainger's favourite part of the day.

Just shy of four o'clock, it felt like she existed in a part of the world that was designed only for her. Every single shop on the high street was closed, the shutters pulled down, each displaying a mural of graffiti. The streets themselves were clear, meaning there were no people to shoot leering glances at her as she strode by. There was no constant buzz of traffic, be it impatient drivers honking their horns or large buses whooshing open their doors.

It was peaceful.

Tranquil.

Hers.

And as she lit her cigarette, as had become her routine, she allowed the smoke to filter into her lungs a few feet from the back door of 'Paradise' before she blew a plume of it into the gentle breeze. As always, the gentleman's club was the only business still awake at this time of the morning, and once again, she had enjoyed a profitable night. Her seven-hour shift involved her standard three dance routine, where she would parade onto the stage in a revealing outfit, usually to the cheers of the pathetic men who comprised the membership. A raunchy song would hit the speakers and underneath the strobe lighting, she would take to the pole, looking to outdo her fellow dancers with her expertise and upper body strength, swirling around it in ways that defied gravity. As the song progressed, her clothing fell to the stage, and she gladly displayed her immaculate body to the leering punters, snapping up the money they desperately threw onto the stage.

She considered that a tip.

Five minutes' work would usually result in over one hundred pounds that she had no intention of sharing with either her manager, Mr Sykes, or the tax man. But in reality, all that dance was for was advertising.

It was the most enjoyable part of her job, as she enjoyed the healthy competition with the other dancers.

The rest of the night was spent in the company of the pathetic men who paid for her attention, sidling up to their tables and allowing their drunken urges to pour out. On that night, however, she'd been a little distracted. She could have sworn she'd seen her ex-boyfriend in the crowd when she emerged for her first dance, but as the evening went on, she couldn't locate him anywhere.

The last thing she wanted was for her personal life to spill into her professional one. Especially if it meant the other punters could learn more about her.

Part of her allure was her mystique. And a lot of that mystique came from her anonymity.

Lauren was the star of the show, although none of them would know her by that name.

They knew her only as Athena.

Named after the Greek goddess of war, Lauren knew she symbolised something that should be unattainable to the many men who threw money her way, and it was no surprise that she racked up the most private dances. At the back of the club, which was immaculately decorated with a long, well-stocked bar, and numerous booths, were three private areas, watched over by Benny, the bouncer, and Sykes himself. The men could only pass Benny once they'd paid Sykes, and then they allowed five minutes alone with their chosen dancer.

Lauren had rules.

They could touch her breasts and her buttocks, but not her vagina, nor could they kiss her. Inside the booth, the dance was tantamount to a dry hump, with her writhing over the trousers of her punter, taking them to the brink and sometimes over the edge of ecstasy.

That was their problem to deal with and, judging by the number of men who touched her with a hand with a wedding ring attached to it, an explanation they'd need to give to their wives.

All they were to Lauren were cash machines, and as she drew the most business, she got the biggest cut and Sykes, who, despite the odd, inappropriate comment, looked after his girls well enough, made sure she was handsomely rewarded. She was making over three hundred pounds a night, including her tips, which for a woman of twenty-three years of age, with little to no education, wasn't bad going. In the near two years she'd been dancing at Paradise, Lauren had been able to save for a mortgage.

She'd been able to work on her future.

In fact, she found the whole thing empowering, especially as she'd witnessed her mother achieve nothing in her life besides substance abuse before Lauren was taken into care at fourteen years of age.

Now, she was a working woman, mastering her craft, and becoming one of the most revered dancers in High Wycombe. She planned to continue for as long as she needed to, until she could open her own dance school and hopefully, empower as many women as possible.

'Good night, Benny.' Lauren smiled, and the burly bouncer, his arms thick with tattoos, offered her a wave. The summer morning was mild and knowing it would add another ten minutes to her walk home, she decided to take in the glorious setting of Wycombe Rye at dawn. With the cigarette wafting in her hand, she meandered down the silent high street, past the slew of popular shops, as well as the giant Eden Shopping Centre that housed many more.

Food chains.

Clothes shops.

Mobile phones.

Games.

Everything you'd expect from a town centre, and considering the train to London was less than a half hour journey, Lauren thoroughly enjoyed living in the humble town. It wasn't flush with cash, but she found the enterprising buzz infectious.

As she finished her cigarette, she turned under the underpass, wanting to avoid walking down the main street where High Wycombe Police Station was situated. A stone's throw from the Rye, the Thames Valley Police had always been polite on the few occasions they'd crossed paths, but Lauren had failed to meet a police officer who looked at her with any ounce of respect.

It was, unfortunately, one of the pitfalls of being a dancer in a strip club.

Judgement.

She cut across the magic roundabout, taking advantage of the empty roads. The giant roundabout, surrounded by six smaller ones, was a magnet for traffic and every time Lauren's taxi approached it, she appreciated the fact that she didn't drive. Finally, she came to the entrance of the Rye and then lit another cigarette. The magnificent park was bathed in a dull shadow, as the rising sun was slowly trying to edge its way through the thick clouds to illuminate the stunning vista. Usually, the place was alive with families and animals, all of them swarming upon the wide-open fields to play games of football, or to cram into the two recreation parks. Beyond both was Lauren's favourite part of the Rye.

The lake.

As she approached it, she walked past the kiosk, which offered pedalo boat rides and overpriced snacks. It was closed.

Everything was closed.

Asleep.

The Rye was hers.

As she stopped to enjoy her cigarette, she heard the unmistakable sound of footsteps shuffling beyond the trees, which shielded the winding road that ventured through the woodlands on the other side of the lake. Lauren felt her muscles tighten, her mind darting back to the sighting of her ex in the crowd.

Visions of the abuse flashed in her mind.

The punching.

The spitting.

The forcing her down onto the bed.

As the figure emerged around the final tree, she realised she'd been holding her breath and she released it with relief. A smile spread across her face, one of joy, and as the person approached her, she flicked her cigarette away.

'What are you doing here?' she asked politely, and then she grunted, and her eyes bulged. The instant pain of the knife ripping into her stomach stopped her world. Everything went still.

Colour faded from everything, and with her final few moments of strength, she turned and stared into the eyes of her killer, trying to ask for a reason.

Her arm feebly flailed.

Warm blood gushed from her stomach, and she felt the knife slide out, and then bury itself into her again.

And again.

As the world faded to black and she felt herself falling, she thought about the beauty of Wycombe Rye when the sun hit it, and how there was no better place to die.

CHAPTER TWO

'Ah, crap.'

Jack Townsend uttered his disappointment as he stepped into the garage that ran along the side of their new house, and his eyes fell onto the pyramid of boxes that still hadn't been unpacked. The move to Flackwell Heath had been relatively smooth, but the upheaval for his family wasn't something he'd enjoyed.

Especially as it had undone the work he'd put into his relationship with his daughter, Eve.

It was necessary, though.

Born and bred in Edge Hill in Merseyside, Townsend had grown up navigating the rough streets of Toxteth. What could have been an easy path into a life of crime and hardship was corrected by his father, Malcolm, who had proudly served the Merseyside Police Service as one of its most respected police officers. Townsend would often think back to the awe in which he had regarded his father back then, knowing that his dad would be out on the streets, fighting crime, and stopping the bad guys. It was only when he himself became a police officer in his early twenties did he realise the amount of red tape and paperwork that came with it.

But his father had never moaned.

Never complained.

Even when he suffered a life altering injury during the Toxteth riots in the early 80s, something he kept hidden from Townsend for most of his childhood. As one of the first on scene, his father had been set upon and ended up with a stress fracture to his lower spine. Although he recovered enough to walk the beat for another decade, the long-term effects soon caught up with him, eventually confining Malcolm to a desk and a severe bout of depression that soon saw him separate from Townsend's mum. A few days after Townsend's seventeenth birthday, his father lost his battle with cancer.

With no guidance or clear career path, Townsend came agonisingly close to betraying his father's memory, and had it not been for his wife, he was certain he'd have spent most of his adult life behind bars.

But Mandy was his angel.

Smart. Driven. Caring.

She had pulled him from a rough crowd, and as their instant connection grew, he found himself wanting to be a better person.

To be like the man he used to regard his father as.

It was why he had joined the police, and it was why now, on his first day of his new life as a detective sergeant in the Thames Valley Police Specialist Crimes Unit, he was frantically looking for his father's watch.

He wanted to bring him along on this journey.

After rummaging through the first box, Townsend lifted it up, shuffled across the garage, and plonked it down against the far wall. They'd been in the house for just over three days, and although Mandy had worked her magic on turning the shell into something they could call home,

Townsend had failed to introduce any sort of order to the garage. The only thing he'd unpacked and set up was his weight bench and punching bag, and as per his morning routine, had already used both that morning. He'd found discipline in boxing, although after the years that had threatened to rip his family apart, Mandy had insisted he never step in the ring competitively.

They both couldn't trust that he'd put that side of himself fully to bed.

With an anxious sigh, Townsend threw open another box, rolled up the sleeves of his crisp, white shirt to reveal his muscular forearms, and began searching once more.

Knock. Knock.

His head snapped to the door of the garage.

Mandy smiled at him.

'Tea delivery,' she announced in her scouse accent, plonking the steaming mug down on the messy work bench as she stepped in.

'Thanks, love,' Townsend replied. He sighed. 'Any chance you know which box my dad's watch is in?'

Mandy looked at the chaos before her.

'I'm not sure. I don't think I understand your system.'

'Ah, well it's *dump everything in one big pile and hope for the best*,' Townsend said dryly. He ran a hand through his short, dark hair. Mandy noticed and stepped forward and slipped an arm around him.

'Hey, look. You'll be great.'

As always, she knew when there was something wrong. She could read him like an open book.

'I don't know, Mand.' He shook his head. 'Maybe this was all a mistake?'

'A mistake?' She stepped back. 'We've moved a long way for this to be a mistake, Jack.'

'I know. But detective sergeant? I barely feel like a police officer, let alone a fuckin' detective.'

'Hey, first thing, language. Second, you're a police officer through and through. What you did to bring down Kovac…what you sacrificed…'

Mandy's words trailed off as her voice began to choke. Townsend cursed himself for allowing it to creep into conversation, as Mandy had made it a condition of moving away from Liverpool.

They didn't talk about Kovac.

They didn't talk about the three years he had spent undercover, risking his life to infiltrate the gang of one of the most dangerous arms dealers in the country. It should have been a six-month assignment working inside a dangerous gang in Liverpool. Townsend's handler, Inspector Sanders, allowed greed to take control, and he manipulated Townsend into something worse.

Something that stole him away from Mandy and their daughter for three years, and something that, in the two years since, had hung in the background of their lives like an unwanted echo.

It was why the Merseyside Police fast-tracked him to detective, by way of an apology.

It was why they had to relocate as far away from Liverpool as possible, due to the dangers of running into his fake life.

It was why Townsend struggled to sleep, thanks to the memories of the violent things he had to do to keep his cover.

And it was why, despite two years of work, Eve still hadn't fully embraced having her father in her life.

Noticing his wife trying to breathe away the tears, Townsend stepped to her, and kissed her gently on her blonde hair.

'I'll make this work,' he said firmly. 'I promise.'

'You better…or else I'll find that watch and stuff it up your arse.'

The two of them chuckled, and Townsend wrapped his arms around her. They swayed together until a cough at the door interrupted them.

Eve.

'Hey, Pickle,' Townsend said with a smile. She was the spitting image of her mother, pasted onto the slight frame of an eight-year-old gymnast.

'Can we go to the park today?' she asked hopefully.

'It's my first day at work, love,' Townsend responded. Eve, however, looked past him to her mother.

'Yes, of course. We'll find a good one.'

'Thanks, Mummy.' Eve turned and ran back to whatever she'd pulled herself away from. To the surprise of both her parents, Eve had embraced the move to a new part of the country and was keen to explore.

Townsend sighed. Mandy rubbed his back.

'She'll come around, Jack.'

'It's been two years.'

'I know. But you were gone for three.' Mandy popped up onto her tiptoes and kissed him on his chiselled, stubble covered jaw. 'Now, get going, or you'll be late.'

'I will.' Townsend turned back to the box. 'I just need to find my watch.'

Mandy nodded and headed to the door. Just before she went to step back into the house, she looked back at her husband.

'You've got this, Jack. Do you know why?'

'Because I'm good at bullshitting people?' Townsend shrugged, not looking up from the box as he rummaged through it.

'No. Because you don't know how to quit.' Mandy smiled. 'It's why I love you so much.'

Townsend pulled his hand out of the box, his fingers grasping the strap of his father's watch, and he looked at his wife.

She was the most beautiful person he had ever known.

'Love you too, babe.'

'Now, go. Fuck off,' she said sternly.

'Language.'

She chuckled as she disappeared into the house. Townsend wriggled his hand into the watch and fastened the strap. It was snug, but it offered a modicum of comfort. As if his father was watching over him. He stepped back into the hallway of his new home, closed the garage, and then called out his goodbye. Somewhere in the house, his two reasons for existence were too busy to hear him. He snatched his jacket from the coat rack by the door and stepped out into the mild morning and unlocked his black Honda Civic. He dropped into the driver's seat, tossed his jacket into the back, and let out a big sigh.

He looked at himself in the mirror.

Reasonably presentable. Clearly bricking it.

He'd looked down the barrel of a gun. He'd been beaten half to death by one of Kovac's men.

He'd survived it all.

As he brought the engine to life, Townsend kept his wife's kind words at the forefront of his mind, and rolled slowly off the driveway, hoping that he'd be able to swallow the imposter syndrome before he made it to the station.

Before he started his first day as DS Jack Townsend, of the SCU.

CHAPTER THREE

Detective Inspector Isabella King knew her reputation within the Thames Valley Police.

In an environment where people were urged to put their strongest foot forward, she'd always tried to remain calm and seek a positive solution. Her empathy was often misconstrued as weakness and people would often try to take advantage of it.

She didn't care.

It was also why she didn't hesitate to speak her mind.

As far as she was concerned, her colleagues' ambitions shouldn't be put before the victim of a crime, and if someone needed to hear the truth, she would deliver it without hesitation. If she believed that her superiors were playing political games, or trying to absolve themselves from any responsibility, she would call them on it. Never to instigate an issue, but more for the collective good of the people they were serving. Too many people focused more on their careers than the justice they were employed to seek. As a proud black woman, she refused to allow anyone to play the political game with her, especially as she'd fought against a multitude of prejudice to get to where she was. It only added to the weight of her conviction and her reluctance to back down on what she perceived to be unjust.

It made her unpopular.

But it made her one of the most effective detectives working in the organisation.

Now, as she sat opposite her boss, Detective Superintendent Geoff Hall, she could sense his hesitation as he weighed up his answer to her accusation.

'I'm not sure what you want from me, Izzy.' Hall offered, shrugging his shoulders. 'We're not flush with cash.'

'Oh, come on, Sir. How long have we been working together? Nearly three years or so? I know when I smell your bullshit.'

'What do you want me to say?' Hall said sternly, reasserting his authority. '*You* came to me, remember? You came to me asking for an opportunity. Asking for anything to get out of CID and this is what I'm offering you. CID are overworked and under-resourced as it is, so you asking to step away didn't exactly go down well with them. Besides, you seemed pretty pleased about that a week or two ago.'

'That was before I got all the details.' King sighed. 'And with all due respect, sir, it was either this, or I stepped away completely.'

Hall went to respond and thought better of it. Inwardly, King scolded herself for allowing her personal feelings to slip into conversation. It was an unwritten rule within the police service that the job came first, but that rule became blurry when your personal life and professional life collided.

Especially when your ex-husband had just been promoted to head up CID.

Her relationship with DCI Marcus Lowe had been as

exhilarating as their jobs. Both young and ambitious police officers working in the London Borough of Brent for the Metropolitan Police, their love and careers grew in tandem. Lowe was as good at the political game as he was solving cases, and he combined his handsome looks and his silver tongue to climb the ladder quickly.

King took the scenic route, spending a few years in Armed Response before following her husband into CID, always a rank, and at times, a few footsteps behind him. At work, it was strictly business, and there had been times when he had chewed her up in front of the rest of the team for a rare mistake.

But it was all part of the job, and although they made a comfortable living, soon the adrenaline of the job was replaced by an aching for more.

Together, they decided to leave the Met, transferring from the hotbed of activity that was one of the most crime-filled boroughs in the capital city, to the sleepy suburbs of Buckinghamshire.

The plan was to start a family, but after eighteen months of failure, Lowe soon found himself in the arms of another woman, and King was left with a big mortgage and a broken heart.

A whole year had passed since the divorce had been finalised, and despite the frosty work environment and the constant, underhanded negging off her ex-husband, she'd refused to quit.

Refused to rise to it.

But she needed to be moved away from him, and DSI Hall had offered her a new division for her to make her own.

The Specialist Crimes Unit.

What had started out as an exciting opportunity had begun to reveal itself as a busted flush, and like a rotten onion, the smell only increased with every layer that King had pulled back. The term 'Specialist' had been an oversight, and what had been presented to King was a never-ending-conveyor belt of paperwork, and some unsolved cases that had no dots to be connected.

Lowe had backed the move, and now it was easy for King to see why.

Silence sat between her and Hall, who sat behind his desk, which was littered with manila folders. He was a doughy man, who had long since given up a life on the streets for the comfort of the desks, but he was sharp. Trusting.

One of the good guys.

His greying hair was neatly brushed into a side parting, and he looked at King with the warmth of a hug.

'Look, I know things have been shit for you for a while, Izzy. I do. And lord knows, after what DCI Lowe did, nobody would have blamed you if you'd cut his nuts off. But this is a place of work. The public relies on us for so many things, so that can't be a factor anymore, okay? Lowe may be a bit of an acquired taste, but he's still a powerful man in this building, and to be fair to him, he has agreed to the SCU.'

'Because he wants me locked in that basement you call an office.'

'We're short on space,' Hall answered curtly. 'I know you feel hard done by, but we can't just magic these things out of thin air. Half of these files on my desks are reports from some auditor telling me to cut costs. We just have to manage with what we've got.'

'A wet behind the ears DS and a broken DC?' King said dryly. 'Lucky me.'

Hall frowned.

'That's a bit harsh, isn't it? I remember, not so long ago, a detective looking for an opportunity turned up in my team and she turned out to be pretty good.'

King smiled appreciatively.

'I also hear she turned out to be a pain in the arse.'

'Well, I didn't want to hurt your feelings.' Hall smirked. 'Speaking of your new DS, it's Townsend's first day today, isn't it?'

'It is.' King sighed. 'I guess I'll add babysitting to the list of jobs the SCU provides for the Thames Valley Police.'

'Send him my way when he gets here, will you?' Hall said firmly, ignoring the remark.

'Guv?' King raised her finely shaped eyebrows. Hall waved his hand dismissively.

'Oh, I just need to check a few things. Usually, we wouldn't share this kind of information, but considering you'll be his superior, you needed to see his file and I need to make sure his undercover work and any of the outcomes of that have been taken care of.'

'As long as he doesn't bring it into the office,' King said. 'I actually think a man getting therapy to deal with past issues is a brave thing.'

'I agree. You can question his legitimacy as a DS, Izzy, but you can't question the man's bravery. What he did a few years ago was very commendable.' He smiled at her and nodded. 'Give it time, Izzy. And give it your best.'

'Yes, sir.' King stood and blew out her cheeks, shaking her head. 'Specialist Crimes, eh? The scheming bastard.'

Hall chuckled.

'Yeah, I did question DCI Lowe on exactly what constituted a "specialist" crime. He was pretty vague about it.' Hall stood, signifying the end of their meeting. 'Still, I've thrown you the ball, Izzy. Up to you whether you run with it or not.'

King nodded her thanks to her boss and stepped out of his office. The hallway of the third floor of the High Wycombe Police Station was the same as all the others.

Narrow.

Dimly lit.

Lined with shoddily made posters spouting HR policies and needless acronyms.

The claustrophobic feel was only intensified by the windowless doors that led to small, stuffy offices, all occupied by specialist teams, working diligently against the constant budget restraints and waves of public disapproval.

It really was a thankless place to work, but King wouldn't want to be anywhere else.

Hall was right. She had been given the opportunity not just to stick two fingers up at her repulsive ex-husband, but also to forge her own path away from him. By handing her the 'specialist crimes', of which there were hardly any, it was clear that Lowe was trying once again to put a fork in her road. As she was processing the idea, she walked past the door to the larger, open-plan CID office. At seven thirty in the morning, it was quieter than the usual hub of activity that she'd called her home for the previous few years. Only a few of the desks were occupied, with the detectives either scanning through the police database on their computers or filling out the endless sea of paperwork.

Beyond them, she could see Lowe in his office, leant back in his chair and his thumbs hammering the screen of his phone.

Just the sight of the man made her blood boil, and at that moment, with Hall's semi-effective pep talk still echoing in her mind, King made a silent promise to Lowe that she would prove him wrong.

She would make the Specialist Crimes Unit work.

As she headed towards the stairwell, she nearly collided with a few police constables, who quickly stepped out of her way.

Her reputation preceded her.

Now she needed to live up to it.

CHAPTER FOUR

As he pulled his car into the narrow gap of the High Wycombe Police Station car park, Townsend breathed a sigh of relief. His journey to the station was relatively smooth, due to the pre-rush hour traffic and the summer holidays ensuring the roads were clear. He'd done the journey a few times over the past few days, wanting to commit the route to memory and, as he'd driven down the country roads that connected Flackwell Heath to the city centre, he had found the drive pleasant.

It was a world away from the tight, crushing feeling of Liverpool, which, like London, was fast becoming over-crowded with as much housing as possible spouting up from every spot available.

His journey took him through a few newly created residential plots, with their identikit houses baffling Townsend due to their lack of character or identity. They were stylish enough, with neat, and tidy driveways and pristine doors, but the idea of hundreds of people living in identical houses just felt wrong to him.

A home was unique to every family, and he doubted, based on the eye-watering cost of each house, that the occupants would have much left in the coffers to put their own stamp on it. Also, with everything being brand new, the desire to change a brand-new kitchen to one you actually want would feel redundant.

As he made his way beyond 'plastic avenue', he found himself on a winding road that led to Marlow Hill, and set back from the high gates were large houses and expensive cars.

Millionaires' Row.

He knew that there were some very affluent parts of Buckinghamshire, such as Marlow and Hazelmere, but seeing such wealth less than half a mile from the city centre was surprising. Eventually, he turned off the road and onto the dual carriageway, following it down past High Wycombe General Hospital until he hit the 'magic roundabout'.

This was the bit he had practised, and the part of his journey that caused his sigh of relief.

He'd never seen anything like it in his life, and as he approached the first mini roundabout, he second-guessed another driver, drawing a large beep of the horn and a foul-mouthed tirade from the lowered window. Townsend raised an apologetic hand and successfully whipped around the next two roundabouts, the green fields of Wycombe Rye catching his attention before he turned on to Queen Victoria Road. At the top of the road, which began a sharp incline after the traffic lights ahead, was the railway station, but Townsend squeezed through the tight gap in the wall that surrounded the police station and approached the barrier. A young officer, barely into his twenties, approached, and Townsend gave his name and credentials. The man spoke into his radio and a moment later, lifted the barrier, and waved him in. The car park was deceptively deep, and after weaving beyond a fleet of police cars and vans, he pulled into a vacant spot by the far wall. A few other officers were stepping from their cars, arching their necks at the unfamiliar face of Townsend.

He pulled his mirror down and quickly checked his appearance.

His short, dark hair was set in a rough side parting, and his stubble was trimmed neatly to run across the line of his jaw. The scar, which he'd received from one of Kovac's henchmen, dominated his right eyebrow, but beyond that, he looked presentable. He'd decided against wearing a tie, more for his disdain for the item than for safety reasons, and he retrieved his black jacket from the back of the car and headed around the side of the building. Some of the other officers slipped in through the back entrance, but without his pass, he'd need to sign in at the front. Townsend nodded to the young officer as he walked by, and he stepped out onto the street. The police station itself was a wide, dull-looking building, with the Thames Valley Police logo that sat proudly above the door now thick with grime. Neighbouring the station was the Town Hall, with its grand archway that sat on two pillars. Opposite was the High Wycombe City Council Office, which looked as depressing as it sounded. Slightly further up the street, approaching the traffic lights, was the main Post Office, with a fleet of red vans and lorries already roaring into action.

The small street was the hub of High Wycombe, and Townsend took a few seconds to breathe it in and welcome his new surroundings, then turned, and pushed through the front door of the station. It was as dreary and basic as every other station he had stepped foot in, and he wasn't sure why he expected any different. A row of uncomfortable looking plastic chairs ran across the far wall, underneath a corkboard that was strewn with flyers offering everything from support and advice helplines to the local neighbourhood watch. An elderly lady sat in one of the seats, clutching her bag as if her life depended on it, and she looked at Townsend with concern. As he approached the front desk, he nodded to her with a warm smile, but she just turned away.

Behind a thick, bulletproof pane of perplex glass, a middle-aged officer turned to him, her hair in a neat bun and just the slightest hint of make up on her face.

'Can I help, sir?'

'Err, yes. Detective Sergeant Jack Townsend. I'm here to—'

'Ah, the new fella.' The woman smiled warmly. She cast her eye over him and raised a suggestive eyebrow. 'Younger than I expected.'

'I wasn't given any instruction on who to ask for—'

'No worries. I'll let them know you're here. Just take a seat and someone will be up for you in a minute.'

Townsend nodded, went to step away, and then frowned.

'Up?'

But the officer had turned away and Townsend shrugged and took the nearest seat. The old lady in the corner had clearly been eavesdropping, and she lowered her guard slightly, and Townsend once again offered her his warmest smile.

'DS Townsend?'

A voice caused him to snap back, and he stood to attention. Looking up at him was a young woman with fiery ginger hair, glasses, and a smile that would light up any room.

'That's me.' Townsend extended his hand. She took it firmly.

'DC Nic Hannon. Great to finally meet you. Love the accent.'

'Err thanks. It was my father's.'

Hannon chuckled, turned, and beckoned for him to

follow. She handed him a lanyard with his new police badge attached to it, and as she used hers to open the next door, Townsend did the same. The digitalisation of the world meant that he now had access to whatever permitted areas of the building his rank dictated, and it also created a digital footprint of his movements. Despite the older guard continuously ranting on about *'the way things used to be'* or what they did *'back in my day'*, Townsend was a huge proponent of the use of technology.

Anything that could help them do their jobs.

As they approached the lifts, Hannon greeted a few other officers, and then pushed open the door to the stairwell.

'This way,' she said cheerily, and it was only as she descended the first step that Townsend noticed her slight limp. It wasn't obvious, but her distribution of weight and her grip on the banister told him that she struggled slightly.

'Downstairs?' Townsend asked as he followed her, looking beyond at the gloomy corridor that awaited them.

'Oh yes. We have the best seats in the house.' Hannon chuckled as they reached the bottom of the stairs. A few doors looked bolted shut, and further down the dim corridor, light burst through an open door. As they approached, Hannon stopped at the coffee machine posted outside. It was the standard multi-type machine that promised a difference between a latte or a mocha, but in truth, just pumped out bitter sludge. She reached for the mug that sat beside it, put it in place, and kicked it into gear.

'You want one?' she asked.

'I'm fine, thanks.'

'Are you sure?' Hannon raised her eyebrows. 'It's really awful.'

Townsend smiled, already liking his new colleague. Her mug, emblazoned with 'World's Best Detective' filled with a milky coffee and she turned to the door marked 'Specialist Crimes Unit'.

The office was barely bigger than a storage cupboard.

'Ta da!' Hannon sarcastically said, before heading towards one of the two desks that comprised the office. It was neat as a pin, and she put her mug down, dropped onto her seat, and swivelled to Townsend. 'Welcome to the Specialist Crimes Unit. That's your desk, there. I made sure all your profiles were working. I've got a friend in IT.'

'Thanks,' Townsend said, frowning slightly as he approached the cramped desk. Already, there were a number of forms laid out for him. The usual documents, such as his next-of-kin, health plan, etc. 'It's…cosy.'

'It's a bit a snug.' Hannon shrugged. 'But we get a lot of quiet.'

'But fuck all sun.' A voice cut through, and both of them spun to the door where DI Isabella King stood. She slipped her arms out of her suit jacket, draped it over her arm, and took a step to Townsend. 'DS Townsend. Nice to meet you.'

'Ma'am.'

'Guv will do.' She turned from him quickly, looking at Hannon. 'Did you get him set up?'

'He's good to go.' Hannon gave the thumbs up, then took a sip of her coffee and grimaced. 'I think I'll do a coffee run. Guv?'

'Usual, please.' King was shuffling between the two desks, to the tiny, private office that had clearly been knocked through to accommodate a senior officer.

'Jack?' Hannon asked with a smile.

'Err, flat white, please. Cheers.'

'You got it.'

'Oh, Townsend. Boss wants to see you first thing,' King called back from her office.

'Okay. Now, guv?'

'First thing.' King leant back through the door. 'So yep, right now.'

Already, he could feel a slight bit of doubt from the woman, and hoped it was nothing more than a light hazing. Townsend stood and draped his lanyard over his head. He cast his eye over his desk, and then Hannon's, noticing the back support for her chair and footstool under the desk. After a few more seconds, he sighed, took a breath, and then stepped to King's door and knocked.

'Yes?' She didn't look up from her desk.

'Sorry, guv. Where am I going exactly?'

'DSI Hall.' She looked at him with a forced smile. Something told him she was having a rough morning. 'Up in CID.'

Townsend nodded and stepped back, shaking his head as he weaved past the desks and trying to swallow his imposter syndrome. As he stepped out, Hannon was waiting for him.

'DSI Hall. Third floor.'

'Thanks. Appreciate it.'

The two of them walked back towards the stairwell.

'King can be a tough nut to crack, but she's okay. Once you get to know her a bit.'

'Until then?'

Hannon looked at Townsend with pity.

'Just don't fuck anything up.'

At the top of the stairs, Hannon patted Townsend on the shoulder and headed to the exit. Eager to ensure he didn't spend his whole day sitting at a desk, Townsend decided to take the stairs, wondering how hard he was going to have to swim to avoid sinking.

CHAPTER FIVE

Stretching over fifty-three acres, Wycombe Rye was an oasis of green in the middle of the town of High Wycombe. Usually, it was alive with activity, with families descending upon it for days out, with the facilities offering ample entertainment for children. There was a toddler park, surrounded by a metal fence, that was filled with everything from roundabouts to swings. On the other side of the mass stretch of grass, which was sliced into numerous football pitches, was a tree-top adventure park, designed for the older kids to test their balance and nerve. Rope bridges that ran from elevated platform to elevated platform, as well as a large metal slide. The whole thing overlooked the kiosk, where refreshments and hot food were served at extortionate prices, but the surrounding seating area would always be packed.

The kiosk also presided over the pedalo hire, where families and couples could venture out onto the lake that shimmered under the sun.

A real heartbeat of the community.

But before rush hour, and before the kids could converge on the Rye, it was a peaceful route that many a jogger, dog walker or cyclist enjoyed, and on that morning, Craig Murray pulled into the car park, ready to beat his personal best. He'd been goaded into running the London Marathon the following year by a fitness fanatic, and although part of him regretted his decision, the other part secretly enjoyed it.

The idea that, at the age of forty-two, he could push himself to such a level of improvement and achievement was something his career as an accountant couldn't offer, and he was surprised his wife was as supportive as she was. But she thought it was a good example to set for their two boys, especially as they were approaching their teens.

Craig had never been much of an athlete. The furthest his sporting endeavours went were a few rounds of golf at the weekend.

But as the weight began to drop off his middle-aged body, his times improved, and the struggle dissipated, he found himself slowly becoming addicted to running.

The entrance to the Rye car park was down a side road that then cut through the fields and snaked its way through the trees and then opened up behind the lido. By nine o'clock, the outdoor pool would be packed, but Craig knew he'd already be sitting at his desk and dreaming of a calf massage by then. Once he'd parked his car and paid for the parking, he slotted his earbuds in, hit his favourite true crime podcast, and began at a decent pace. A nice, flat pathway ran around the edge of the lake, parallel with the grassy fields up until the kiosk, where it would then bend, incline, and lead him through the woodlands. It was one big loop, and one that he would run five times every other morning.

A cool breeze followed him as he ran, promising another bright and warm summer's day. As he made his way towards the kiosk, Craig gave a respectful nod to a jogger heading the other way, an unspoken appreciation that he wasn't the only one out that morning.

Across the fields, he could see two dogs running around maniacally as their owners rushed towards them both apologising. His boys wanted a dog, and while his wife wasn't averse to the idea, Craig was worried about the amount of work it would actually be.

Eventually, he would be the one who would have to walk it every day and while he could haul the dog along with him on his run, he wouldn't be able to take it to the office afterwards. It was selfish, but Craig had very little time to himself, and he didn't want to spoil it with further responsibility. The pedalos gently rocked on the lake as he rounded the corner, pushing his effort levels up as he hit the incline and began to climb. As he entered the shaded path that cut through the woods, a cyclist whipped past, sticking to the clearly marked cycle lane.

Craig gave the man a nod.

He received one back.

A nod of respect, as if he was an athlete. It was something he'd never thought would happen and at that moment, he doubled down on the idea that a dog was out of the question. If the boys complained, he'd get them a fish instead.

The thought made him chuckle out loud, and as he looked around to ensure nobody saw him, he looked to his left, where through the gaps of the trees, he could see the shimmering water.

He did a double-take.

Was that a body?

Craig brought himself to a stop, tapped his earbud to pause his show, and then looked up and down the path.

There was no one.

He was completely alone.

Tentatively, he stepped off the pathway, his feet

pushing through the surrounding shrubbery, and he made his way towards the trees. His stomach felt heavy, and his hands were shaking.

'Hello?'

Craig called out, leaning against the first tree and peering round.

It was a body.

His heart sank, and with a courage he didn't know he had, he rushed through the rest of the trees, snapping the branches that were in his way until his feet squelched in the mud of the embankment.

It was a woman.

'Oh, Jesus,' Craig exclaimed, as he stared down at the young lady, who was face down on the water, her body pressed against the muddy bank below him. Involuntarily, Craig turned to the nearest bush and felt the entire contents of his stomach rush up through his throat and explode onto the leaves. He stumbled back up and held onto the tree for support. His hand was shaking as he pulled the phone from the holder that he'd strapped to his arm and with his fingers trembling, he dialled nine-nine-nine.

'Emergency Services. How can I assist you?'

'Err, yeah, I need police, please. And an ambulance.'

'Is everything okay, sir?'

'She's dead. This woman, she's dead.'

'What woman, sir?'

Craig felt woozy, and in the back of his mind, he knew he was stumbling over his words. He needed to take charge of the situation.

'I was jogging, in Wycombe Rye, and I saw a body in the lake.'

'The body of a woman?'

'Yes. Please send the police. Send everyone.'

'Have you checked that she is breathing?'

'No.'

'Are you able to do that safely, sir?'

'There's no point.' Craig said, his eyes filling with tears. He looked down at the body once more, at the reason he had vomited so violently. 'She's covered in stab wounds.'

'Police are on their way, sir.'

Craig let the phone drop from his hand as the shock began to set it, and as he scrambled back towards the pathway, two cyclists had stopped, and were peering towards him with intrigue. By the look on their faces, he wasn't a pretty sight, and as the female cyclist helped him to the nearest bench and offered him her water bottle, her husband followed his own curiosity and headed through the trees to the water.

Craig took long, concentrated breaths.

Seeing a dead body wasn't something that he had prepared for.

Seeing one that had been so violently maimed would haunt him for the rest of his life.

CHAPTER SIX

Townsend took a second to compose himself before he rapped his knuckles against the glass panel on the door.

'Come in.'

DSI Hall's voice radiated authority, and as Townsend stepped in, the senior officer peered up over his glasses at his newest detective. He regarded him intently for a few moments, a well-rehearsed power move that put Townsend on the spot with the hope of making him squirm slightly. It was nothing personal, it was just one of Hall's ways to get the measure of a man. Townsend certainly matched the description. Tall, strong, rough around the edges. From the way the man stood, with his back straight, his shoulders wide, and his strong jaw set, Hall could tell the man lacked fear.

He may have lacked experience, but there was impressive grit to the man, and Hall's blank expression formed into a smile. He stood, stepped around the desk, and extended his hand.

'Ah, DS Townsend. Welcome to the team.'

Townsend took the firm handshake and reciprocated.

'Pleasure to be here, sir.'

'Please, take a seat.'

Townsend did as he was told, and Hall made his way back to his desk. It was evident by the man's bulk that in his younger years he had been an intimidating presence. Now, Hall's intimidation came from his standing and his reputation, as half a century had seen him pile on a few pounds. He took his seat, slid his glasses onto his nose once more, and lifted a file.

Townsend quickly realised it was one about him.

'So…you can understand I may have a few concerns.' It was less of a question and more of a statement. 'Should I?'

'Concerns about what, sir?'

'About you.' Hall spoke curtly. He lifted the file. 'I'll summarise, but three years undercover, with a litany of offences during that time, betrayed by another police officer, almost beaten to death, and apparent ties to a wanted vigilante. Does that sum it up?'

'They also kidnapped my wife…' Townsend shrugged.

'That's a lot for anyone to go through.' Hall's tone changed to that of a concerned father. 'I'm assuming there were no barriers put in your way by Merseyside on your path to DS?'

'No. They saw it as compensation for everything I've been through.'

Hall could sense the frustration in Townsend's voice and leant back in his seat.

'And you don't like that?'

'I don't like the notion that I didn't earn my spot. That I'm a fake detective.' Townsend could feel his fist clench. 'They fast tracked me to DC, and for eighteen months, I paid my dues. I wasn't even allowed to go out to any calls because my cover was in Merseyside. So I spent that time locked in a crummy office, trawling through paperwork…'

'That's the job of a DC, son.'

'Exactly. I did my time as a DC, so I want to just be given a fair crack of the whip. That's all I ask.'

Hall sighed and lifted Townsend's file once more and then casually tossed it onto the cabinet behind his desk.

'You've completed your therapy?'

'Every session, sir.'

'Settled into the area? Flackwell Heath isn't it?'

'Yes, sir. And we're getting there. Few teething problems, but we'll soon feel at home.'

'Good. It's a nice little village.' Hall leant forward and clasped his hands together. 'Look, I'm willing to give you a shot, Townsend. As far as I'm concerned, everything that's happened before, we draw a line under it. I don't want to hear about your past, I certainly don't want to hear the name Sam Pope, and as far as you being *ready* to be a detective sergeant on my staff, you need to not fuck this up. Is that clear?'

'Yes, sir. Thank you.'

'DI King is one of my best detectives. Don't tell her I said that.' Hall smirked. 'But she's had a shit time of things these past few years, none of yours, or my business, but she needs the SCU to work. I'll be honest, she wasn't pleased to have you dropped into her team. So, I'm not the only one you need to prove yourself to. I trust her, I trust her judgement, so make a fan of her and hopefully, I won't need to have you back in my office.'

'I appreciate the heads up, sir.'

'Good.' Hall leant across the desk and extended his hand. Townsend took it. 'Now, off you pop.'

With a polite nod, Townsend stood, just as a heavy fist rattled the door and then it flew open. DI King stepped into the room, slightly out of breath, and her eyes wide with apparent excitement.

'Sorry to interrupt, boss.' She held an apologetic hand up to Townsend and then looked to Hall. Hall also stood, removing his glasses, and dropping them on his desk.

'What is it?'

'Call's just come in. A body's been found in the lake at the Rye. Uniform are already there to close the scene off.'

'Foul play?' Hall asked with concern.

'Multiple stab wounds,' King said. 'So yeah, some pretty fucking foul play. CID are swamped…call came through to Hannon.'

'I see…' Hall frowned. His mind was racing as he navigated the political minefield. After a few seconds of deep thought, he looked at the two detectives before him.

One of them was an asset to the force but had been through the ringer.

The other was effectively a try-out.

A smile spread across his face. A chance to shake things up. King's eyes narrowed as she regarded him.

'Guv?'

'Right, you two, get on it.'

'But what about CID…'

'I'll handle Lowe. You want to prove your team can get shit done around here, Izzy. Then it's time to do just that.' King nodded and stomped back through the door. Townsend went to follow until Hall called after him. 'Time to prove it, son.'

Townsend shot him a glance back and appreciated the encouraging nod from his superior. He smiled, stepped through the door, and hurried down the corridor to catch up with Detective Inspector King.

'Who called it in?' Townsend asked as they bounded down the stairs.

'A jogger. Saw her body passing by.' They reached a small landing midway between the second and first floor and King stopped and turned to Townsend. 'Look, we don't know each other yet. And I know it's going to take some time for us to get through the weeds, figure each other out, and so on. But I need to know I can trust you to carry out orders.'

'Guv, I just want to have a good first day.' Townsend smiled. He saw a slight twitch of one in the corner of King's mouth.

'Well, you've picked a good day to start.'

They made their way down the final flight of stairs, an excited energy buzzing between them.

'You seemed surprised that DSI Hall gave this to us,' Townsend said with interest. 'Isn't this considered a specialist crime?'

King pushed open the door to the station, and they stepped onto the forecourt. The traffic was bumper to bumper, and Queen Victoria Road was a different beast to the quiet street he'd seen earlier. King stopped for two seconds, dipped her hand into her jacket and pulled out a thin, black vape. She took a deep puff on it and then blew out a plume of fruity smelling smoke.

'Do you play the political game, Jack?'

'Excuse me?'

'You know. All the back-slapping and favours people pull to move up the corporate ladder. Is that for you?'

Townsend scowled and shook his head.

'No, guv. I just want to help people.'

'Me, too.' She took another puff and then pocketed it. 'And *that* is why we have this team. It's a a way for them to bury those who just want to do good work. Now, keep up.'

Instead of turning towards the car park, King strode through the entrance to the forecourt and out onto the jam-packed street.

'Guv. We're walking?'

King laughed.

'I need to get my steps in.' She then pointed across the

roundabout to the mass of trees on the vista. 'Besides, we're only heading over there.'

Townsend fell into step alongside his boss, his adrenaline pumping for his first case on the team. But there was a dark feeling emanating from the back of his mind.

The thought that someone had been murdered a stone's throw from a police station sent a shiver down his spine.

Time to prove yourself, Jack.

With opportunity waiting, Townsend followed DI King as she headed to the underpass that would lead them to the entrance to the Rye and the location of a murdered woman.

CHAPTER SEVEN

As they approached the entrance to the park, King was happy to see it had already been taped across by an officer, who was keeping watch. With so many entrances to the park, it would be impossible to keep the most voyeuristic of the public away, but so far, it seemed like the officers had done a reasonable job of preserving the scene.

'Ma'am.' The officer nodded to King as she approached. She didn't need to show her badge. Townsend did, but in an effort to build good relationships, he smiled happily as he presented it. 'First day?'

'Yup.'

'Good luck, mate.'

A number of police officers were on the woodland side of the lake, doing their best to preserve what little of the crime scene they could. On the opposite side, passersby had stopped to watch, under the watch of another officer, who was sternly telling a few teenagers to put their phones away.

'Fuck,' King uttered. 'This will be all over social media before we even see her body.'

Townsend grunted his agreement. Social media was a

concept that was alien to him. He wasn't a wildly private person, but he found little gain in the appreciation of strangers. The idea that someone would post something pertaining to a murdered woman for the sole reason of 'engagement' turned his stomach, and it took everything within him to stop himself from marching over and tossing their phones into the lake. With his mind wandering, he almost collided with King, who had come to a standstill.

'Everything okay, guv?'

He followed her gaze to the concrete on the loop of the pathway, just before the incline into the woods.

Blood.

'Wait here. I'll send an officer over to block this off.' King ordered, and she quickly jogged up the incline to the nearest officer. Sure enough, the officer, a greying man with a paunch hanging over his belt, swiftly relieved Townsend. King waited for Townsend to catch up, and then they marched towards the crime scene. 'Right, this is game time. We can't fuck this up, okay? Just follow my lead.'

The area had been cordoned off, with a line of police tape slinking from tree to tree, providing a loose perimeter. In the small clearing between the trees and the embankment, the body of the woman had been laid flat on her back, her clothes sodden, and her skin a ghostly shade of grey. One of the other officers was looking through the nearby overgrown shrubbery as another approached. The officer was an Indian woman who, despite being short in stature, radiated the authority that her twelve years of service deserved. She smiled at King, and then nodded to Townsend.

'Glad you guys are here.' She shook Townsend's hand. 'PC Shah.'

'DS Townsend.'

'He's my newbie.' King clarified. 'What's the situation?'

'Nothing new, I'm afraid. Jogger found her body this morning. We've counted over fifteen stab wounds across her body, but there could be more.' Shah shook her head. 'Poor girl.'

'We found a puddle of blood over by the kiosk.' King nodded in the direction. 'Safe to say it was hers.'

'Did the jogger not see it?' Townsend cut in. They both looked at him. 'The blood, I mean.'

'He's in a pretty bad state of shock. One of mine is with him right now, but you're welcome to take over.'

Townsend looked at King, who nodded.

'Get what you can and then invite him down to the station for a statement,' King said. She turned back to Shah. 'Anything else? Any ID?'

'Not yet.' Shah shook her head. 'Poor girl. She's so young.'

As they both cast their eye over the dead body, the officer who'd been relieved by Townsend approached. A grumpy-looking man in his early forties, he looked like he hadn't slept for days.

'CID are finally here.' He then looked like he noticed King. 'Come to check up on our work?'

King scoffed and shook her head. The man clearly had a woman sized chip on his shoulder and she held her hand out to display the body before her.

'I've come to find out what's happened to this poor girl. But if you want to have a discussion about your problems with a female superior, I'd be happy to catch up with you later, Constable Boyd.' She shot him daggers, and he looked away. 'And we aren't CID. This investigation is now with Specialist Crimes.'

PC Boyd ran his tongue against his bottom lip and then thought better of running his mouth. Especially to DI King, who had never been afraid of confronting a problem head on. He held his hands up and stepped away. The officer in the shrubbery called out excitedly.

'I've got a bag.'

King and Shah rushed to his location, and the officer, caked in dirt, emerged from the weeds holding a small leather clutch bag. King was already wrapping her hands in latex gloves, and was thrilled to see he had done the same. He handed it over to her and then stepped away. Drawn by the excitement, Townsend sidled up next to King.

'Is it hers?'

'I'm just checking.' King popped open the clasp and slowly moved the bag to shuffle its contents. 'Anything from our jogger?'

'Nothing. No.'

'He's not our killer, then?' King raised her eyebrows, a dry smile on her face.

'Look, it was a genuine question. He ran up in that direction, but just didn't notice the body or the blood. Was in the zone, apparently.'

'Don't beat yourself up, newbie,' King said, holding the bag up at eye level. 'I'd rather you put everyone under the microscope than nobody. Ah ha.'

Carefully, King slid two fingers into the bag and pulled out a card holder. The leather sleeve had space for multiple cards, and she tucked the bag under her arm and then slipped the driver's license out.

'Lauren Grainger,' King said sadly. 'Christ, she was only twenty-three.'

Townsend was already pulling his second latex glove on when she handed him the license.

'Call Hannon. Get her looking into Lauren immediately. Address. Job. Family. Friends. I want to know everything there is to know about her before I get back.'

'On it, guv.' Townsend pulled his phone out of his pocket and then paused. 'What's her number?'

King frowned, fished out her own phone, unlocked it, and then made the call. She shot Townsend a frustrated glance, and he made a note to update his phone the second he got back to the office. As King relayed her orders to Hannon, Townsend took a few steps towards the lake and looked out across the water. The gathering crowd was growing by the minute, with a few more police officers joining the thankless task of keeping them at bay. Beyond the water and the green fields, traffic was slowly inching its way down London Road, the concrete vein that cut through the town and connected the town centre to the M40. All the drivers and passengers had their heads turned, intrigued by the strong police presence in the usually tranquil park. The whole place was so different to the concrete maze that was Toxteth, where he'd grown up, where the appearance of a police car on a street was as regular as the postman.

But he wasn't on Merseyside anymore.

Buckinghamshire was an enormous, yet quaint county, that spread from the Chilterns to the edges of Berkshire. People were used to the country walks, the rolling fields that surrounded the major towns, and just a quieter way of life. Many families, priced out of London, had set up home in the many villages dotted around the town centre, and young professionals had found their way onto the more affordable property ladder.

This wasn't a place of real crime.

Murder was reserved for the inner cities.

But a woman had been killed. Brutally murdered.

And Townsend could sense the fear that would likely spread through the town when the news spread.

His eyes landed on the entrance that he and King had arrived at, where the officer was removing the police tape to allow the SOCO van to drive through. As soon as they'd passed, he refastened it around a tree and took up his post once again, as the van crawled towards the kiosk. To Townsend's appreciation, the officer standing watch on the blood puddle waved it down, and two of the scene of crime officers hopped out, already in their white overalls, and began to lock down that particular part of the path.

King hung up the phone.

'SOCO's here.' She nodded, following Townsend's gaze. 'Let's let them do their job and we'll start doing our own digging. Come on.'

King turned and headed back towards the butchered body of Lauren, and she squatted down beside her. Townsend watched intently, moved by the anger that seemed to be coursing through his boss's body.

'Who did this to you, Lauren?'

Before Townsend realised the question wasn't meant for him, he spoke.

'Someone she knew.'

King's head snapped up, and she stood.

'What makes you say that?' She was testing him.

'It wasn't a robbery.'

'There could be something missing from her bag…'

'They'd have taken the whole thing and dumped it later. And judging by the number of stab wounds, whoever did this, did this with passion.' Townsend shook his head. 'I've seen people get robbed. This isn't it.'

'You think she was targeted?' King said, rubbing her chin with interest.

'I think she was murdered,' Townsend replied, his eyes focused on the corpse before him and his words full of purpose. 'And I want to find the sick bastard who did it.'

After a few seconds, King nodded her agreement and then made her way back through the trees to the pathway, greeting the SOCO team as they made their entrance and began to erect the necessary tent and station to do their work. Townsend kept his eyes on the body, the young woman who had been brutally snatched from the world, before turning and following his boss out of the woods, knowing that catching her killer would become his obsession.

CHAPTER EIGHT

'What've you got for me, Hannon?'

King was only halfway through the door to the SCU office when she called out to the young detective, who swivelled in her chair with a welcoming smile across her face.

'Hello to you, too.' Her smile fell when the joke fell flat. 'Quite a bit actually.'

King stepped to the small space behind Hannon's chair and looked down at the two screens on the desk. Townsend leant against his own desk, his arms folded across his chest. The room felt tiny with all three of them in it. He looked down, saw the now cold cup of coffee on his desk, and thanked Hannon for it.

'Let's hear it, then,' King said, agitated.

'Right…so I've been trawling through our databases and there wasn't too much about Lauren. She appeared twice, once in a report about an incident at Paradise.' She looked up at Townsend. 'The local strip club. And she was also referenced in a report about a domestic dispute two years ago.'

'Was she the victim?'

'To be honest, guv, it doesn't say much. It's a pretty lazy report.'

King sighed. A regrettably common theme when it came to domestic abuse.

'Figures.'

'But I've been through her social media accounts and also done some digging on Paradise. Lauren Grainger has been a dancer there for nearly two years, but in that time, she's moved into her own flat not far from the Rye, bought a car, been on holiday…'

'So she's earning well?' Townsend interjected.

'She was pretty stunning,' Hannon said. 'Seems likely she'd have got a lot of business.'

'Have you got her financial records yet?' King asked.

'Not yet. I've sent off the request, but will take some time.'

'Chase them up. Tell them this is a murder investigation and we want to see her history. See if there's anything out of the ordinary.' King turned to Townsend. 'When I get back, we'll hit up Paradise, see if anyone is about and find out who was there last night.'

'You think the killer was a customer?'

'Possibly. Men can get pretty possessive over women, especially ones they pay for.' The tone in King's voice told Townsend her mind was heading down that avenue. 'Also, we may find out if she had any issues that she wouldn't post about.'

'Drugs?' Townsend frowned. 'There was nothing of note in her possession was there?'

'No, but we have a young woman dead in a lake and we don't know why. So we need to cover *every* possible angle and eliminate them as quickly as possible. Okay? The quicker we eliminate those, the quicker we get on the right track.'

'Yes, guv.' Townsend held his hands up and King

nodded. Already, she seemed pleased with his hunger to learn. She then turned back to Hannon.

'When SOCO finishes up, they'll be bringing her phone back here. We need to get everything that's on it… who she was calling, texting, what websites she was visiting.'

'I'm all over it.' Hannon scrawled a note onto the pad beside her keyboard. 'What about her home? Do we need to get anything to get in there?'

'I'm going to go see her mother. She needs to know about her daughter and maybe she has a key?' King shrugged. 'If not, Hall will sign off on anything we need to search her premises. In the meantime, Townsend, I want you going through CCTV of last night. I'll give them a nudge to get the footage sent to you right away.' Townsend nodded, but clearly struggled to hide his hesitancy at CCTV work. 'Look, I know it's a slog, but right now, we need to figure out her last movements, the last people to see her, the last people to contact her and eliminate as many reasons for her murder as possible. Hall will be all over me for progress, and we need to have made some.'

'Yes, guv,' Townsend and Hannon said, practically at the same time, which drew a smile to Hannon's face. King's, too.

'We'll regroup when I'm back, pull together whatever we discover by then, and start piecing together what the hell happened. Hannon, you have the mother's address?'

'Pinging it to you now.'

'Thanks. Let's get to work, guys. Let's find out who did this.'

King marched out of the office, a determined stride that would ensure everyone would step out of her way. Townsend watched her leave, and despite the initial hesitancy, found himself already respecting her. It was as if she'd taken the death of this young woman personally, which meant she would fight tooth and nail to find the killer.

It was a mutual feeling, and he turned to Hannon and blew out his cheeks.

'So...coffee?'

'You mean *another* coffee?' Hannon chuckled. 'Yeah, I could go for another one. As long as you're happy to order an oat milk frappuccino?'

'It's my go-to drink.'

Hannon burst out laughing and then grimaced with pain. She stretched her back and tried to hide the discomfort on her face. Townsend thought better than to pry.

'I'll check your access when you're gone, but you should be up and running when you're back. Oh, and the best coffee shop is up the hill.'

'Noted. Thanks.' Townsend lifted his jacket from the back of his chair. After marching out with King earlier that day, he'd forgotten it, and had been surprised by the brisk breeze that had accompanied the sunny day. 'Need anything when I'm out?'

'Just your safe return.' Hannon spun round. 'And some biscuits.'

'Will do.' Townsend slipped his muscular frame into his jacket and then raised his eyebrow. Hannon looked perturbed. 'Hey, everything okay?'

'Yeah, it's just...this poor girl, you know? I mean, I know we didn't know her, but she was only twenty-three and she must have been so scared. Like, there would have been a moment when she knew she was going to die, and she would have been alone and in the dark, and watching this person kill her.'

It only struck Townsend then that Hannon couldn't have been that much older than the victim, and whereas he, and King were looking at Lauren Grainger as a poor girl stricken from earth, Hannon was seeing herself in the woman.

A young woman, brutally killed in the dead of night.

It could have been anyone.

But it was their job now, whether it was meant for the Specialist Crimes Unit or not, to prove that it couldn't have been just anyone. They needed to find out exactly why poor Lauren Grainger had been marked for death.

Townsend leant down and rested his hand on the arm of her chair.

'Hey, listen. What has happened is fucking evil, okay? We know that, but that's why we turn up, right? To put things like this right and to bring these people to justice.' He offered her a warm smile. 'As first days go, this is a bit intense, but I already know that the guv will hunt this fucker down to the ends of the world, and so will I. So let's just get working and do what we can?'

Hannon took a deep breath, as if Townsend's rousing speech had had an instant effect. She seemed to re-calibrate, straightened her shoulders, and then turned back to her screen.

'Let's do it,' she said firmly. Townsend made his way to the door, and just as he was about to step out of their dingy office, she called after him. 'Don't forget my biscuits.'

Despite the horror of the morning, Townsend found himself smiling as he headed to the stairwell.

CHAPTER NINE

Although it was only a twenty-minute drive to Great Missenden, DI King was thankful for the headspace. It was against her better instincts to leave two inexperienced detectives to do the urgent work, but she had no other choice. DSI Hall had made it clear she needed to make it work, and that meant getting over her doubts about their capabilities. From the few weeks she'd spent with DC Hannon, she'd already noted that although she had a cheery exterior, there was a woman who had built up walls to protect herself lurking behind it.

It was hard to detect, Hannon hid it well, but King was well trained in reading people, and when she looked beyond the sparkle in her youthful eyes, King saw fear.

But the girl was game. That much was clear, and Hannon's enthusiasm was a trait that King didn't want to quash.

Townsend was a different matter entirely.

The man looked as tough as his backstory suggested, but he was a fish out of water. The man didn't know the area, and although that would come with time, she needed him to get up to speed as quickly as possible.

A young woman had been killed.

Brutally.

And the last thing she needed was the SCU dragging its heels because her team wasn't capable.

With her mind pre-occupied with the case and the hurdles they'd need to jump over, she didn't even acknowledge the officers or staff who passed her in the hallway. She would always offer a smile or a friendly word, but today her mind was elsewhere.

It was with Lauren Grainger.

Lying by the lake, with her body shredded to pieces.

It wasn't until she'd given the young officer by the car park barrier a wave and pulled out of the car park did she let her guard slip. The anger came swiftly and relentlessly, and as she shot up the hill past High Wycombe Railway Station she let out a guttural roar of rage.

It was good for her to let it out.

After her marriage to DCI Lowe broke down, she'd fallen into a rage filled depression that had resulted in a few outbursts, one of which had seen her strike her ex-husband after he had callously remarked about her inability to have kids.

He'd deserved it, but she was lucky he didn't press charges.

Since that moment, she'd strived to improve, and her weekly therapy sessions had been a godsend, if not one that she'd worked hard to keep hidden from her colleagues.

Through her sessions, she'd found ways to control her pain and to channel it into being more empathetic to those around her. To work hard not to rise to provocation and to treat people with respect.

It was tricky, especially when it came to her ex-husband, but she didn't want him to have any further impact on how she felt about herself.

Even if he'd worked to give her a duff hand with the Specialist Crimes Unit.

As the city centre faded into her rearview, she navigated the winding, residential roads until she came to Hazelmere, passing her own street as she carried onward.

As a detective in London, it had been painstaking trying to traverse the traffic-logged streets, adding hours onto her days. Out here in the countryside, it was quick and easy, and soon the greenery rolled by her window. King turned off her air conditioning and rolled down the window. As the fresh air filled her car, she took a few puffs on her vape and blew the smoke out of the car, before turning off the main road and heading toward Little Kingshill.

Spread among the rows of trees and vast fields was the odd street of houses, each as quaint as a postcard. She passed the odd local newsagent, or a small hairdressers, but just fifteen minutes from the busy town centre was like being in a different world. She knew she should appreciate it more, but her mind had never quite allowed her to.

It didn't matter where they were, people were still capable of evil. Of acts of extreme brutality.

TV and fiction had almost rendered such crimes exclusively to London or vague, Scandinavian cities, all of them handed over to a reckless rogue in a trench coat, or a tough woman that fit her own description.

But these crimes happened in the quietest of spots, and at some point the night before, as she walked alone through the dark, Lauren Grainger had found that out to the most heartbreaking of costs.

King passed the sign welcoming her to Great Missenden, and she pulled her car into the car park of a small supermarket and composed herself. The small town was a picturesque monument to the British countryside, with its elegant cottages and high street consisting of small, local businesses. There were posters affixed to the street railings, advertising the school fête, offering family fun, and a chance to help the school raise money. It was the sort of place that was completely alien to someone who had spent their entire lives within the M25, and King, despite having lived in Buckinghamshire for a few years, still found the difference startling. Great Missenden even had its own Food Festival, which she was certain would be the sort of place where she would stick out like a sore thumb. Her satnav said she was two minutes from her destination, and she needed to be the personification of calm. It would do Lauren's mother no good, regardless of what their relationship was like, if King couldn't hold it together.

She needed to be composed. Direct. Caring.

But she also needed to display the authority of someone who would bring justice for her daughter.

King looked in her mirror. Her eyes were a little red where the anger had threatened to draw a tear, and she shook her head.

'Pull it together, Izzy.'

She pressed the button to fire up the engine, and then pulled out of the car park, following the satnav the final few streets until King pulled up outside the home of Rebecca Grainger. As she stepped out of her car, she saw the curtains at the front window of the cottage twitch. With a deep breath, King straightened her jacket, stepped through the metal gate and walked up the cobbled steps to the front door.

It opened before she knocked.

'I'm not interested in anything. Thank you.'

Rebecca Grainger's aggression was staggering, and King held up her lanyard.

'Sorry to intrude, Ms Grainger. I'm Detective Inspector King from the Thames Valley Police. Can I have a word with you?'

A sudden panic spread across the woman's face, and King marvelled at how, despite the age, Rebecca looked startlingly like the dead girl she'd seen that morning.

'Look, I haven't had any trouble with your lot in years. I'm clean, okay. Please…I have a life here.'

'Ms Grainger, if I could just come inside?' King said with a forced smile. 'It's about your daughter.'

'Oh, what has she done now?' Rebecca rolled her eyes, stepped to the side, and ushered the detective in. Before she closed the door, she gave a quick glance up the street and then slammed it shut.

Telling the woman that the murder being widely reported across the news platforms was her own daughter was heartbreaking, and King felt sick to her stomach when the woman collapsed back onto the sofa in shock. Any words of comfort that King offered seemed to bounce off the woman, as if she was bulletproof, and then the devastation took over. Cradling a cushion, Rebecca rocked onto her side and wailed, tears flooding down her cheeks as her heart fell to pieces. King stood quietly, allowing the grief to sweep over the bereaved mother, and then, when she finally sat up, King fetched her a glass of water, from which she sipped with shaking hands.

'I know this is a difficult time for you, Ms Grainger, but I need to ask you some questions. Anything you can offer could help us find the person who did this.'

'Oh, I know who did this.' Rebecca shook with fury as she placed the cup down on the coffee table. The living room to the cottage was modest but had a homely feel to it. 'It was that little shit.'

'Who?' King said, flipping open her notebook. 'Who do you mean?'

'That little runt. Dean Riley. I always told her he was a fucking criminal.'

'A criminal?' King scribbled. 'How so?'

'Drugs. Burglary. He's just a complete shit. Knocked her about. But she wouldn't listen.' Another wave of sadness crashed against Rebecca. 'I should have done more…'

'I take it Lauren didn't appreciate your opinion on her choice in men?'

'Oh, she didn't give a shit.' Rebecca looked down at her feet with shame. 'Things were hard for her. Growing up. I was a single mum. Her dad was never about. I had to do whatever I could to put food on the table and that broke me.' She tapped the side of her head.

'I understand.'

'No, you don't. Look at you. A high flying, fancy police officer turning up here in a sports car. You don't know real struggle.' Rebecca didn't apologise for her bluntness. King didn't expect her to. 'I turned to drink. A lot of drink. Then to drugs. By the time Lauren was fourteen, she was begging for social services to take her away. I didn't stop them…'

Rebecca's voice trailed off, and she collapsed in on herself, the tears as frequent as the groans of heartache. King closed her notepad. She could fill in the blanks herself, and she logically guessed that when they looked further through Lauren's history, they'd find no relationship with her mother. Now, the woman would spend the rest of her life broken by the death of the daughter she'd abandoned.

'Thank you for talking to me, Rebecca. I know it's hard, but this is helpful.' She stood. 'I know there is nothing I can say that can stop what you're going through, but just know that my team and I will do *everything* to catch whoever did this.'

Rebecca turned to her, her eyes a bright red. Behind the pain was a fury that would chill anyone to the bone.

'Just find that fucker and throw away the key.'

'I'll do my best.' King pulled a card from the inside of her jacket and placed it deliberately on the coffee table. 'You call me if you need anything. In the meantime, a Family Liaison Officer will be here shortly. They'll be on hand to help you with whatever you need, okay? I'll be in touch.'

The information didn't seem to get through to Rebecca. Leaving the grieving woman to her pain, DI King let herself out, closing the door gently behind her before stepping back down the cobbled steps to her car. As soon as she dropped into the driver's seat, she scrambled for her vape, taking a few long hard puffs and sighing out the smoke.

She'd need to ask Hall to sign off on them entering Lauren's flat, but that wouldn't be a problem.

Telling a parent that they'd lost their child was one of the hardest parts of her job, and remembering the soft words of her therapist, she knew she had to let the pain of it all flood out. As she pulled her car away from the curb, she recognised the FLO who was stepping out of her own.

At least Rebecca would have support.

She kept the heartbreaking scream of the grieving mother in her thoughts for the entire drive back to High Wycombe Police Station.

She had to find the killer.

She just had to.

CHAPTER TEN

'Catch.'

Townsend looked up just in time to see the cardboard packaging of the sandwich hurtling through the air towards his head. He shuffled erratically and managed to snatch it out of the air just before it splattered against his skull. Hannon chuckled sheepishly and shrugged.

'Thanks,' Townsend said, setting it down on his desk. 'A new meaning to the word fast-food.'

'I aim to innovate,' Hannon said, lowering herself uneasily into her seat. She popped open her packet of crisps and set them to the side of her keyboard and then went about tucking into her sandwich. A few bites in, she turned to Townsend. 'So, how's it going?'

His dual screens were filled with multiple boxes, all of them filled with grainy CCTV footage. Townsend sighed, rubbed his eyes with the palms of his hands, and turned to face her.

'Thrilling.'

'Yeah, well, we gotta trawl through the shit to find silver,' Hannon said and then took a bite.

'You like all this stuff, huh?' Townsend asked as he

ripped open the packaging of his tuna sandwich. 'All the office work.'

'Busy work, you mean? Come on, if you're going to belittle it, do it properly.'

'I didn't mean to offend…'

'I'm kidding.' Hannon flashed a cheeky smile. 'I know most detectives and police officers want to be out on the street, chasing bad guys through alleyways or kicking down doors. But ninety-nine per cent of the case will be figured out in these walls, on these computers. I just like the challenge, is all.'

Townsend couldn't help but smile. There was a maturity to Hannon, despite her cheeky quips, that he thought belied her twenty-five years of age. The woman seemed as dedicated as any police officer he had ever met, but her mind seemed to be wired differently. Her excitement came in the detail, and he wondered why she hadn't been snapped up to work in the main CID office upstairs.

'Well, hopefully some of that enthusiasm finds its way to this side of the room, because this is grating,' Townsend said, turning back to his screens. 'Over thirty-five CCTV cameras were operating and functioning last night in the town centre, but not one of them on the alleyway where Paradise is.'

'Have you managed to find Lauren?' Hannon asked, as she scoffed another mouthful of crisps.

'Yeah, but we only have her as far as the overpass.' Townsend minimised a few of his tabs and pulled up the street map of High Wycombe. 'The biggest problem is that I don't know this bloody town yet.'

'Yeah, I guess that's a shitter.' Hannon shunted along on her chair, wiping the grease from her hands on her trouser legs. 'Let's have a look.'

Townsend shifted to the side and allowed Hannon to take control of the computer, and was instantly envious of how quickly she navigated the files to pull them together. Townsend wasn't illiterate when it came to technology, but he was certainly a beginner. Hannon's fingers glided across the keyboard in a blur, and with her eyes glued on the screen, seemed to be connected to the computer herself. As he tucked into his sandwich, he watched as she began to position some of the CCTV around the screen, the camera angles beginning to make sense as she essentially mapped them out in conjunction to their street positions.

'Right…there we go.' She smiled. 'These are the seven main cameras that focus on the high street. Look, there's the entrance to Eden Shopping Centre there, and that's the road that goes down to Paradise. I've also pulled through the CCTV of the underpass, which is on your map here.'

Hannon tapped the screen where the map of High Wycombe was still open. Townsend finished a quick swig of his mineral water and twisted the cap back on.

'Thanks, mate. I owe you one.'

'Payment in biscuits is always appreciated.'

The two of them returned to their screens and Townsend began the painstaking task of playing through each clip of the CCTV footage. But thankfully, the software allowed him to play them all at the same time. Although there was nothing to be thankful for in a murder investigation, it certainly helped that it had occurred at such an early hour of the morning. The streets were empty, which meant when any movement appeared on one of the cameras, he could draw his attention to it and pause the others.

A car here or there.

A group of drunken louts, disappearing past the shopping centre to their inevitable destination of Paradise.

A few homeless people.

Then Townsend sat up, his eyes wide.

Loitering near the overpass, he saw a hooded figure.

Shrouded in the darkness of the shadows, the figure was decked out in all black, making it impossible to discern whether they were male or female. But there was someone there. Townsend checked the times.

Two twenty.

He scribbled a note down in his notepad and then continued trawling through the footage once more. Again, apart from the drunken patrons stumbling back into the town centre after their seedy evening had ended, there was nothing of note. With his back aching and his eyes burning, Townsend began to contemplate yet another coffee run when he saw it.

The hooded figure.

Frantically, he tapped the keys to pause the footage and then, using his intuition, managed to zoom in on the shadowed area beside the Eden Shopping Centre. He rolled the footage back, and sure enough, for a brief two seconds, a hooded figure stepped out from the darkness and disappeared out of view.

He checked the time.

Three forty-two.

Although they hadn't spoken to the management of Paradise yet, Hannon had been able to confirm via the phone call that Lauren had left the club just before four that morning.

The time synced.

Townsend scribbled another note in his pad and then sat back, staring at the grainy outline of the person on his screen.

Are you the killer? Townsend thought, his knuckles whitening as he clenched his fists. Just as he turned to update Hannon, the door to the office opened and in marched DI King, each step more purposeful than the last. Without even offering a greeting to her team, she approached the far wall and began to strip the corkboard of all the leaflets and flyers that had been pinned there by HR. Then, she took a photo of Lauren Grainger and pinned it to the top of the board, and then turned to her team of two.

'Right. Lauren Grainger was murdered this morning, that much we know. But what else do we know now?'

King sat on the edge of Hannon's desk and looked at the young DC.

'It seems that Lauren was receiving some pretty nasty private messages on her social media accounts. Facebook and Instagram. The usual slut-shaming messages, but also some pretty graphic threats of sexual abuse.'

'Fucking hell,' Townsend said involuntarily.

'My thoughts exactly.' King agreed. 'Do we know who from?'

'Sadly, they're dummy accounts. No name. All registered with newly created, generic email accounts. I've asked DS Murray in Cybercrime to try to link the IP addresses. Hopefully, he comes through quickly.'

'Good work. Murray's one of the good guys up there. Any update on the financial records?'

'Still waiting to hear back from the bank.'

'Keep chasing them.' She turned to Townsend. 'Anything on the cameras?'

'Yeah, this...' Townsend turned back to his screen and King strode across and leant over his shoulder. Hannon scooted up next to him. 'Nic helped me plot the cameras so they lined up with the town centre, but if we look at this footage of the overpass here, you can see this figure.' He pulled the video to the correct time. 'That was about an hour and a half before Lauren left the club, but on this camera here, right next to the alleyway...'

He clicked the play button and then paused on the second the hooded figure was visible.

King's eyes lit up.

'The same person?' she asked.

'Perhaps.' Townsend nodded. 'Certainly wouldn't hurt to find out who it is.'

'Great work.' King smiled and then stood, leaving Townsend to smile inwardly. She approached the board.

'Lauren's mother, as you can imagine, is broken by the news. But they didn't have much of a relationship. She was in a dark place a long time ago – drink, drugs, worse – and Lauren was taken into care when she was fourteen. I think her mother kept tabs on her, but they didn't seem close.'

'Possible motive?' Townsend shrugged. Hannon looked shocked, but Townsend dismissed it. 'All possibilities, right?'

'Right,' King agreed. 'But no, I highly doubt it. She mentioned an ex-boyfriend. Dean Riley. Apparently, he's been in our bad books a few times, so Hannon, I need everything on him as quickly as possible. When we get back, fill us in.'

'Right you are, Guv,' Hannon said, spinning in her chair, and then shifting back to her desk.

'Get back?' Townsend asked as he stood. He lifted his jacket as King stepped by him and headed to the door. 'Where are we going?'

'To the most ironic place on Earth,' King replied dryly, seemingly enjoying her own joke. It took Townsend a second to get it.

Paradise.

They were heading to the last people who saw Lauren Grainger alive.

CHAPTER ELEVEN

The walk from the station to the Eden Shopping Centre took less than five minutes, something that Townsend was surprised to find he quite enjoyed. Having grown up on a rough estate in the concrete jungle that was Toxteth, the idea of the police station being so close to action was a bizarre notion. He'd seen police cars lured to cul-de-sacs for the express purpose of being pelted with bottles or for police officers to be attacked.

Yet here, in the quiet town of High Wycombe, he and his Detective Inspector could stroll leisurely down the high street with the only real problem being someone dropping their cigarette butt on the ground. There were bad people who lived in the town, of course there were, but there wasn't a clear anti-police agenda like the one he'd grown up with.

Like the one he'd ignored when he'd watched and idolised his father all those years ago.

The high street wasn't as equipped as the expensive shopping centre, with the outlets comprising shops that sold phone cases and baseball caps, to budget home stores that offered household goods at cheap prices. The street itself was blocked off from vehicles, allowing for a row of pop-up food carts that smelt incredible and stalls where small businesses could pedal their wares. It had an energy to it, one that wasn't entirely positive at times, but it felt like a town that could survive on its own, away from the grasp of the capital city, and the high street stores that comprised the shopping centre.

As they walked, King idly puffed on her vape and she pointed out a couple of sandwich bars that would be worth Townsend's attention. They hadn't really discussed anything on a personal level yet; he was certain that type of connection with the woman would be hard earned, but whatever coldness she'd displayed to his arrival had quickly dissipated. As they approached the shopping centre, the streets became familiar to Townsend, having stared at them for a few hours on his monitor. King led them down the alleyway, and sure enough, the neon pink "P" hung above a small door between two fast-food chains. It was an inconspicuous entrance, one that was easy to miss, which Townsend guessed was the point.

Nobody wanted to advertise that they were heading into a strip club, and he wondered if that was why the CCTV around the area was completely absent.

'This is the place,' King said with a sigh. She shuddered and then reached into her jacket to pull out her phone. It was DSI Hall. 'Give me a few minutes.'

Townsend gave her a thumbs-up and scanned the surrounding area, looking for any sign of CCTV. The fast-food outlets, all reasonably cheap knock-offs of high street staples, couldn't even afford proper signage, let alone security cameras. Across the alleyway, a dirty pub was stuffed into the corner, but judging by the decaying benches and missing letters on the signs, he doubted he'd have much luck there. He glanced over to King, who looked in deep conversation and pulled out his own phone and tapped out a message.

How's girly been? X

He clicked send, and within seconds, Mandy had texted back.

Good as gold. Went to the park. It's really nice around here. How's your day going? Xx

The message filled his heart with joy. Although his daughter had still locked herself off from him, the thought of her enjoying the new life he'd forced upon the family was all he could hope for.

Busy. You wouldn't believe what I'm working on. Have you seen the news? Xx

As the phone indicated his wife was responding, he looked up to see King, a few metres away, finishing up her phone call amidst a cloud of vape smoke.

The message came through.

The body!!?? Babe, that's crazy.

Mandy was still typing.

Another message came through.

I'm so proud of you. You've got this. Xxx

Townsend smiled at his phone screen. Mandy was his rock, and through his years undercover, she never abandoned him. Never berated him for what he was doing. For those who knew what Townsend had been through, they regarded Townsend as one of the toughest people they'd ever met.

But he drew his strength from his wife, who, without a doubt, was the toughest woman he'd ever known.

She believed in him. Now, he needed to generate the same belief in himself.

'Something funny?'

King's voice pierced his concentration and Townsend looked up from his phone. Realising he had a goofy smile spread across his face, he shook it away, and pocketed his device.

'Sorry. Just the wife.'

'Everything okay?' King asked.

'Yeah. Just...you know, kid update.' He sheepishly shrugged. 'Won't happen again.'

'Don't be silly. Family first. Right...let's get some answers.'

King balled her hand into a fist and slammed it against the door of Paradise. The thick wood was jet black, with no windows or security pad. It was just a black void between the two shops.

No answer.

She slammed it again, this time with enough force to turn a few heads of those passing by.

No answer.

'Fuck,' King uttered, stepping back with her hands on her hips. 'A warrant will take too long.'

'We could come back later?' Townsend suggested. He checked his watch. It was only half two, but the day had begun to hang heavy on him.

'We need to speak to the manager now.' King sighed. 'This is the last place Lauren was seen alive, as far as we know, and we need to know who was here and if anything happened. Plus, I've got Hall on my case asking for some progress. Let's get back to see what Hannon has for us.'

Townsend fell in line beside his superior officer, and as they began to head back up the alleyway, he tried to envisage the CCTV. The angles of the camera and the brief second that he saw the figure down the side of the alleyway. With his mind racing, he stepped away from King who turned.

'What are you doing?' she asked, intrigued.

Townsend didn't respond. He stepped across the wide alleyway to the metal bins beside one of the back entrances to the shopping centre. It was the exact spot that he saw the figure flash by, and he looked up at the wall, praying for some sort of camera.

Nothing.

He turned, scanning the unfamiliar high street, peering beyond the pedestrians that scuttled among the food stalls. Directly across from them was a respectable high street bookshop, and Townsend squinted, homing his vision to the doorway.

A CCTV camera.

Excited, he set off across the street, weaving through the public, who had no idea there was a murder investigation among them. King followed as Townsend burst into the shop and marched up to the till, his lanyard raised.

'DS Townsend. I need to speak to the manager.'

The young woman looked at his badge, nodded, and then rushed to the back. King caught up, and Townsend explained the CCTV. Whatever system the council had in place was neither correctly positioned nor offered a good enough picture. He was hoping that the bookshop would be the opposite.

'Hi, I'm the manager. I understand this is a police matter?'

The woman offered her most cooperative smile, something Townsend always found funny from the public. There was no doubt in his mind that the woman led a squeaky-clean lifestyle, but whenever a police presence entered a normal world, people over-egged their helpfulness.

'Yes, we are investigating an incident last night…'

'Not that poor girl I saw on the news, I hope?'

'We can't discuss an ongoing investigation, I'm afraid,' Townsend said, his scouse charm oozing out effortlessly. 'But would it be possible to review your CCTV footage from last night?'

'Yes, of course.' The woman beckoned as she headed to the door at the back of the shop marked 'Staff Only'. 'Follow me.'

Townsend and King obliged, and soon they passed into a narrow corridor, and then a stockroom packed with boxes of books. The manager's office was no bigger than one of the boxes, and as Townsend squeezed his muscular frame into the room with the woman, King glanced over the latest batch of books. She scolded herself for not making more time to read. It was something she enjoyed immensely, but had seemed to sacrifice for the job.

The woman sat at the cramped desk, clicked through a few files, and then the screen was filled with the eight camera angles being recorded in the shop.

There was one on the front door and it offered a clear picture of the street opposite.

More importantly, it offered a view of the bins.

'That one there.' Townsend pointed. 'Can you roll it back to three forty this morning?'

The manager nodded firmly and then began to rewind the footage. As the screen began to speed backwards, Townsend watched as the people sped by, the stalls were deconstructed, and eventually, the midnight hush fell upon the screen.

'There,' he said, and sure enough, the figure could be seen. Clearly male, the hood covered the details of his face, but they caught a brief glimpse of his white skin. 'Can you zoom in?'

'I'm afraid not.' The woman sounded embarrassed.

'Can you take a print of this image?' Townsend asked, and the woman nodded. 'And then, please send the footage of that camera to...'

He turned to the doorway, and an impressed looking King smiled and gave the manager her email address. She then glanced to Townsend with a look that told him that he needed to learn his own.

It was duly noted.

Before they left, Townsend and King asked for her to play the footage one more time, and as the clock at the bottom of the video passed 3.42 a.m., the figure glanced down the alleyway in the direction of Paradise, clearly saw what he was waiting for, and moved swiftly.

King thanked the woman and headed back towards the shop, and Townsend did likewise, with an urgency in his step.

They needed to know who that figure was.

CHAPTER TWELVE

With his pass in his hand, Townsend felt a strange sense of belonging as he followed DI King around the side of the High Wycombe Police Station to the staff entrance. It was only earlier that morning that he'd been gormlessly walking in through the front door, trying his best to wrestle his imposter syndrome from his mind.

Now, he was striding in alongside a respected Detective Inspector, in the throes of a murder investigation.

With pride, he lifted his lanyard to the security panel, and felt himself smile as the light turned green and beeped him through.

He belonged here now.

King hadn't eaten lunch yet, and Townsend followed her to the poorly stocked canteen, casting his eyes across the tables where groups of officers spoke over their lunches. Friendships that had been forged on the beat, based on trust that they always had each other's back. Although the police came in for a lot of stick from the public, it was those unspoken moments of togetherness that made it such an incredible career. Townsend, for the first few years after his father's death, was routinely checked up on by some of his father's old colleagues. That trail went cold when he went deep undercover, but the fact remained that through the time they spent with his father on the beat, they felt tethered to the man's family afterwards. King took a sad looking roll from the fridge, a bottle of water, and then paid at the till.

'We'll see if Hannon can get the image through the system. You never know, we might get lucky.' King shrugged as she opened her bottle and took a swig. 'But good work out there.'

'Thanks, Guv,' Townsend said, battling to hide the smile. King noticed it and smirked.

'So…how's your first day going?' She laughed, and the two of them stepped through the door to the corridor and collided into two other men.

One of them was DCI Marcus Lowe.

'Whoa…come on now, Izzy. Not at work.' The man quipped, turning to his colleague for an approving laugh. It arrived swiftly, if a little forced.

'Let's not do this now,' King said curtly, looking at the ground. 'We have work to do.'

'Oh yes…that's right. The murder investigation that you stole from my team.' Lowe turned to his hanger-on again. 'I guess I didn't get everything in the divorce.'

Townsend looked at the two men as they chuckled, acting like high school bullies, and then glanced to his colleague. For all the strength and resilience the woman was clearly filled with, he could quickly piece together what was going on. Private lives were never considered a good idea within any profession, least of all the police. But to watch his DI, who had been such a steady hand for the day, squirm uncomfortably made Townsend's blood boil.

'Hey, why don't you just go and get your lunch and let us get on with our work, eh?' Townsend suggested, a little forcibly.

'Eh, scouse. Calm down. Calm down.' Lowe chuckled again, his white teeth gleaming under the halogen bulbs. Lowe was tall and handsome, with neat black hair, and a trimmed beard speckled with grey that stood out against his dark skin.

'That's an original joke. Well done.' Townsend rolled his eyes. 'You find that funny?'

Townsend directed the question to the detective beside Lowe, who seemingly panicked.

'Err…' He shot a worried glance to Lowe.

'Oh, I'm sorry, should I ask your boss?' Townsend said, turning to a clearly agitated Lowe. 'Does he find your joke funny?'

'Watch yourself, newbie,' Lowe spat through gritted teeth. 'Remember the chain of command.'

'Apologies. Does he find your jokes funny, sir?'

'Jack, leave it. We've got work to do,' King interjected, but Lowe held up his hand.

'No, no. Big man here has been a detective for one day and thinks he's hot shit.' Lowe took a step towards Townsend, who didn't bat an eyelid. 'I'll tell you what is funny. My ex-wife showing the decency to at least pretend you're a detective, when we all know you're the furthest thing from one.'

The two men stayed still, their eyes locked, neither one of them giving an inch. King sighed and pulled Townsend's arm.

'Dick swinging's over lads,' King said. 'Sorry, Marcus, but we *do* have a murder investigation to be getting on with.'

Lowe cockily smirked and stepped aside.

'For now.'

Townsend bit his tongue, allowing the man to have the final word, and he followed King down the corridor to the stairwell, feeling Lowe's eyes burning into the back of his skull. As they hit the stairs, it seemed like King had been holding her breath and she let out a deep sigh.

'Sorry about that,' she said.

'Don't be.' Townsend shrugged. 'We all have shit, right?'

'Right.' She looked at him and smiled. 'Thanks for having my back.'

'Anytime.'

Another nod of approval and another step closer to their trust being forged. King marched with a renewed purpose through the corridor and pushed open the door to the SCU office. Hannon spun on her seat to welcome them.

'Any luck?' Her eyes were wide with hope behind her glasses.

'No dice,' King replied, plonking herself in Townsend's chair and unwrapping her roll. 'I have an email to send to you. Sherlock Holmes over here found a camera that gave us a better shot of our mystery man.'

'Well, while you two have been out for a little walk, I've been digging up some information on Dean Riley.' Hannon shook her head.

'Bad?'

'Prolific. Nothing too bad, but let's just say the guy has stronger links to the police than Sting.'

The joke fell flat, as Townsend looked to King and shrugged. Obviously, it was a regular thing and King, with her mouth full of cheese and bread, motioned for the young DC to continue.

'He's been nicked six times over the past few years. Drunk and disorderly, few times with possession, but never with intent to sell. A few scraps at kicking out time. A report of domestic abuse, which I guess we could draw a line to the one that we linked to Lauren.'

'He knocked her about?' Townsend spat angrily.

'Possibly.' Hannon turned back to her screen. 'He spent six months in HMP Aylesbury for a burglary two years ago...'

'Right around the time Lauren began working at Paradise?' King asked.

'And got her own place,' Hannon added. 'Now, he's back at home with his mother and...well, he just seems like the best guy.'

Townsend scoffed and stepped closer to the screen to look at the file. Beside the litany of offences was the face of a man who had given up on trying to live a lawful life. It was like looking at every single member of the Bell View Gang that he'd been undercover with.

Shaved head.

Eyebrow piercing.

Acne scars.

A tacky tattoo of curved writing along the side of his neck.

But it was the eyes that told Townsend the man had no remorse for whatever crime he'd committed the day they took the picture. It wasn't so much defiance behind them, but apathy.

He just didn't care.

'Bring him in.' King decided as she vacated the chair. 'I think we should find out what Dean Riley was up to last night, don't you?'

'Yes, guv.' Townsend turned to Hannon and raised his eyebrows. 'You want to drive?'

A wave of panic seemed to wash over Hannon, who went an even paler shade of white. She looked to King, who offered her a reassuring smile.

'Does it need both of us?'

'I have a call to make,' King said sternly. 'Besides, I can't send him out alone on his first day. He'll probably get lost.'

Hannon nodded weakly and then began to lift herself up from her chair. Townsend could sense his colleagues's apprehension, and when King disappeared into her own tiny office, he put his hand on her shoulder.

'You okay?'

'Yeah, just...'

'Don't worry.' He smiled. 'I'm a good driver. Although what the hell is with that roundabout?'

His attempt at levity fell on deaf ears, and as he followed Hannon out of the SCU towards the stairwell, his mind wandered to what the issue was. It was too early to ask such a prying question, the same when it came to her obvious disability.

All he could do was build up enough trust that she'd share it with him.

And the only way to do that was to help her and King solve Lauren Grainger's murder.

Two minutes later, Townsend was pulling out of the station car park and heading towards the 'magic round-about', thankful that the traffic was non-existent.

CHAPTER THIRTEEN

After surviving another trip around the 'magic roundabout', Townsend felt near unbreakable. Having successfully navigated his way around three of the mini roundabouts, he turned off and flew up and over the flyover, shooting glances over the stone walls at the streets below. He could see the Eden Shopping Centre, where he and King had been just an hour or so ago, and then he filtered through the traffic and was soon shooting down West Wycombe Road and into the residential maze that was the rest of the town. Hannon sat quietly, peering out of the window at the passing world and clearly doing her best to keep herself calm. As they passed a petrol station, Townsend looked to Hannon for guidance, and another half a mile up the road, she directed him left.

He turned down a road marked 'Sands', which was another small suburb that clung to fringes of High Wycombe. It was no different from the streets they'd just passed through. There was a large school, one that would be out of their catchment area, and a large industrial unit, surrounded by excavators, and bulldozers, all of them sufficiently sprinkled with rust. They passed a row of the usual convenience shops and then a large pub that had seen better days.

The Hour Glass.

Hannon pointed it out to Townsend as the watering hole for the Wycombe Wanderer's Football Club supporters on match days, and then directed him down a side road that led towards the large industrial estate where their home stadium, Adam's Park was tucked away. Townsend tried to broach the subject of football with her, but again, she seemed distracted.

Finally, they turned left at a roundabout and were presented with nothing but trees and a national speed limit sign. Townsend put his foot down, and as the speedometer shoot upwards, they thundered up the hill and through a tunnel forged by the overhanging trees. The road was narrow, but Townsend kept the car steady and, as they rounded a tight corner, the road widened, and welcomed them forward. There was nothing but trees and bushes, and as they ascended slightly, the view broke out into another serene picture of green fields and the odd collection of cows or sheep.

Townsend was slightly taken aback by the beauty of it, as he had been on some of his other drives.

The notion that people needed to escape the country to visit beautiful countries was driven by profit, as the stunning vista offered as much beauty as you'd see on any other continent.

You just needed to look for it.

The road to Lane End, aptly named Lane End Road, was long, and winding. As they drove, Townsend turned to Hannon, keeping one eye on the road in front.

'Do I smell or something?'

'Excuse me?' Hannon was shaken from her thoughts.

'Do I smell? It's just you didn't seem keen to get in a car with me.'

Hannon chuckled, and Townsend noted a small personal victory on being able to break the tension.

'No, it's just…never mind.'

'Okay, cool,' Townsend said as he drummed his fingers on the steering wheel. 'We've all got our shit.'

'Really?' Hannon turned to him. 'You've got shit?'

'Oh yeah. Major shit.' Townsend grinned, drawing another chuckle from his colleague.

'Tell me, DS Townsend, apart from being in a new area, what shit do you have? You're in good shape, you're good looking, you've got a wife, and a kid, I assume a nice house?'

'Don't forget my relatively new car,' Townsend replied. Hannon nodded. She was playful with her frustration.

'What possible shit do you have?'

Before Townsend could answer, they rounded a corner, and then crossed over a bridge that loomed over the M40. Then, a shooting range, followed by a sign welcoming them to Lane End. With their conversation momentarily halted, Hannon directed Townsend down the hill and then to take the first few turns that led them quite swiftly from an affluent street of large houses, to a cramped and neglected estate that was stuffed away at the back of the village. It was a sharp transition, and Townsend was taken aback by how stark the difference between the streets was.

Gone were the large gardens and expensive cars, replaced by thin houses that were linked together in long rows, all with criminally small gardens that the residents were still trying to maximise. Between each strip of houses was a narrow alleyway, the wooden panels of the fences either broken or rotten. Townsend slowed his car as he got near the top of the hill, and Hannon pointed towards number fifty-two.

Riley's mum's house.

Turning sharply, Townsend crawled into one of the

cramped parking areas and reversed his car next to a broken-down Punto that had a smashed window, a missing tyre, and a litany of foul words sprayed on it.

'Well, this is nice?' Hannon said dryly.

'Reminds me of home,' Townsend said, killing the engine. 'Don't judge people because they live differently to you.'

Hannon could sense the seriousness in her colleague's words and then regarded him carefully.

'So, what shit do you have?'

It dawned on him that his file wasn't likely to have been shared around the police service. DSI Hall had seen it. HR had obviously thought it prevalent that he knew what he was accepting.

There was a strong chance he'd shared some of the information with his senior detectives, such as King, and Lowe. But Hannon seemed none the wiser. She believed he was a stable guy who had just moved to the area.

She deserved to know more.

The truth.

He tapped the scar that sliced through his right eyebrow.

'See this? I got this when a Croatian arms dealer's right-hand man near beat me to death. A few years ago now, but I remember it clear as anything.'

'What the fuck?'

'Long story short, I was undercover for more than three years. First in Liverpool, then I got moved to Suffolk to infiltrate an arms dealing gang. The officer who handled me turned out to be a fucking snake, and it nearly cost me and my wife our lives.'

'Holy shit. Jack, I didn't know—'

'It's not really common knowledge. The Merseyside Police, they wanted to "make things right" and fast tracked me to detective. But it's hard to be a detective in a town where you've been undercover, so after eighteen months, I got detective sergeant, and was told they'd find me somewhere to go. I guess you guys pulled the short straw.'

Silence sat between the two of them for a few moments as Hannon processed the snippets of a life story she'd just heard.

'Well, if it's any consolation, you're doing a pretty good job today.'

'Thanks. I know I can be good at this. I just…' Townsend pulled his lips thin and shook his head. 'Like I said, we've all got shit, right?'

'Yeah.' Hannon took a deep breath. 'Four years ago I was working the beat. Usual routes, usual team. I loved it. I really did. Then one night, we get a call to a potential drug incident. Just kids smoking weed. So we turn up and turns out it's some prick with an axe to grind against the police and a baseball bat. He gets the drop on my partner, knocks him out in one go and then goes to town on me. I mean he beats the living shit out of me. Broke five ribs, my collar-bone, and he stamped on my back so hard that I've still got issues with it.'

'I'm so sorry.' Townsend could feel his muscles tighten with rage.

'Well, I'm still breathing, and that fucker is four years into a very long jail sentence. But you're right, we've all got some shit and I'm now terrified every time I have to leave that office.'

Townsend nodded and then threw open his door.

'You'll be fine this time.'

'Why?'

'Because you're with me.'

Townsend stepped out of the car and straightened his jacket. Hannon pulled herself up, grunting quietly with discomfort, and then they walked back towards the main street. As they did, a few kids shot by on their bikes, glancing backwards with concern.

Townsend knew they stood out, but it didn't matter. They weren't there for trouble.

At least he hoped they weren't.

Hannon was first to the door, and she pushed the bell, and then panicked as she fished her lanyard from her jacket pocket. Townsend coughed, and as she turned, he flashed his lanyard mockingly.

The door opened before she could respond.

Karen Riley sighed, already knowing who they were and the likely reason they were there. She looked tired, as if life had been hard since day one, and she took a puff on her cigarette as she motioned to their badges. Townsend and Hannon duly obliged and lifted them up for her.

'What's the little shit done now?' she asked, her voice croaky from the smoking.

'Nothing,' Townsend said with a smile. 'We just need a word with your son. Is Dean home?'

'Why do you want to talk to him if he's done nothing?' Karen spat back, clearly not a fan of the police.

'It's important we speak to him—' Hannon began.

'Sorry, love, but how old are you? Is it bring your daughter to work day?'

Beyond the woman, Townsend glanced down the hallway that was cramped with furniture and random mess. He saw into the kitchen which needed a good clean, just in time to see the wiry figure of Dean Riley burst through the back door.

'He's making a run for it.' Townsend was already turning onto the street. 'Head back to the car and try to follow.'

He tossed the keys to Hannon and burst forward into a sprint, rounding the corner of the street just in time to see the navy clad figure disappear into one of the alleyways.

Fearlessly, Townsend pursued, launching himself between the wooden fence panels and pushing himself to full speed. He turned a sharp corner, just in time to see Riley scale a fence.

Townsend followed.

Over the next one and they dropped down into another alleyway. Riley was running for his life, and as Townsend began to gain on him, he could hear the desperate gasps for breath from the man.

They emerged out of the alleyway onto a small green, where a rusty old swing set and climbing frame stood, along with a derelict basketball court that hadn't seen a net in years. A few of the local teenagers, clearly with nothing to do, were sitting on the bench smoking, and their eyes all locked on the two men who were racing towards them. Riley slowed, and the second he did, Townsend barrelled into him, sending him crashing into the mesh fence of the basketball court and drawing some noise from the teenagers, who were reaching for their phones.

Townsend took a few steps towards Riley, then glared at the young group.

'Phones away, lads. Otherwise, you'll lose them.'

One of the boys, decked out in a tracksuit similar to Riley, kissed his teeth, and stood up.

'You can't take our shit, mate.'

Townsend stared at him.

'And I'm pretty sure you can't smoke weed on that bench. So how about you make my problem go away and I'll make yours.'

The bargain seemed fair enough, and the bullish teen was soon talked down by his friends as Townsend turned to Riley, who was gasping for breath with his back against the fence.

'Why'd you run, Dean?' Townsend asked. He wasn't one iota out of breath, a testament to his fitness regime.

'I ain't done nothin',' Riley said with a sneer.

'So why'd you run?'

'Because you pigs are always trying to fuckin fit me up for stuff, init?'

'Well, we need to talk to you about something. So why don't you come with me? We'll do that and then this will all be over.'

Townsend glanced around the green, noticing a few of the local curtain twitchers had walked round to see the commotion. A scene was beginning to be caused.

'Fuck you. Am I under arrest?'

'No. Do you want me to arrest you? Running from the police and all that.'

Realising his defiance was pointless, Riley sighed, and agreed. Townsend took him by the arm, squeezing firmly enough to educate the man on what would happen if he tried to break free. The group of teenagers called out after Riley, with one of them calling him a legend, which Townsend found depressing. Hannon pulled the car up at the end of the pathway, and Townsend shoved Riley into the back of it, warning him to behave. As he and Hannon switched seats, Hannon fastened her seat belt and spoke quietly.

'Thanks, Jack.'

Townsend shot a glance to Riley in the rearview, and the young man had his head pressed against the window and a bored look on his face. He started up the engine, turned to Hannon, and smiled.

'Don't mention it.'

CHAPTER FOURTEEN

The interview rooms at High Wycombe Police Station were identical to those in any other station. A dark, dingy room with little natural light. A metal table, along with four chairs, two on either side.

No personality.

No niceties.

The way it was supposed to be.

Townsend stepped through the door holding two plastic cups of water and all heads turned to him. King smiled her appreciation as he placed one down in front of her on the table, and then he reached across and popped the other in front of Dean Riley. The young man sneered at Townsend, flashing his stained teeth. After the initial submission at the basketball court, Riley had snapped back into his aggressive, confrontational self, and had been a nuisance since they'd been back at the station.

'Here you go,' Townsend said, gesturing to the water. 'Now, let's talk, shall we?'

'I need a piss now,' Riley said cockily.

'Then I suggest you piss your pants, because until I get some answers from you, you're not going anywhere,' King cut in, her eyes burning a hole right through Riley. The young man acted tough, but she could see she made him nervous.

'You can't deny my right to the bathroom,' Riley protested.

'I can do whatever the hell I want,' King said, impressing Townsend with her sharp tone. 'I've been here for nearly twelve hours today, and my patience is wearing a little thin. So, unless you want to be known by your friends as the guy who pissed himself when questioned by the police, maybe we should hurry up and get on with it. That okay?'

'Fine.' Riley sighed. 'What the hell do you guys want?'

'Lauren Grainger.'

'That bitch,' Riley scoffed, drawing a glare from King. 'What's she said I've done now?'

'Nothing.' Townsend's turn. 'Her body was found this morning in the lake across the road. Twenty-two stab wounds in all.'

The colour drained from Riley's face, the panic already setting in as his eyes bulged.

'She's fucking dead?'

'I'm afraid so.' King clasped her hands together. 'DS Townsend and I are investigating her murder, and your name has come to our attention.'

'Y-you think I did this?'

'We don't know who did it. Yet,' King said with authority. A promise for justice. 'But right now, we are trying to eliminate as many possibles from the list so we can get this young girl some semblance of justice. I had a horrible chat with her mother earlier today…'

'I bet that was fun,' Riley said, clearly over his grief.

King slammed her fist on the table, snapping Riley up straight, and alerting Townsend.

'Answer me this, have you ever had to look into the eyes

of a parent and tell them that their child had been murdered? That someone so evil, so vile, had the drive to end their life?' Silence. King continued. 'No. After the woman managed to find her breath again, she mentioned your name. Dean Riley. You dated Lauren, didn't you? Right before you went to HMP Aylesbury?'

'So?'

'So tell us about it. Were you happy together?'

Riley shook his head and leant forward, his hands on the table.

'She was a bit wild. Enjoyed the party scene. Drink. Drugs. Same as me. Same as most people with a bit of fucking fun in them. Then I got sent down, and she started selling her fucking pussy to whoever paid enough.'

'She began sex working?' Townsend asked with a raised eyebrow.

'Not as such. But you think there's a difference between taking your kit off and gyrating on dirty old men in a club than there is in a hotel room?'

'I think there is a big difference between dancing for an audience and selling your body for money,' King stated firmly.

'Good for you,' Riley spat back. 'But I don't agree with that feminist bullshit. I went down, I came back, and Lauren had become a dirty whore, so that was that.'

Townsend could sense the anger trembling through his superior officer's body, so took the lead.

'You say that was that? You never saw her again.'

'What, for like a cheeky fuck? I couldn't afford her anymore, mate. You could, probably. Well…could have.'

Townsend locked his eyes on Riley, meeting the arrogant gaze head on. The man clearly didn't care that his ex-girlfriend had been brutally murdered, and was now seemingly revelling in showing it. King was sitting, arms folded, her eyes on Riley, and her mind racing.

'Just to clarify, Dean....and this is very fucking important...' Townsend's anger was creeping through. 'You didn't see her again?'

Riley leant across the table.

'Nope. Can I go now?'

'Where were you last night?' King finally spoke.

'Last night. Dunno. Out.'

'Out where?'

'I don't know, I was off my nut wasn't I?'

'So you can't account for your actions last night?' King nodded and then turned to Townsend. 'I'd say that's sufficient enough to hold him till at least tomorrow. What do you think?'

'I agree, guv.'

'What? You can't keep me here. I'm not even under arrest.'

'Do you want me to arrest you?' Townsend asked with a shrug. 'No.'

'I didn't think so.' Townsend stood, as did King. 'Guv?

'I'll send one of the uniforms to see him out. And Dean, I want you to have a really long think tonight about where you were last night.'

'Fuck off'

"Atta' boy. I'll be speaking to you soon.' King headed to the door and yanked it open, and Townsend followed her through. King motioned to one of the uniforms sat at a desk across the room and then jutted her thumb towards the door behind her. 'Get rid of him, will you? Feel free to take your time.

The officer gave a thumbs up and King smiled and walked off.

'He's a bit of a knob,' Townsend added.

'They usually are,' the officer said dryly, much to Townsend's amusement.

After a quick stop at the canteen for a coffee that

wasn't complete sludge, Townsend followed King back down the stairs to their office. He glanced down at his father's watch.

He'd been at work for just under twelve hours.

And it clearly told.

'You should head home, Jack,' King said as they walked down the corridor. 'It's been a long day.'

'What about Paradise?'

'Nothing. Their website has little to no information and the mobile phone number we have for Sykes, the owner, keeps going straight to voicemail.'

'Should they be open today?'

'I'd have thought so. It's a bit strange. The news of Lauren's death isn't public knowledge yet, so why would he have closed up?' King said with a frown. 'I've got uniform hunting him down, but until we can locate him, we're up slack alley.'

'Want me to stay behind and try to find him?'

King contemplated it for a moment and then shook her head.

'No, get yourself off home. It's been a busy first day. But tomorrow, we need to speak to that man and find out what happened in that club last night. Speak to the other dancers. Check if they have CCTV. Any dodgy customers. Everything.'

'Agreed.' Townsend awkwardly nodded and smiled at the same time. 'Thanks, guv.'

He followed her into the office. Hannon had already left, although she'd stuck a Post-it note to Townsend's screen of a smiley face. He shook his head and showed King.

'She's a funny one,' King said with a wry smile.

'You heading home, guv?'

'In a bit. Few things I need to handle. Hell of a first day, huh?'

'Yeah, if I knew it was going to be this busy, I'd have stayed back home.'

'Well, you did some good work today. Thank you.' King looked a little concerned.

'Thanks. You, too.' His compliment seemed to land and he could feel a bond being forged. They were a small team, up against it, but all three of them had shown that finding Lauren's murderer was their only concern. As the compliments hung in the air, Townsend tucked his chair under his desk. 'Same again tomorrow?

'Oh yes,' King said. 'We've got a killer to catch.'

Townsend left his boss to it, headed towards the stairwell, and put Mandy and Eve in his mind's eye.

He needed to see them.

It was time to go home.

CHAPTER FIFTEEN

As he turned onto the street that was now his home, Townsend took a moment to savour the surroundings. The semi-detached, three-bedroomed houses were all set back from the street, tucked behind well-kept gardens, or neatly paved driveways. There were a few cars parked on the street itself, but what struck Townsend most was how quiet it was.

Not just his street, but the entire village.

Heck, the entire town.

Having grown up and then started a family in Liverpool, the tranquillity of village life was something he knew he'd have to adapt to.

He enjoyed it.

But he'd need to get used to it.

Townsend pulled his car up onto the drive, pulling up snugly behind Mandy's Ford Fiesta, before killing the engine. He looked up at the house, the building that didn't quite feel like home yet, but he knew what was waiting on the other side of the door.

His entire world.

As he walked from his car to his front door, he looked

across the street to a neighbour who was dumping a packed bin liner into their rubbish bin. Townsend raised a hand and received one back. The neighbourhood had a tight-knit feel to it, and he knew that Mandy was keen to get involved in it. That was where their opposites came to the fore.

Although Townsend was good with people, he wasn't one for idle small talk or forced social situations. Mandy, on the other hand, loved to make friends and throw herself into events with the confidence that he found endearing.

So much so, in fact, that as he stepped through the front door, he had a beaming smile on his face, one that only intensified when he smelt the food cooking in the kitchen.

'Smells good,' he called out, shuffling out of his jacket and dumping it on the banister. He stepped past the flat-pack box of the hallway table Mandy had designated to him and into the kitchen.

'Here he is,' Mandy said gleefully. 'DS Townsend.'

'Eurgh, don't call me that here, please. I get that enough at work,' Townsend said with a grin, wrapping his arms around his wife and then pressing his lips against hers.

'Eurgh. Don't do that in here, please. I've just eaten.'

The snappy comment came from behind him, and he turned to the kitchen table where Eve sat, her elbows on the table and her chin on her hands. In front of her was her tablet, playing the final few scenes of Frozen.

Her favourite.

'Let it go, Pickle. Let it go.' Townsend joked, and although she tried to stifle it, a little grin spread across her face. 'Is that a smile?'

'No.'

Townsend took a few steps towards her.

'Are you sure? I'm a detective, I can tell these things.'

As he took another step towards her, she tried not to smile again. To bring it on home, Townsend began to sway terribly and burst into a full rendition of the widely popular song from the film. Behind him, Mandy cackled at his off-key singing, and sure enough, Eve cracked too.

Just hearing her laugh was worth the embarrassment. He stopped behind her chair, and peered at the screen and then leant down and kissed her on the top of the head. He then took the seat next to her.

'You're in a good mood, all things considered,' Mandy said, scooping the spaghetti out of the saucepan and into the new, stylish round bowls she'd bought as a 'moving present'.

There had been a lot of them.

'Well, I get to come home to you two, don't I?' He winked at Eve, who turned her attention back to the screen. 'Besides, I think I made some progress.'

'On the investigation?' Mandy asked, topping the pasta with the bolognese sauce and then a generous helping of parmesan cheese. 'That poor girl…'

'I know. Horrible.'

'The fact you had to see it.' Mandy shuddered. 'I don't know how you do it.'

'Someone has to. And besides, I think I might be quite good at it.'

She placed the bowl down in front of him, along with a fork, and then opened the oven. A waft of smells emerged, and she took out half a stick of garlic bread and put it on a side plate and as she sat down opposite her husband, she put the plate next to his dinner.

'I know you're good at it, Jack. Doesn't change the fact you have to see some horrible things.' Mandy sipped from her glass of wine. 'But here you go, your favourite dinner.'

'You mean the easiest dinner?'

'Listen here, mister detective. If you think I'm going to

be doing this every day, you can think again.' The two of them smiled at each other and she watched with a warm smile as he tucked in. 'So, you made some progress?'

'Yeah. Well…' Townsend finished his mouthful, then continued. 'Baby steps on the case. But I think I got on quite well with the team.'

'That's good.' Mandy stood and went to the tall standing fridge, and pulled out a beer. She popped the cap off on the magnetic opener affixed to the fridge door and then handed it to her grateful husband. 'To new beginnings.'

Townsend lifted his beer and clinked the glass.

'New beginnings.' He took a swig and set it down. 'How was your day? How was the park?'

He looked to Eve, but she was lost in the movie, so he turned back to his wife.

'All good. She had fun…made a few friends. She's good like that.'

'Gets that from you,' Townsend said, then stuffed another forkful into his mouth.

'Speaking of new beginnings, I have some news.' Mandy opened her mouth wide as if in shock. 'I have an interview next week for a VA position for a marketing start-up in Oxford.'

'Oh, well done…' Townsend's smile quickly shifted to confusion. 'Two things…what's a start-up and what's a VA?'

Mandy laughed and took a sip of her drink. Townsend couldn't help but marvel at her. Every feature on her face was perfect, from her ice blue eyes to the perfect curve of her nose.

They were facial features he had memorised and thought about everyday he was undercover.

'I forget that you don't really exist in the modern world.' Mandy chuckled.

'I do. I just don't do all this social media shit.'

'Language,' Mandy said with a laugh. Eve looked up cheekily, seemingly pleased at the swear word. Townsend raised a hand to his mouth, pretending to be shocked.

Eve giggled again.

He was breaking through.

Mandy sat back in her chair and continued.

'It's a new marketing agency. Just got off the ground. It's not huge, but they have some big clients now and are looking to grow.'

'Ah, they've just started up. Gotcha.' Townsend put his fork into the empty bowl and went about polishing off the remnants with garlic bread. 'And a VA is?'

'Virtual Assistant.'

'Virtual?' Townsend frowned.

'I'll work predominantly from here. So I work virtually. Come on, detective. Keep up.' She finished her glass of wine and watched adoringly as her husband finished his dinner. 'But it's good. I think. I'll get to work from here so can dip in and out for school runs and once or twice a month I get to go into the office and actually work with people.'

Townsend finished the last slice of garlic bread.

'People are overrated.'

'Well, considering I took three years off to be a single parent, and the last few years I couldn't really go out for my own safety, working with people, overrated, or otherwise, is very appealing.'

Townsend stood, collected his bowl, and then gave his wife a big kiss on the top of the head.

'Well done, babe. I'm proud of you.'

Mandy leant back into him for a few moments and then took his bowl to the dishwasher. As he then began to gather the other dirty pots and utensils, Mandy clapped her hands together and snatched their daughter's attention.

'Right, miss. Time to get ready for bed.'

'It's still sunny outside.' Eve protested.

'Yeah, well, it won't be in your room. Now, off, and up them stairs.'

Townsend turned around from the dishwasher.

'Do you want me to read you a book, pickle?'

'No, Mum can do it.'

Mandy shot a sorrowful glance to Townsend, and then a reassuring nod that he was getting there.

Eve then hammered it home.

'Goodnight, Daddy.'

It was the first time since they'd moved that she'd said it, clearly taking down some of the barriers that had been put up ever since his absence. Townsend felt his heart melt, composed himself, and called out after her as she ran up the stairs.

'Goodnight, pickle. Love you.'

There was no response, but there didn't need to be one. Mandy disappeared up the stairs behind her, and Townsend finished loading the dishwasher and then made sure to switch it on. Too many times he'd come down in the morning, only to find he'd stacked the machine but not actually set it in motion.

As it rumbled to life, Townsend picked up his beer and headed to the back door, stopping to hear as his two loves giggled together.

It would take a while before he could join in, but he still smiled warmly.

They were getting there.

Slowly but surely.

He took a seat on one of the wicker chairs that sat neatly on the patio, took a sip of his beer and then sat it on the glass-top table. The sun was beginning its decline beyond the trees, but the warmth of the evening was welcome.

He closed his eyes.

Willing himself to switch off and enjoy the new life he was starting with those he cared most about.

But all he could think about was the mutilated body of Lauren Grainger, and how they needed to find that bastard in the dark hoodie.

As he finished off the bottle of beer, he headed back inside for another, already accepting that her death had consumed his mind.

CHAPTER SIXTEEN

The next morning started like any other for DC Hannon.

She woke ten minutes before her 6 a.m. alarm, her body clock so well-tuned that it didn't need the assistance. After a few moments to gather herself, she switched her alarm off, allowing her partner the extra half hour of uninterrupted sleep as she went to the spare room of their quaint, two-bed house in Chesham. There, she laid out her yoga mat and then put herself through her thirty-minute stretching routine, gritting her teeth through the discomfort that her physio had said would be permanent.

Two of her vertebrae had been cracked in such a way that they'd healed as much as they could, but would forever cause a locking sensation at the base of her spine. At twenty-six years of age, she was certified disabled, but she refused to allow it to define who she was.

Shilpa's alarm went off just as Hannon put herself through her final stretch, and sure enough, her girlfriend appeared at the doorway, rubbing the sleep from her eyes and asking if she'd fed Beans yet.

And, as always, it had slipped Hannon's mind.

She wasn't much of a cat person, but Shilpa had

brought her kitten with her when Hannon had asked her to move in with her on their first anniversary. In the seven months since, she'd become fond enough of the little guy, but not enough to make him a priority.

It was only one of two points of contention that their otherwise loving relationship faced.

As Shilpa made her way downstairs, clicking her voice for the cat to join her, Hannon stripped off, and stepped into the shower, standing for ten minutes to allow the warm water to filter over her body. Then, after quickly brushing her teeth, she sat at her dressing table and dried her hair, before pulling out a white shirt and black trousers from her immaculate wardrobe. It was the mirror opposite of Shilpa's, which was a mishmash of colours, all thrown into a pile, and it gave Hannon an anxiety crisis just to look at it.

But it was why she loved her with all her heart.

When she'd been assaulted all those years ago, it wasn't just her spine that had been permanently damaged. Her mental state had been forever altered, and the carefree, action seeking girl of the past had been replaced by one who saw the world for how terrifying it was. Where excitement had once resided, fear now stood in its place. Risk wasn't a positive for her anymore, and she found that Shilpa's carefree attitude was the perfect counterbalance to her caution.

After running a brush through her thick, curly ginger hair, Hannon stood and then shuffled down the stairs towards the gorgeous smell of a fresh coffee and the humdrum of Radio One playing off their smart speaker.

'Morning,' Shilpa said with a smile. Beans sat at her feet, tucking into his breakfast. 'How's your back?'

'Same as ever.' She kissed her and smiled. 'Sleep well?'

'Yeah, not bad. Although I couldn't stop thinking about the meeting today.'

Hannon nodded, faking interest in the constant stream of meetings that Shilpa had to attend as a Health and Safety Manager for a big corporation. It was as mundane a subject that she could think of, but she always ensured she listened intently to be able to ask questions that would prove she cared. She was pretty sure Shilpa knew that, too.

Another reason to love her.

'How about you?' Shilpa asked, sipping her coffee. 'Feeling better after yesterday?'

Hannon smiled meekly. She'd left the office before Townsend or King had returned, and the moment she'd pulled out of the car park, she'd broken. The photos of Lauren Grainger's body were imprinted on her mind, and although she knew it was all part of the job, it was a haunting ordeal to be one of the people responsible for finding her killer. The pain and devastation that had been caused, but also the fear that the poor woman would have experienced as she died in the dark.

When Shilpa had arrived home from one of her trips into the London office, she'd found Hannon sitting in their modest garden, already halfway through a bottle of red. The bottle was sat on the kitchen side, along with the empty pizza box they'd had delivered.

'I'll be fine.' Hannon waved dismissively.

'Come on now, Nic. You can tell me.'

'Honestly. I think I just need to get my head round the gravity of it all. Usually, I'm chasing up traffic offences then suddenly. BAM! Murdered woman. It was just a lot to take is all.'

'Does Izzy know?' Shilpa said, crossing her arms.

'No. As much as I love DI King, I don't want her to see how much this got to me.' Hannon frowned. 'I should give her more credit, but I don't know…I don't want to appear weak.'

'Yeah, I know.'

'What's that supposed to mean?' Hannon snapped, out of character. Shilpa frowned at her.

'I'm just saying, there are things you don't like to share with the people closest to you because you care too much what they think.'

'Oh, not this again...' Hannon waved her hands and began to gather things – her phone, her lanyard, etc.

The other point of contention had reared its head again. As she snatched her keys from the kitchen counter, she turned, and marched through to the living room, past their plush corner sofa that sat opposite the wide-screen TV where they loved nothing more than binge-watching numerous critically-acclaimed TV series.

Shilpa followed her.

'I'm not having a go, babe. I'm not.' She looked defeated. 'But we've been together for nearly two years now...'

'My parents wouldn't understand,' Hannon uttered, feeling her shame. 'They just wouldn't.'

'But would Izzy?'

'I don't know...'

'Because you're too scared to be yourself. I'm sorry, but I don't understand why you're ashamed to be gay.'

'I'm not...'

'I get that it's hard to tell people, but there comes a point where it begins to hurt. I know this isn't about me, babe, but it's not good for you to keep it hidden.'

Hannon could feel a lump growing in her throat, and a silent rage building in the back of her mind for having to confront this the day after her murder investigation had begun. How had they even got onto the topic? It felt like Shilpa had it primed in the chamber and it was clear that Hannon's lack of courage in coming out to those closest to her was beginning to have a negative impact on their relationship.

Their home was one of happiness, and a real haven from the world outside.

The last thing Hannon wanted was to upset the equilibrium of her life.

She opened her mouth to answer, when her phone buzzed in her hand. She glanced down at the title of the email.

It was First Direct.

Lauren's bank.

Her bank statements and logins were attached.

'Oh shit,' Hannon said involuntarily.

'What is it?'

Hannon stepped towards Shilpa and kissed her. Despite the argument, Shilpa returned in kind, and the two of them held each other with a little extra firmness. Neither one of them wanted to let go of the moment, or their relationship.

But there were obstacles to clear.

Barriers to break down.

Hannon stepped back and felt the calmness flow through her body as she looked into her beloved girlfriend's brown eyes.

'I have to go. But let's talk later.'

'Okay.' Shilpa, to her credit, never held Hannon's job against her. She understood.

'I want to be better.' Hannon smiled, then kissed Shilpa once more and then pushed open the door. The narrow street they lived on was a nightmare to park on, with none of the houses offering any sort of driveway. It was a free-for-all when it came to parking, and Hannon had found a spot a good three-minute walk from their house.

Then, it would be a twenty-five-minute drive to the office, especially if she missed the M40 build-up around Beaconsfield.

She wanted to be there in twenty.

With a spring in her usually laboured step, Hannon banished any of the negativity of the morning out of her mind and concentrated on two things.

Finding something to help track down Lauren Grainger's killer.

And getting home to Shilpa and making things right.

CHAPTER SEVENTEEN

Another easy journey into the office had already filled Townsend with a better mood, that, and the memory of Mandy's naked body on top of him from the night before. After she'd put their daughter to bed, Mandy had joined him on the decking of their garden with a beer of her own and they'd spoken about the future.

About her new job.

Then, about the case.

As Townsend spoke with such purpose about finding justice for Lauren Grainger, Mandy had taken his face in her hands and kissed him passionately. That kiss had led the two of them to stumble up the stairs to their bedroom, where they'd made love and then fallen asleep in each other's arms. Waking up before his alarm, Townsend had shut it off, quickly showered, and then headed off to work, allowing the two most important people in his life to sleep in.

It had put a spring in his step, and after he had parked his car behind the police station, he had bypassed the side door and headed to Hannon's coffee shop where he recounted the order from yesterday and picked up three coffees before heading back to the station. A few officers nodded their greetings to him, which he returned in kind, before he delved underground to their office.

'Morning,' he said with a smile.

Hannon turned to greet him and eagerly took her coffee. King was already in her office, on the phone, but she waved. He held up the coffee, and she soon hung up the phone to collect it.

'Thanks, Jack. Much needed.'

King looked a little worse for wear.

Tired? Stressed? Hungover?

Townsend could speculate all day, but instead, he turned on his computer and took a seat at his desk. King leant against it, sipping the hot drink.

'Ready for day two?' she asked.

'If it's anything like day one, I doubt it.'

'Fair point. We'll stop by Paradise at midday.'

'Can't we go knock down the door now?' Townsend asked.

'Not right now. If Sykes is hiding anything, or if something did happen there that night, the last thing we want to do is get off on the wrong foot,' King said, her experience shining through. 'Apparently, they do a lunchtime show on Tuesdays, so let's just go when the doors open.'

'I bet that's nice,' Hannon said without looking away from her screen. 'Beats a Tesco meal deal.'

Townsend chuckled and then leant forward, peering at Hannon's screen.

'Is that Lauren's bank statements?'

'Yup,' Hannon said proudly. 'I got the access this morning. So that's me done for the day.'

'Boring as it may be, the clue to her murder might be one line on one statement,' King interjected. 'It's important work.'

'I know, I know. It's just…it's hardly ransacking a strip club, is it?'

'First off, we aren't ransacking it. We're just going to go ask some questions. Last thing we want to do is put the manager's back up when we have information we need to gather. And second, I didn't think you liked going out of the office?'

Townsend sipped his coffee before interrupting.

'That was before she got to go out with me. We had a hell of a time, didn't we?'

'Oh yeah. Nothing like watching you chase an upstanding citizen through an estate.' Hannon swivelled in her chair. 'Speaking of which, are we following up with him today? He was so charming.'

'No. We don't have anything else to ask him right now.' King shrugged, ignoring the smart comment. 'He'll undoubtedly tell us to fuck off again if we ask where he was on the night.'

'We could bring him in for another afternoon?' Townsend suggested. 'That might break him.'

'We don't have the resources. Besides, we've got more important things to deal with. Let me know if you find anything, okay?'

Hannon nodded to King, who went to turn to her office. Townsend, hands behind his head, stopped her in her tracks.

'I don't think it's to do with money.'

She turned, perched on the edge of her desk and folded her arms.

'Go on.'

He could see she was coaching him, affording him the opportunity to spread his detective wings.

'I've read the SOCO reports. No sign of anything missing from her bag. Debit cards still in there. Phone still in there. If she owed someone money, they wouldn't have killed her, because they'd never see a penny of it. It wasn't a robbery gone wrong, otherwise they'd have taken her stuff.'

'Perhaps they panicked?' King offered. She watched Townsend intently as he shook his head.

'What? And stabbed her twenty-two times? Hell of a panic attack. I know I'm new to this team, but I've been a detective for eighteen months, and in the police for over ten years. People don't butcher people like this for a smartphone. They kill for one of three reasons – desperation, passion, or revenge.' Townsend looked to King who encouraged him to continue. 'A desperate person is someone looking for money or whatever else. They didn't take anything. The post-mortem isn't back yet, but I don't think we'll find any sexual assault. This wasn't desperation.'

'Revenge?' Hannon asked, turning in her chair.

'Perhaps. But for what? What could a twenty-three-year-old dancer have done to someone that would make them brutally kill her in cold blood?'

'Theft?' Hannon asked after a short pause.

'Maybe. So yeah, you might find the motive in those bank statements. But again, if she'd stolen something from someone, they won't get it back if she's dead.'

King nodded along.

'So passion?' she finally asked.

'That would be my gut reaction. The number of stab wounds, the public place. Someone waited for her. We know that, we've seen the footage. Someone waited for their moment alone with her in the dead of night and they stuck a knife in here. And whatever the reason, it was enough for them to do it again and again and again while they got whatever evil out of their system.'

Townsend's harrowing account of the murder hung in the air for a few uncomfortable moments, as the severity of their task became clear. King took the final sip of her coffee and then pushed herself off the desk.

'Good work. I like your thinking and I don't want us to discount anything, but I think you're on the right track.'

'Thanks, guv.'

'Hannon, get into those records, and try to pick out anything unusual.'

'Like what?' She lifted her notepad.

'I don't know. Irregular incomings or outgoings. Something that isn't a regular payment or doesn't seem like it connects with our victim. Even if it is nothing, it could be something.'

'On it.'

Hannon swivelled in her chair and immediately lost herself in the screen before her. King headed to her office, but then dipped her head back out.

'Townsend.'

'Yes, guv.' He turned to face her, sipping his coffee. She motioned for him to follow her. He stood, took off his jacket which he realised he hadn't removed, and then stepped into her tiny cupboard she called home. 'Everything okay?'

King had been issued with a laptop, something clearly above his paygrade, and she spun it round with a frown.

'No matches for our guy in the hoody.'

'Damn. It was a long shot.'

'Yes, but another dead end. We can put out a notice for a man of reasonable build in a black hoody, but I doubt we'll get much.'

'Still, we know it's a man, and that whoever did this was lying in wait.'

King sat back and put her fingers together. Again, she looked a little under the weather, but Townsend knew they were not at the point in their relationship where he could pry. It was only their second day as a team, but he needed to build up that trust.

'Everything okay, guv?'

King seemed to snap back into the room.

'Yes. Sorry. I didn't get much sleep.' She shrugged. 'These things become all-consuming, you know?'

'We'll catch whoever did this.'

'We have to.' King's words were as serious as they were desperate. 'I've got some bullshit red tape to cut through, but we need to be good to go by twelve. Back to work.'

'Yes, guv.'

'One last thing…' He turned to her and was immediately caught off guard by her forced smile. 'Can you write up a report on our little chat with Riley? I know he was an ignorant little shit, but we need to do this properly.'

'Sure thing.'

Townsend took the two steps that were needed to reach the door back to the slightly bigger office, when King looked up once more.

'Oh, and Jack…be nice.'

Townsend smiled.

'I'll try.'

CHAPTER EIGHTEEN

It had been clear to DCI Marcus Lowe from an early age that he could own any room he walked into. He was tall, dark, and handsome, but he possessed the wit and charm to go with it. It made him a leader in the eyes of his superiors and during the early stages of his career in the Metropolitan Police, he was able to produce great results by channelling all his skills into his work.

The public loved him.

Criminals were scared of him.

The superiors respected him.

It all came so easily. It took him only a few years to make detective, while his fiancé at the time, Isabella King, searched for her fix of adrenaline in the Armed Response Team. Their romance had been one built on intense pressure, with both of them finding an outlet for the stresses of the job between the sheets. What had started off as a white-hot fling soon grew into a deep connection, one they couldn't find outside of the force. In separate teams, the higher ups and Human Resources didn't see too many problems, but when King made her way to CID after a few years, things started to become a little strained. Lowe had already been promoted to detective sergeant and not long after his now wife had joined the team, he was Detective Inspector. To her credit, King had never wanted any preferential treatment and Lowe was just as happy to drag her across the coals as he was to compliment her for a job well done.

And that happened a lot.

King was one of the finest detectives he had ever worked with, and as they approached their mid-thirties, the couple decided the time was right to start a family. Having spent over a decade policing the streets of London, they landed on Buckinghamshire as the place to do it, moving to a four-bedroom house in the popular Marlow. King had just secured a promotion to Detective Inspector, and the husband-and-wife detective team transferred to the CID of Thames Valley Police.

But as with all good rides, the wheels soon began to fall off and after eight months of trying for a baby, the stress began to set in.

Planned sex lacked the thrill of the spontaneous passion filled romps of their past, and soon, all their conversations were about conception and possible changes to their lifestyle to help it along. It drove a wedge between them and as far as Lowe was concerned, it was what drove him into the arms of Keeley.

He'd never intended to be the type of man who would cheat on his wife, but like father like son, he had done. He'd met her during one of his cases, as she'd known the victim of an assault outside a nightclub in Maidenhead that he'd been called in to investigate alongside the Berkshire branch of CID. Keeley was a marketing manager for a tech firm, a job that he still hadn't been bothered to feign any interest in.

But there was a spark.

The same spark that he'd shared with King all those years ago.

For six long months, he'd hidden his deceit from the woman he'd sworn his loyalty to, but then the day came when King pushed for them to seek medical assistance for their conception that he broke down and told her of his infidelity. He'd wept for hours, ashamed of the man he'd become and the one that he would hide from the colleagues who idolised him at work. To them, he was an alpha male, and he knew that they'd never believe King if she told them of how he had cried his pathetic apology out to her as he packed his bag and left their home for good.

A year had passed since that night of weakness, and he, and Keeley were as passionate as ever. His promotion to Detective Chief Inspector and head of CID had seemingly poured fuel on their flame and every evening that he got home to her, he felt invincible. At work, he had hit his stride, even managing to offload his ex-wife into a newly created division that would keep her locked in the basement, busying herself with cold cases and menial tasks.

Life had been great.

Until Lauren Grainger had been murdered.

The death of the young woman had finally reached the local news, and all eyes were on the High Wycombe Police to find her killer and deliver justice for the poor girl.

Except they weren't looking at him.

They were looking at his ex-wife.

Fate had handed the case over to his wife, who despite the horrific few years she'd been through, was still as resilient, and frustratingly headstrong as she'd always been.

She was also still a tremendous detective.

Professional rivalry shouldn't interrupt their duty to the public, but Lowe knew how the game was played, and if King and her preposterous team managed to deliver, then his authority would be questioned. He'd be shown up, and for a man who was held in such high regard by the rest of his department, he couldn't contemplate that happening.

He also couldn't show it.

Which was why, despite the anxiety that had begun to nestle at the back of his mind, he was boorishly striding through the police station, followed by two of his junior detectives who clung to his every word. He'd just taken them to the on-site gym facility, where he ran a weekly boxing class, as well as sparring in there every morning without fail. As a youngster, he had enjoyed the sport, but his career, and lifestyle had taken him away from achieving any real level of skill at it.

But it was more than most, and combined with his towering height and impressive physique, being the boxing expert in the station added yet another layer of macho credibility to his name.

'Don't worry, Jay. I'm sure you'll figure out how to punch by next week.' He joked, and one of his followers laughed at the other. 'Maybe focus less on beating your meat and hit the bag a little more, eh?'

The crude joke drew another forced laugh from one of the junior detectives while the other feebly smiled.

It was all hazing.

A few female police constables walked past, and Lowe offered them a smile, ensuring that his exposed arms were tensed, flexing his impressive biceps. One of them gave an impressed glance and then he stopped outside the gents' toilets and turned to the two men who were shadowing his every step.

'You ladies coming in with me? Or are you going back to work?'

The young detective who had been the butt of the jokes took the opportunity to scamper off, while the other followed Lowe into the bathroom. In silence, the two men stood at the urinal, their eyes facing the grim tiles before them as they abided by the socially accepted bathroom etiquette. As they both finished up and approached the sinks to wash their hands, Lowe began bragging about his exploits once more when the door to the bathroom opened.

Jack Townsend.

Lowe grinned as the newly arrived detective saw him, rolled his eyes, and then approached one of the urinals. Lowe finished washing his hands and then smiled at the young detective who seemingly worshipped his every move. As the urine began to clatter against bowl before Townsend, Lowe stepped behind him, a few centimetres from his ear.

'Day two, huh?'

'Boundaries.'

'Excuse me?' Lowe frowned.

'Sorry. Boundaries, sir.'

Lowe scoffed. He wasn't used to having his authority ignored.

'You know, an ego is a really bad trait for a detective sergeant.'

Townsend kept his eyes dead ahead as he answered.

'And a Detective Chief Inspector.'

Lowe stepped to the side of the urinal to look Townsend in the eye, offering the new detective his most intimidating glare.

'You need to watch your fucking mouth, scouse. You understand me.'

Townsend smirked, shook, and then zipped up his trousers.

'Show's over.' He winked at Lowe and then headed to the sink, but the other detective stepped in his way. Townsend smiled and shook his head. 'What is this, guys? Are we really going to do this?'

Lowe stepped behind Townsend.

'What, teach you some manners? Or teach you how things are run around here?'

'Is this because I didn't laugh at your terrible joke yesterday?' Townsend turned around, going almost nose to nose with the DCI. 'I'm sorry. I'll make sure I do next time. It won't be hard, because I assume all of them are just as bad.'

'You got a smart mouth, Townsend. But let me educate you about how the next few weeks will go for you. You and your little team will make fuck all progress and Hall will hand the case over to me and my more qualified team. King will go back to filing away my paperwork with her little helper and you will be out on your arse as just another guy who couldn't hack it.' Lowe gave a self-satisfied smirk. 'I've read your file. Perks of being a senior detective around here. You're not a detective. You're just a guy who was owed a favour.'

Lowe barged past Townsend and nodded at his subordinate to follow him. Townsend sighed and turned to the sink to wash his hands and called out after him.

'If you read my file, sir, you'll know that I don't back down from anything.' Townsend flashed a glance up into the mirror, meeting Lowe's gaze. 'Anything.'

Sensing the challenge, Lowe stepped to Townsend once more, puffing out his chest, and trying to make himself as big as possible. He was taller and broader than Townsend, but it annoyed him that the detective showed no fear.

'It also said in your file that you used to box.' Lowe rolled his shoulders in a needless act of intimidation. 'If you ever fancy it, every Tuesday at midday.'

'You inviting me to lunch?'

'Yeah, if you like the taste of your own teeth.' Lowe looked at the other detective who acknowledged the threat. 'Either that, or just stay the fuck out of my sight.'

Townsend let the threat linger for a moment, refusing

to offer Lowe even the smallest of recognition. He balled up his fist, lifted it, and then slammed it against the metal button of the old hand dryer affixed to the wall. The clang made the younger detective jump and Townsend dried his hands and then headed to the door.

'I've got a murder to solve.' Townsend parted with, before pulling open the door and leaving the bathroom, where Lowe slammed his own fist down on the porcelain sink with frustration. He angrily yelled at the young detective to fuck off and for the next few moments, he tried to calm himself down with the sobering thought of the inevitable failure of DS Jack Townsend.

CHAPTER NINETEEN

As Townsend and King walked the same route to Paradise as the day before, she took a few puffs on her vape before engaging him in conversation.

'Did you write up that report?'

'Oh yeah Was great fun.' Townsend smirked, his hands stuffed into his pockets. The warm summer's heat of yesterday had been replaced by an overcast sky that had brought with it a chilling breeze.

The British summertime.

'All part of the job I'm afraid.' King popped her vape stick away. 'Do you think he did it?'

'I wouldn't rule it out. He didn't seem too fussed that she was dead, and it didn't sound like they'd the best relationship. He clearly had a problem with her dancing.'

'Jealousy?' King mulled it over. 'It's a powerful motive.'

'Yup. Plus, he's a little shit,' Townsend said through his teeth, drawing a chuckle from King. As they walked past a few high street banks and great-smelling food stalls, Townsend contemplated recounting his run-in with DCI Lowe to King, but thought better of it. Her mind was clearly on the case in hand, and the last thing she needed was to know her ex-husband was trying to cause cracks in her team. The lunchtime rush had hit High Wycombe high street, with long queues weaving through the pedestrian pathway, with hungry locals waiting for their chosen meals. Townsend's stomach rumbled, but he pushed it to the back of his mind. As they made their way down towards the pink signage above the door of Paradise, Townsend noticed the large man standing outside. Casually leaning against the door, the bouncer was clearly in place to keep non-members out. As the duo approached, his eyes flickered with excitement, and he pushed himself off the wall and somehow managed to make himself seem even bigger.

'Can I help you?' he said with a sneer. Both King and Townsend lifted their lanyards. From the bouncer's reaction, he wasn't a fan.

'We need a word with your boss,' King stated firmly.

'You have a warrant?'

'We don't need one,' Townsend said. 'We just want a word. If you want us to get a warrant, we can, but I'll make damn sure we leave a hell of a mess behind.'

The man seemed to appreciate the challenge and turned to Townsend, his eyes daring him to do something. King held a hand up to defuse the situation.

'The young girl who was found dead yesterday…'

'Nothing to do with us, love.' He winked at King.

'Well, she worked here. Went by the name of Athena.' The name clearly meant something to the man. 'So, it is something to do with you. Now, let's stop wasting time, shall we?'

The man rubbed his stubble covered chin and then yanked open the door with considerable force. A waft of sweat escaped, and he ushered the two of them in before slamming it shut and returning to his role. The landing was dimly lit with a dull, pinkish light, and Townsend led the way down the staircase, where the volume of the music rose with every step. King followed closely behind, and they stepped past the cloakroom and into the main floor of the strip club.

Despite the promise of decadence, it was poorly lit, and numerous booths, and tables were dotted around the main stage, where a woman, half naked, was writhing across the floor towards the few desperate men who sat in the front row. King shook her head and then followed Townsend as he marched across the venue to the bar that ran along the far wall of the club. Behind it, an older gentleman stood, watching the performance with a proud smile on his face. As the duo approached, he drew his eyes away from the stage and greeted them.

'Good afternoon, detectives,' he said, and Townsend, and King looked at each other. The man chuckled. 'Come on, now. You couldn't be more obvious.'

'I'll take that as a compliment,' King said.

'Take it however you want, love. We don't judge people in here.'

'DS Townsend and DI King.' Townsend went through the needless introduction and even lifted his lanyard.

'Fuckin' hell. Is he new?'

'We're here to speak to the manager. Graham Sykes.'

'Guilty.' The man held up his hands. 'Oh shit. I shouldn't say that to your sort should I?'

King humoured the man with a grin. Behind her, a modest round of applause went up from the few patrons in the audience as the dancer finished her performance and collected her clothes.

'Can we talk in your office?' King asked with the clear indication that it wasn't actually a question. Sykes held his arms out.

'Can't I'm afraid. Solo shift. Can I get you a drink at all?'

'No thanks,' Townsend said.

'I was asking the lady,' Sykes spat. 'You're not from round here, are you?'

'Wow. You should be a detective,' Townsend said. 'Lauren Grainger. She worked here, right?'

'Worked?' Sykes frowned. 'She's my best girl. You haven't nicked her, have you? Because I'll tell you now, that girl is a sweetheart.'

King looked at Townsend and then back at Sykes, who seemed genuinely concerned.

'Perhaps we should go sit down for a moment.'

'Why?' Sykes turned to the King, a sense of acceptance in his voice.

'Mr Sykes, Lauren Grainger was the woman who was found in the Rye yesterday morning. She'd been murdered.'

Like the colour from his face, all the tension between the trio drained away and the club manager wobbled a little on his feet. He was in his fifties at least, and a lifetime of drinking and drugs had taken its toll on his skin and teeth. But judging from his reaction, both King, and Townsend were surprised at how genuine it felt.

The man cared.

'Fucking hell. She was so young,' Sykes uttered, his forearms resting on the bar. 'A good kid, too. Ambitious.'

'Ambitious?' King probed.

'Yeah. Wanted to start up a dance academy or something.'

'Do you know where?'

'She didn't talk too much. Only when we had the odd cigarette together. Beyond that, she was all business. Focused. Brought in a lot of business.' He blew out his cheeks. 'I don't really read much of the news. Murdered? Do I want to know how?'

'She was stabbed twenty-two times,' Townsend said. The information seemed to sicken the owner, who bowed his head, and shook it, his thinning hair flopping from side to side. King nudged Townsend, indicating the need for more tact. 'I'm sorry for your loss.'

Sykes' demeanour changed. Suddenly, the sadness was replaced by anger, and he glared up at the two of them.

'Who did this?'

'That's what we are trying to find out.'

'Was it that prick? The one who wouldn't leave her alone?'

King leant forward, her brow furrowed.

'Dean Riley?'

'Maybe. Some loser she dated before he went inside. He'd been sending her all kinds of shit.' Sykes stood up straight, recomposing himself. 'He came in here one night and tried to march her off the fucking stage.'

'When was this?' King scribbled in her pad.

'Not too long ago. Benny helped him out.'

'Has he been back since?' Townsend asked.

'I don't think so. Lauren never said anything about it. She just apologised.' He shook his head again. 'Like I said, she was a good girl.'

'Well, if you don't mind, we're going to need your member logins for the past few weeks, as well as two nights ago.'

To both Townsend and King's surprise, Sykes began to chuckle.

'Come on. Do you think I'd have such a successful business if I tracked who came in? We don't have memberships here. You pay at the door every time.'

'Well, we'll need bank transactions and…' King was cut off as Sykes lifted his hands.

'Sorry, I want to help. But let's just say some pretty powerful people in this town might be a bit pissed off if they knew we were handing out their bank details.' He looked to Townsend and shrugged. 'Most people don't want certain people to know they come here. You get my drift?'

King squeezed the bridge of her nose in frustration.

'I can come back with a warrant.'

'You do that. Well, you can try. Depends who's signing it off, right?'

The implication was clear, and King shuddered at the thought of senior members of the Thames Valley Police Service frequenting such a place. Townsend looked around the club.

'No CCTV?'

'Secrecy, pal. It's the second-best thing we offer these guys. Why do you think there's no camera covering the street? You think that was my idea?' He leant forward. 'Look, I'm sorry I can't be more help. Lauren is – was – a good kid. Like I said, she wanted to give back. But I can't turn my business upside down for her. I've got too many other girls who depend on this place to make ends meet.'

'And your own bank account…' Townsend scoffed.

'Fuck you.'

'Sorry.' Townsend held up a hand in apology. 'That was out of line.'

Sykes seemed to accept the apology, and King smiled at Townsend, clearly happy he'd done it. She turned to Sykes.

'I know this is a trying time for you, but I need to know your whereabouts yesterday morning and why you were closed yesterday.'

'Oh, come on…' Sykes chuckled. 'You think I did this?'

'Just dotting i's and crossing the t's,' King said tactfully.

'I was here for another hour or so after the place closed. Some of us had a few drinks as I cashed up. Standard.'

'And you're usually closed on a Monday?'

Sykes shook his head.

'Not always. But every few months or so, I take the ball, and chain on a spa day.' The two detectives looked at Sykes with surprise. 'What? I'm an old romantic. I can give you the details of the spa if you want?'

'We'll have uniform come along shortly to take full statements and they'll collect all those details. Also, I appreciate you protect your dancers, but you will need to share their contact details so they can chase them up.'

'They might not like that.' Sykes shrugged. 'Some of them aren't necessarily fond of you guys.'

'Well, one of their co-workers was murdered yesterday. We need to speak with them.' Sykes nodded that he understood. 'Thank you. We'll be in touch.'

Townsend turned and walked back across the club to the stairwell. A few of the customers kept their heads down, clearly trying to hide their faces. King reached into her jacket and pulled out a card.

'If you need to contact me.'

She slid it across the bar to him and then turned and followed Townsend, as Sykes lifted the card, flicked it once with his fingers and then slotted it behind the bar.

The music ramped up again and another young lady emerged from behind the curtain, and as she began her routine, Sykes felt an overwhelming sense of sadness that he'd never watch Lauren Grainger do likewise again.

CHAPTER TWENTY

When the call came in to book the viewing, Natasha Stokes couldn't believe her luck. The estate agency she'd started a few years ago was doing enough to keep its head above water, in spite of the rocky housing market and the government-led clusterfuck that was the mortgage crisis.

Somehow, they'd survive.

Stokes Homes was one of the smaller players in High Wycombe, battling for a slice of the market against some of the bigger, more national companies. To establish themselves, Natasha had taken on as many properties as possible, using her fifteen years of experience in the industry to turn them around quite quickly.

Houses went up for sale.

Buyers were found.

The commissions came in.

After the COVID pandemic, with the stamp duty freeze in full effect, business had boomed to the point that she'd made one of the most stupid decisions of her life.

A decision that had cost her not only her marriage but also a number of her friendships. People she'd loved and known for years, who couldn't believe that she, Natasha

Stokes, happily married, and a mother of two, would have an affair with a man a decade younger than her. In hindsight, she knew it was a bad decision, but she'd been so miserable in her marriage that the comfort she sought had come in the most unexpected place.

Tyler had been one of the top members of her team, working extensively with letting properties. He was smart, handsome, and spent every lunchtime in the local gym. Natasha was an attractive woman, albeit with signs of her late thirties beginning to creep in around the edges of her eyes and a few errant grey hairs scattered among her blonde bob. She looked after herself through regular Pilates classes and a strictish diet. When Tyler had begun to notice her, and offer a few inappropriate comments, she felt a twinge of excitement.

One that would change her life.

Her sexual exploits with Tyler had been a reawakening for her, and with her thirteen-year marriage to David fizzling out, she found herself wanting to move on. To have the freedom to experience other men and other pleasures.

It meant telling a good man that she'd been unfaithful, and it meant ripping a stable home life apart. Their two girls, Maisie, and Callie, were too young to understand why their father left, but she wouldn't lie to them. For now, telling them that she'd made him upset would suffice and she would have to deal with consequences of her actions as the girls grew older and asked more detailed questions.

The fling with Tyler had been exhilarating, but when he wanted to end things and move on with the rest of his twenties, Natasha soon found herself filled with regret.

She'd lost a lot.

But not her business.

But the market had slowed, and just before a disastrous government announcement brought it almost to a standstill, she'd taken on a run-down house on London Road. It had turned into a regret as big as her infidelity.

The house, while in a decent location, not five minutes from the motorway, was beyond saving. The price had been lowered countless times, but the cost of getting it to a liveable state had scared away buyer after buyer.

Even one of the town's leading developers had turned down the chance to take on the project and flip it.

It would be a heavy anchor around her neck, and the seller, a middle-aged man who had been left it by his now deceased mother, was badgering her with calls to get it sold.

So when the call came in the previous day from a cash buyer who wanted to start their own property portfolio, she fist pumped the air. The house had never been priced lower and with a new and potentially naïve developer on her hands, she could finally be rid of it. The buyer, Jeremy Willis, sounded older than her, but judging by his line of questioning, he wasn't particularly knowledgeable about the business.

There was a good chance she would be able to rid herself of the cement shoes that was the house on London Road.

She'd arrived half an hour earlier than the appointment and had stopped in the nearby business park for a coffee. She'd tried calling David to ask how the kids were, as they'd been staying with him for a few weeks of the summer holidays.

He didn't pick up.

A twinge of guilt and regret echoed through her at the thought of the three of them having fun, while she sat on her own, lost in her own decisions.

She wanted to see them. Maisie and Callie.

She wanted to see David.

The idea had been festering in the back of her mind

for a while, but had now planted itself fully. If there was any way she could build a bridge to David, then she would.

She saw the potential sale of the house as a sign.

That even the most lost causes could be redeemed.

If he picked up the phone, she'd say sorry right then and there, tell him she still loved him and rush straight to them.

But there was no answer.

And she deserved that.

As she finished her drink, she stepped out of the coffee shop and, with the late afternoon offering a nice breeze and the promise of a brisk walk, she decided to leave her car in the business park and stroll up London Road to the property. The appointment was just after five, and as she arrived outside, it was a few minutes beforehand.

He'd be there any minute.

She cast her eyes over the garden, which was horrendously overgrown, with branches hanging over the wall that separated the property from the main road. You could barely see the house through the overgrowth, and she cursed the seller for not at least making an effort to sell the place.

Perhaps Jeremy wouldn't mind.

Natasha pushed open the gate and made her way through the neglected garden when she stopped.

The door was open.

With a frown across her face, Natasha pulled out her phone and checked her emails. There was nothing from the owners to say that they would be stopping by.

Nothing from them at all.

She found the homeowner's number in her contact list and pressed dial as she approached the door. With the shoulder of her navy jacket, she nudged it open, calling out to see if anyone was there. There was a small chance that the office manager might have allocated the viewing to another member of her small team. Perhaps Aidan?

There was no response.

If the owner didn't pick up the phone, she would call the police.

The phone was ringing in her ear, and combined with the traffic, did just enough to cloak the footsteps that crunched on the dried grass as the figure emerged from the overgrown garden.

Natasha thought she saw something in her periphery.

She definitely heard the homeowner answer the phone.

But all of it seemed to fade from existence as she felt the knife plunge deep into her spine. The blade severed something, and as the searing pain burnt through her body, she felt herself lose her balance.

Somewhere, she could hear the faint echo of someone asking if she was there.

Shock set in, which helped quash the pain as the blade slid out of her spine and then ripped into her side.

Then again.

And again.

Then it all went black, as Natasha's final thought was of her kids, and how she wished David had picked up the phone.

CHAPTER TWENTY-ONE

'So, anything?'

King rubbed the bridge of her nose in frustration. Not at her team, but at the situation. They had nothing. A young woman was dead, and despite their second day of intense investigation, they had nothing but a dodgy ex-boyfriend who they'd already questioned. With an understanding smile, Hannon gently shook her head.

'Not really, guv,' she said, spinning back to her screens on her chair. Across all of them were rows of financial records. A display of white with black lines. 'She led a pretty frugal life. Shopped at the cheaper supermarkets. Didn't spend too much online. Usual other things – phone bill, Internet. Daily trips to Costa…that's about it.'

'Any one-off payments?' Townsend asked from his chair. He looked as tired as the rest of them.

'A few. Mostly to restaurants. A few trips to the cinema. Again, nothing out of the ordinary. She did make a sizable donation of a few hundred pounds to a local charity. I'm looking into that but again, most people aren't really targeted for their charity work.'

'Good work,' King said, patting Hannon on the

shoulder and then stepping towards her office. 'Both of you. I know it's hard and I know progress is slow, but as long as we don't stop, then we're doing right by that girl. Now, no offence, you both look like crap, so go home, get some sleep, and then back at it tomorrow.'

'Cheers, guv,' Hannon said and began the process of saving her work and shutting down her machine. As she eased herself up from her chair with a gentle grimace, she said goodbye to Townsend, who sat in thought.

'Have a good one,' he replied, and as Hannon left for the night, he rose from his chair and approached King's door. He knocked and leant his head in. 'You okay, guv?'

King was mid-yawn and her desk was covered in paperwork.

'Just tired, is all.' She stretched her back. 'Don't you have a home to go home to?'

'I could ask you the same thing?'

'Unfortunately, as nice as it is being a Detective Inspector, Jack, it does come with the heavy downside of a whole shit heap of paperwork. I'll head off after this.'

'Cheers, guv.' Townsend smiled. 'Look after yourself.'

Townsend turned and walked back to his desk, retrieving his black bomber jacket that he pulled over his muscular frame. DI King watched her new detective gather his things, including a few files, and she felt a strange sense of pride. It was more a feeling of surprise, and she enjoyed the notion that she'd been proven wrong. The man was still finding his feet – in the local area, the police station but also as a detective. She'd been granted access to his file before he had arrived, and while the contents of his extensive undercover work had been held back, there was no denying the man's bravery. But as a Detective Constable, he hadn't been subject to anywhere near the level expected of someone becoming a DS. The Merseyside Police, for reasons known to themselves, fast-tracked the young man, gave him a golden handshake and organised his move down to a completely new town.

To a completely new life.

She hadn't given him the credit he was due, especially as he'd moved his young family with him. From what she'd read, he had been kept away from his young daughter and the last thing she wanted was for his new job to do the same thing. But there was a determination to Townsend, a trait that she looked for in any good detective, that told her he was in this until the end.

Until they caught Lauren Grainger's killer.

The summer evening soon set upon the town of High Wycombe, offering a mild breeze that counterbalanced the muggy heat. It would mean the beer gardens would be full, with local businesses thriving off humanity's need for escape. King understood.

There would be a bottle of wine in her very near future. A thought that troubled but encouraged her in equal measure.

With the paperwork seemingly regenerating quicker than she could process it, King eventually slammed her pen down, shut off her laptop, and stood from her desk. Her back felt stiff, and she'd contemplated borrowing Hannon's back support but then remembered that her stiff back paled in comparison to the lifelong injury the young detective was dealing with. Combing that injury with Townsends' lack of experience and past discretions, along with her seemingly daily reliance on alcohol, King had the ironically sobering thought that maybe the Specialist Crimes Unit wasn't best placed to get Lauren Grainger the justice she deserved.

'Bullshit,' she said out loud, banishing the self-doubt from her mind. It was time to leave, and King marched up the stairs as fast as she could, hoping a speedy exit would expel any notions of doubt for good. As she ascended the final step onto the ground floor, she rolled her eyes at the smiling face of the man who was walking down the flight of stairs opposite.

DCI Lowe.

'Izzy.' He held his arms open. 'You look…tired.'

'I feel it. You know, big murder case going on.' King tried her hardest not to sink to his level. 'Have a nice evening.'

As she strode towards the main door of the station and to her much-needed freedom, Lowe called after her.

'How's it going?' King turned to look at him. For once, he looked awkward. Unconfident. 'The case, I mean.'

Throughout the animosity between the two of them, which had been created out of the ashes of their passion, it was easy to forget that Marcus Lowe was a damn fine detective. Cocky. Brash. Full of himself.

But a great detective, with an inquisitive mind, and the enviable ability to connect dots that haven't been discovered yet.

'Slowly,' King admitted, stuffing her hands into her trouser pockets and taking a step back towards him. 'We've got some lines of enquiry we're working.'

'The boyfriend?' Lowe had clearly been keeping tabs. 'Most likely route. Jilted. Jealous. Has a long list of being a fucking scumbag.'

'He's a possible suspect.' King admitted. 'But my team are…'

Lowe's expression changed in a heartbeat, and the cool, calm persona was replaced by a scowl she'd seen a hundred times.

'Oh, come the fuck on, Izzy. Your *team*? You've got a detective who hates the outside world and a fucking newbie with a bad attitude.' Before King could respond, Lowe held up an apologetic hand. 'Sorry. But someone killed this young girl, and I think we need our best people on it.'

'That's what this is? Your little ego is bruised that my team is working this murder.'

'No. *My* ego isn't bruised. It's *your* ego that's the problem.'

'Excuse me?'

'You can't admit that my team is best placed to track this killer down. We made your team as a place to dump detectives who don't quite make the grade, and yet here they are, tracking a killer through our town. Now Hall has said—'

'Hall gave me this case.' King stepped in with authority. 'So get over yourself.'

They both heard the incoming call that crackled through the radio of a passing uniform. It brought their petty squabble to an immediate halt and instigated a wave of anxiety that Detective Inspector Isabella King would never show her ex-husband.

It would bring about a visible sense of panic, not just within the police station, but the entire town of High Wycombe.

Another body had been found.

Stabbed to death.

Without even so much as a reference to their fight, Lowe told King that he would drive, and they both rushed out to his needlessly flashy sports car. Once inside, Lowe roared the engine to life, burst through the small exit to the car park and headed in the general direction of the location that had come through on the radio. As they sped down London Road, King watched the incredible view of Wycombe Rye whizz by, the lake bathed in the shadow of the trees as the sun set behind them.

The place where Lauren Grainger was killed.

And now, to her own horror, it was only the first one.

With a sigh, she lifted her phone to her ear and waited for Townsend to answer.

CHAPTER TWENTY-TWO

Townsend wondered how long it would take for Flackwell Heath to truly feel like home. He didn't worry about that for Eve, who wasn't old enough to have true attachment to their home back in Liverpool. But for him, their new residence was a completely different world. All the streets carried a warm, quaint quality. The houses were all a good size, set back from the road and tucked behind well-maintained gardens. The "high street" was nothing more than a small parade of local businesses such as hairdressers and coffee shops, with a mini-supermarket squashed in the middle of them. Beyond a few well-rated pubs, there was nothing much else to the village.

Townsend was used to the pace of urban living. The estates that he grew up on were swarming with people, most of them fundamentally good, but they were overpowered by the more dangerous residents that patrolled the concrete jungle that was his home.

It was a tough upbringing. It was why his father had encouraged him to box as a kid, and it certainly helped in the few yearly scrapes he'd found himself in. When his father passed away, that was when Townsend had found his calling. The cancer had reduced his father to a husk of the man he once was, but the debilitating injury he'd suffered had already done the damage mentally. Malcolm Townsend was a good man, and Jack wanted to emulate him.

Be just as good.

Or be better.

And as he stepped out of his car on the driveway, he looked up at the large, three-bedroom house, with its pristine front garden and separate garage bathed in the dimming light of the summer evening, and wondered what his father would say.

He'd probably think it was overly fancy.

But he'd be proud.

Proud of the man Townsend had become and the family he provided for.

The front door opened, snatching Townsend from his thoughts, and he was greeted by the welcoming smile of his daughter.

'Daddy, come quick.'

Eve bounded back into the house, and Townsend followed after her, catching a glimpse of her as she disappeared into the kitchen, and again as she dashed out into the garden. The smell emanating from the oven told him he was in for another good meal and as he stepped out onto the decking of their garden, a smile broke across his face.

'What is that?'

His question drew a giggle from Mandy, who stood with a giant plastic racket in her hand. A jumbo tennis net had been erected across the grass, and Eve ran to retrieve her own racket and inflatable tennis ball.

'Look, Daddy. We're playing tennis.'

'I can see.' He stepped down onto the grass and gave Mandy a kiss. 'Having fun?'

'It's quite full on,' Mandy said with a giggle. Eve threw the ball up and walloped it, sending it up, and over the net. Mandy lunged and returned it before Eve sent the ball tumbling down the garden with an errant shot. Mandy handed him the racket. 'Fancy a go?'

For the next ten minutes, Townsend, and Eve hit the giant ball back and forth, with him over-egging the effort he was putting in. By mimicking the usual grunts and groans of professional tennis players, he made his daughter laugh wildly. When she sent a great shot over the net, Townsend dived hysterically to try to reach it.

'I win!' his daughter declared loudly, and Townsend sat up, and celebrated with her. She ducked under the net, and to Townsend's surprise, threw her arms around him and they both fell back on the grass.

Time seemed to stop, and Townsend could feel his heart thudding against his rib cage as his daughter clung to him. It had been a long road to get to this point, and as they laid on the grass, she nuzzled into him. He wrapped his powerful arms around her petite frame and breathed her in.

It was a moment he wanted to keep forever.

'Well, look at you two.' Mandy's voice cut through the moment; her words heavy with emotion. 'Dinner's ready.'

Eve yelled her excitement at dinner, pushed herself from her father's grasp and rushed back to help. Townsend ambled to his feet, very much feeling like a man in his late thirties. Before he could respond to his wife and bask in the moment of reconnection with his daughter, his phone buzzed.

It was King.

'All right, guv?' His face soon dropped, telling Mandy everything she needed to know. 'On my way.'

As he hung up the phone, he turned to Mandy with a sigh.

'Jack. Go.' She smiled. 'We're proud of you.'

With a heavy heart, he kissed his wife goodbye and then dashed into the house. Eve was surprisingly okay with him needing to go back to work, and he promised her another game of tennis tomorrow. Less than two minutes after receiving the call, and fifteen minutes after getting home, Townsend dropped into the driver's seat of his Honda Civic, bashed 'London Road' into the satnav, and pulled out of the driveway. By weaving through Loudwater, home of the business park, he was on the main road within ten minutes. The rush hour congestion to hit the M40 has subsided, and as he drove down the main road, he soon saw the fleet of blue lights around one of the houses. Two police cars had blocked the road, with one of the young officers guiding the remaining traffic through one lane. An ambulance was parked up on the curb, and as Townsend pulled his own car up onto the pavement, he saw DSI Hall deep in conversation with a paramedic. Townsend slipped on his lanyard and stepped out. As he approached the crime scene, DSI Hall noticed him arching his neck to the house where King would undoubtedly be waiting.

As he stepped through the gate of the overgrown garden, he almost collided with DCI Lowe.

'Watch it,' Lowe spat, clearly agitated. Townsend stepped to the side.

'Sir.'

Lowe glared at Townsend, almost daring him to say something else. When he didn't, Lowe shot a glance to DSI Hall, grunted, and then stormed up the road towards his own car. Townsend watched him leave for a few moments, then stepped over the threshold and into the overgrown garden. King stood in the doorway with her arms folded and her back to him. Two uniformed officers nodded to

Townsend as he approached and before he could see much of the body, he saw the blood.

Lots of blood.

He stepped around it and then stuffed his hands in his pockets so as not to interfere with the crime scene. He stepped up behind King and looked down at the brutal murder before him.

The woman was lying on her front, her hands splayed out as if she was reaching out for help. One of her legs was bent at the knee, and her head was tilted to the side.

Her eyes were wide open.

They say in death, the final feeling coursing through your body is imprinted on your eye like a photo.

All Townsend could see was fear.

The woman's smart blazer and shirt had been ripped to shreds, where the knife had been thrust into her body again and again. The pattern of attack was crazed, and through the blood, he could see the deep puncture wounds that had ended the woman's life.

She had been murdered.

Violently.

'You okay, guv?' Townsend eventually asked, as the blue lights from the road behind them intermittently illuminated the dark hallway of the house. The noise of the traffic echoed loudly. King didn't move or respond. 'Guv?'

'Her name was Natasha. Natasha Stokes.' King shook her head and took a deep breath. She revealed a gloved hand that held a small card wallet. 'Her phone was on her person, too.'

'So not a robbery?'

'Nope.' King's voice was laced with fury. 'Whoever did this meant to do this. Planned it. Fuck.'

King turned to Townsend; her brow furrowed.

'You think it's the same guy?' Townsend asked.

'Excellent question.' DSI Hall's authoritative voice

caught them both by surprise. He approached them through the overgrown foliage. 'Because the last thing we need is a serial killer on the loose.'

'Sir, I don't think we can jump to conclusions—' King began, but Hall held a hand up.

'I'm not, Detective Inspector. But the fact is we've had two women murdered within three days.' Hall removed his glasses and sighed as he rubbed them. 'Now I sent DCI Lowe home because you promised me you could handle this, Izzy.'

'I will find the person who did this, sir,' King said with a lack of conviction that Townsend found unnerving. He hadn't known her for more than a few days, but her confidence had seemed unwavering.

Until now.

Hall sighed again and replaced his glasses.

'And you, Townsend. Are you up to this?'

Townsend took one more glance at the brutality in the doorway and felt his fists clench.

'Yes, sir.'

'Then do it. Both of you.' Hall's authority came from his directness. 'Otherwise, I'll have no choice but to bring DCI Lowe and his team in. Understood?'

Both of them nodded and Hall bid them farewell. As he was approaching the gate, the overall-clad SOCO team began to filter through, and King, and Townsend stepped away from the door and into the tall grass of the garden. For a few minutes, as the final shreds of sunlight dissipated for the night, they watched the team begin to close down the crime scene and get to work. Beyond the bushes that separated the outside world from the horrors before them, they could hear an argument between one of the uniformed officers and a reporter.

The press would be all over it within minutes once news broke out of another murder.

A serial killer on the loose.

Townsend glanced at King, whose eyes were locked on the butchered body in the hallway of the house. She was committing it all to memory. The viciousness of the attack.

The feeling of failure.

All of it. Storing it all up as fuel to push on to find the person who did it. King blew out her cheeks, rubbed the tiredness that was clinging to her eyelids and then turned to Townsend with a sense of purpose.

'We've got a killer to catch.'

CHAPTER TWENTY-THREE

'SERIAL KILLER HITS WYCOMBE!'

'WOMEN AREN'T SAFE.'

'IT COULD BE ANY OF US NEXT.'

Townsend was rubbing the tiredness from his eyes as he sipped his coffee. He was sitting next to King, who was showing him the sensationalist headlines being pumped out by local news accounts on social media. An online presence wasn't something he had ever desired, especially after being undercover, and Townsend found the notion of sharing your life with strangers for their approval to be a strange concept. Even worse, by allowing unfiltered posts to be shared, it gave people the voice of authority on subjects that they didn't deserve, and thus, misinformed the people who followed them blindly.

'This isn't good,' King said as she scrolled through the comments, with dozens of local accounts all sharing their dismay and fear that there was a killer in their midst. There was also a groundswell of negativity aimed towards the police themselves, with a number of generically named accounts slamming the police for their apparent lack of care.

If only they knew.

Townsend and King had worked through the night, trying their level best to get ahead of a case that was starting to rapidly escalate. King had already taken the painstaking journey to inform the ex-husband of the deceased of her murder. The man's name was David, and after vomiting upon hearing of her murder, had been very cooperative. He provided answers to his own whereabouts, understanding that he wasn't a suspect, but they needed to eliminate who they could, and seemed to hold back his own pain to focus on the two girls who were asleep upstairs at the time.

By now, both Maisie, and Callie Stokes would have been informed that their mother was dead.

Gone forever.

Townsend thought about having to have that chat with Eve, and it made his teeth clench, and his fists tighten.

They had to catch the sick bastard who did this.

The person who had snatched the life of the two young girls' mother.

Neither King nor Townsend had even suggested heading home once they'd finished up at the crime scene, and as they'd trawled through the necessary paperwork, they'd silently cemented another bond between them.

They were both in this to the end.

There was little time for idle chat, as uniformed officers poked their heads into the SCU office, offering their help, and support. It filled Townsend with pride to see the sense of urgency and togetherness from the Thames Valley Police, and King had no problem delegating work to them upon request.

Even DCI Lowe, who, after what looked like a good night's sleep, seemed a little more respectful when he dipped his head in to inform them that his team had resources to help. King thanked him curtly but didn't follow it up. Townsend got his customary sneer from the senior detective, but nothing else.

They'd written up every report.

King had filled out every form.

Townsend had pulled as much information as possible on Natasha Stokes, with a long list of phone numbers that he'd handed over to uniform to follow up on. They needed to build a picture of the woman, one that was very different to the brutally slain body that they'd tacked onto the wall alongside Lauren Grainger.

They needed to know what connected a twenty-three-year-old dancer and a thirty-two-year-old estate agent who came from very different walks of life.

They needed to find out who was killing.

Neither Townsend nor King had any notion of the time when Hannon marched in, drawing their attention away from King's phone as she put her bag down on her desk and approached King's door.

'Jesus.' Hannon's face already relayed that she knew what was going on. 'Again?'

King nodded.

'Yup. Early evening,' King stood and stretched her back. Townsend did likewise. 'A passerby was walking to the Tesco's not far from the house and caught a glimpse of the open door. Thought it was strange as he walked past that house every day and knew it was abandoned. Poked his head into the garden and…'

King's voice trailed off, leaving both Hannon, and Townsend to contemplate the feeling of shock that must have hit the civilian. Part and parcel of their jobs was to deal with dead bodies, and while it was never pleasant, it was something that eventually became easier over time. For someone who was just popping out for a packet of cigarettes, it can be life changing.

Especially when the body had been mutilated. Hannon

shuffled to her desk and lowered herself into her chair, adjusting the back support slightly. Townsend perched on the edge of his desk as King approached their display wall. At the top of the wall were pictures of both Lauren Grainger and Natasha Stokes. Then, just underneath, the image of their stab riddled corpses. A picture of Dean Riley was also on the wall, just off from Lauren, along with other pieces of information they'd collated in the past few days. All of it something, but none of it anything. King reached up and tapped the photo of Natasha Stokes, who was smiling in front of a sun-drenched backdrop.

'Natasha Stokes. Thirty-two. Divorced. Two kids. Ran her own estate agency just up the road.'

'Stokes Homes?' Hannon interrupted with her eyes wide.

'Yes. You know it?' King asked and Hannon nodded. 'Well, last night, she was murdered in the doorway of one of the homes she was currently selling. Her ex-husband has been informed and the FLO is there to help him tell their two daughters that they no longer have a mother. That's the seriousness of what we're dealing with, okay? Now, logic dictates someone arranged to meet her there, so we need to know who put that phone call in. Jack?'

'I went through her website and found the names of the other employees. One of them, Aidan Hanlan, agreed to meet me at the office at eight, so I'll head up there in about fifteen minutes.'

'Good work,' King said, hands on hips. 'I want to know who made that call. Get a uniform to follow up with the rest of the staff. Where they were, any disputes. The usual. I want to rule them out as quickly as possible.'

'Yes, guv.'

'Now, the biggest question is—' King started but was cut off.

'Who the fuck is doing this?' Hannon said coldly.

'Exactly. But unless they walk up and knock on our door, we need to figure that out. Our best shot…is finding out what connects Natasha Stokes to Lauren Grainger. It might not be a personal connection, but there has to be something.'

'They were both blonde women,' Townsend said with a shrug. Hannon looked at him with a raised eyebrow. 'What? Maybe he has a type? We already know the killer didn't steal anything from either victim. So if this is out of passion…maybe he's targeting blonde women?'

'It's a theory,' King said cautiously. 'But we can't tell every blonde woman in the town to stay indoors. We need more. Something that proves these women were in danger before this happened.'

'I have something,' Hannon interjected and turned to her screen, which she navigated with expertise. 'I ran a few encryption programs last night that our friends at Cyber Crimes approved my license for.'

'That sounds fancy,' Townsend chipped in.

'Incredibly, darling,' Hannon said with a smirk. Then she hit a couple of keys and sat back in triumph. 'Those abusive social media posts that Lauren Grainger was receiving. All from separate accounts, but the same IP address.'

Both King and Townsend leant forward to read the screen. King snarled.

'Dean Riley.'

'Yup. For a man who said he didn't care about the woman, sending her a message that says, and I quote, "*I hope you fucking die you stupid bitch*" seems a little contradictory.'

'It seems very fucking contradictory. Get him in here. Both of you,' King said, as he started back to her office. 'I need to call ahead for the post-mortem.'

'Guv, I need to meet that Hanlan lad at the office.' Townsend objected.

'I'll handle it,' King assured. 'Right now, I want you and Hannon to drag Dean Riley out of his bed in his fucking pyjamas and get his arse in here.'

Townsend stood, stretched out his broad shoulders and then lifted his jacket. He turned to Hannon, who, despite her best efforts, was struggling to conceal her worry. She looked at him and he offered her a warm smile.

'Round two.' He winked. 'Reckon he'll get as far as the basketball court this time?'

Hannon clearly appreciated the levity that her colleague was trying to inject, but her apprehension was still locking her to her seat. She knew it was something she'd need to keep fighting and having Townsend alongside her offered her the best opportunity to overcome her fear. She wasn't sure she was trying to hide it, and if she was, she was clearly doing a poor job as Townsend hunched down so he was eye level with her and he fixed her with a gentle smile.

'I'll buy you a coffee,' he offered.

'Sold.'

She finally agreed, and she took the hand he offered to help him up. As the two headed through the door, they could already hear King on the phone, trying to tick one task off a list that would never end. Hannon didn't envy her, and she turned into the stairwell and followed Townsend up the stairs, Hannon realised she didn't envy herself either.

CHAPTER TWENTY-FOUR

'Haven't you lot got anything better to do?'

Mrs Riley stood in the doorway of her house, cigarette in hand, and a scowl across her face. The early arrival of the police had caught her before she'd got ready, and she stood in her pyjamas, her hair a mess, and her face without the usual make-up.

'Sorry, Mrs Riley, but we need to talk to your son.'

'I read online that you've got another dead woman. Surely you should be looking into that?'

She flicked her cigarette ash out of the door, making little attempt to stop it from falling towards the officers. Townsend stepped back and smiled warmly.

'We are.'

'Let me tell you something. My boy is a prick. I know that and your lot know that. But he ain't a killer.' She took a long drag on the cigarette and eyed both Townsend and Hannon. 'Besides, I've never heard of this Stokes woman.'

'You know her name?' Hannon asked with concern.

'Oh yeah. It's all over the Internet.' She shrugged. 'Why don't you go find her killer instead of bothering me.'

'Look, I really don't have the time to come back here again with a warrant,' Townsend cut in curtly, his authority catching both Mrs Riley and Hannon by surprise. 'So just get your boy down here because I need to talk to him. If he hasn't done anything wrong, then he'll be back for lunch.'

'I thought you'd already said he hasn't done anything.' Riley stubbed her cigarette out on the outside wall and let it drop onto the step beside a number of others.

'Not exactly,' Hannon replied. 'But we now have some evidence of some worrying behaviour from your son to the first victim, Lauren Grainger—'

'That tart,' Mrs Riley said coldly.

'Excuse me?' Hannon said, offended.

'My boy loved that girl. Then he got sent down for a bit, and she decided to start selling her body or whatever for money. Fucking bimbo. I won't cry for her for the hurt she caused my boy.' Realising Townsend was scribbling down notes, she quickly collected herself. 'He ain't here, anyway. Although, you're welcome to come in and have a look.'

Townsend took her up on the offer, ignoring the crass comment she made about taking an extra good look in her room. Hannon watched from the open doorway, battling her anxiety as Townsend disappeared from view up the stairs. A few moments later, he returned, did a quick sweep of the modest downstairs and then marched back to the front door, shaking his head.

'Where can we find him?' Hannon asked.

'Usual place. Social club.'

'Which one?' Townsend asked.

'You're the detective,' the woman said smugly and then closed the front door. Townsend took a step back, smirking at the cheek of the woman. He understood her disdain for the police, especially with an errant child of her own, but surely the worry of her son being involved in murder would at least appeal to her sanity.

'Let's go,' Hannon said, turning and walking back to the car which they'd parked in the same spot as before. This time, there was no audience for them, and Townsend assumed that delinquency didn't begin in the school summer holidays any time before eleven.

'We need to find out what club he's at.'

'We already know,' Hannon said as he lowered herself into the driver's seat and Townsend hoped in as well. On the drive back from Lane End to High Wycombe, she explained the undercurrent of drugs that was rife through Buckinghamshire. If there were numerous pockets of affluence throughout the county, there was still a hard poverty line that the majority lived under.

And where there was poverty, there was opportunity, and a reliance on something to get through the day. Organised Crime Gangs had been running County Lines throughout many towns to move drugs and there were numerous spots throughout the city that were known as potential dropping and sales points. The dedicated Drugs Diversion Unit were focused on stopping as much as they could, but budgetary constraints meant any and all resources were focused solely on making inroads into the OCGs themselves. Uniform were left to police the streets, shutting down sales, but again, their reach was only as far as the government would pay for.

It meant hotspots were left long enough for business to be picked up, before they were shut down again and the cycle would continue.

It was a depressing story for Hannon to relay, and Townsend blew out his cheeks and looked out of the window as they moved from the tree clad country lanes and swiftly into the cramped residential streets of High Wycombe. The nearer they got to the town centre, the more run-down the backstreets became, with houses squished together with little to no parking, and their few feet of front garden reduced to mainly dumping grounds. It made him thankful of his relocation to the quaint village of Flackwell Heath, although the road where the West Wycombe Social Club sat reminded him of Toxteth.

Blocks of flats and small houses, all of them having been neglected for quite some time. A few run-down newsagents that put little to no effort in their presentation and a concrete park that should come with a hazard warning for parents.

'This is it,' Hannon said dryly as she pulled into the car park of a small social club. The paint was flaking from the walls and one of the windows was boarded up. 'Looks nice.'

Townsend chuckled at the joke and, as he released his seat belt, he noticed she hadn't done the same.

'Wait here,' he said with a firm nod.

'What? No, I can't let you go in on your own.'

'I'll be fine.' Townsend smiled. 'Trust me, I've dealt with worse than Dean Riley.'

There was a hint of mischievousness to his voice that told Hannon that her partner had been in some bad situations before and coupled with the allusions he had made to being undercover, she had no reason to doubt him. She took a deep breath, annoyed at her own perceived cowardice.

'Okay. But be quick.'

'Get ready to chase him if he makes a run for it,' Townsend said as he pushed opened the door and climbed out. 'Back in a tick.'

He closed the door and marched towards the social

club, yanking open the front door that creaked on its hinges. The smell of stale smoke filled his nostrils, and he headed towards the bar area, through a corridor that had been decorated decades ago. The bar was a larger function room, with faded red carpet, a row of old tables and chairs, and a wooden bar that clung to one side of the room. There was an old man sitting behind it, reading the newspaper, who glanced over the pages before ignoring Townsend entirely.

Townsend didn't mind.

His focus was on the three young men on the far side of the room, gathered around the battered old pool table. Most specifically the one in the middle.

Dean Riley.

As Townsend strode across the room, his footsteps alerted one of the men who nodded to Riley who turned and sneered. Stopping a few metres from the group, Townsend looked over the group before him. Like Riley himself, his cohorts wore the same smug expressions, with their faces ragged from obvious drug abuse. One of the men pulled his hood up in a lame attempt at intimidation, and Townsend chuckled.

'Come on, Dean. We need a chat.'

'The fuck we do,' Riley said with undeserved confidence. 'I suggest you turn and walk away.'

Townsend sighed. One of Riley's friends stuffed his hand into the pocket of his hoodie, clearly reaching for something. Townsend looked at his father's watch and then back to them.

'I've got a lot on today, Dean. So we can either do this nicely or we can do it another way. Up to you.'

'Fuck this guy,' the other member of the gang yelled.

'I'm married.' Townsend held up his wedding ring. 'Sorry to disappoint you.'

'Look, you scouse cunt.' Riley was clearly enjoying having an audience. 'Turn around and fuck off. Or we'll do you.'

'How about you come with me and I don't have the boys in blue knocking this place down and taking whatever stash you've got back there behind the table? I'm pretty sure your sellers would be pretty pissed off if you lost it right?' Townsend saw the concern spread across the three faces. 'So, let's do each other a favour. Last chance, Dean. Let's go.'

'Seb, fuck him up.'

Riley gave the order to the man beside him, who took a few steps towards Townsend, his hand adjusting the object in the pocket of his hoodie.

'You got CCTV in here?' Townsend called back to the old man behind the bar and was treated to a genuine laugh as a response.

Good.

A few feet from the detective, the young man pulled his hand free, and a box cutter was wrapped in his fingers. But Townsend knew what was coming, and lunged forward, grabbing the unsuspecting man by the wrist and using his superior strength, he wrenched it backwards. The young man squealed in pain as Townsend dug his fingers into his pressure point and the box cutter fell to the ground. Swiftly, Townsend dragged it behind him with his foot and then twisted the man's arm up behind his back and then slammed him face down onto the nearest table. The impact split the man's eyebrow and drew another cry of pain.

'Fuck this.' The other member of Riley's crew bolted to the door, and Townsend shoved the unfortunate Seb to the floor and then approached Riley, who tried to mask his fear by throwing his fist up.

'I wouldn't.' Townsend warned, but Riley ignored him. The right hook he swung was lazy, and Townsend weaved underneath, and then hammered the air from Riley's body with a devastating uppercut to the stomach. Spluttering for breath, Riley fell onto his knees, only for Townsend to grab him by the hood and lift him to his feet. 'Let's go.'

Hannon was already halfway out of the car, having seen the young man burst through the front door. She had called for back-up as soon as Townsend had got out of the car, and one of the two uniformed officers who'd arrived immediately gave chase. The other was approaching Hannon for an update as Townsend pushed a heavily winded Riley through the door, roughly holding the man's arms behind his back.

'Jesus. What happened?' the officer asked firmly.

'There's another one inside with a head injury,' Townsend said calmly, walking past the officer, and pushing the cuffed Riley into the back of Hannon's car.

'A head injury?' the officer said accusingly.

'He fell.'

'Fucking hell,' the officer uttered before turning towards the social club, barking something into his radio as he disappeared. Hannon stood, arms folded, and an accusatory look on her face. Townsend held his hands up.

'I gave them the option.'

'You're something else, Jack. You know that?' Hannon said with a wry smile. 'Did he say anything?'

'Apart from a few limp threats. No. He will, though.' Townsend followed Hannon's gaze to the backseat of the car, where a despondent Riley had his eyes closed as he tried to catch his breath. 'I'll tell you one thing.'

Hannon turned to Townsend as he began to walk around the car to the passenger door.

'What's that?'

‘That boy ain’t a killer.’

Townsend dropped into the passenger seat, leaving Hannon to ruminate on his words. A few moments later, she was back behind the wheel, taking Townsend, and their suspect back to the station, hoping to find some answers.

CHAPTER TWENTY-FIVE

King had left the office not long after the rest of her team, and with the estate agent's office only a few minutes' walk up the hill, she decided to head to the coffee shop where Hannon was a frequent visitor. The young woman was as addicted to caffeine as King was, which was a trait that seemed to be shared by almost everyone in the profession. As expected, the coffee shop had a queue out of the door and King joined the back of it, puffing intermittently on her vape as she kept her eyes on the front door of Stokes Homes office, which was on the other side of the road, a little further back down the hill.

Like clockwork, another commuter hurried through the door, coffee in hand, and then scurried up the remainder of the hill to the train station to begin their journey to London and eventually, it was her turn to order.

Just as she placed her order for a black Americano, she noticed a young man in a tight-fitting suit approaching the door to office. He knelt and turned a key in the lock that lifted the shutter, and then one in the main door and then let himself in.

King collected her coffee, thanked the owner, and then

marched down the hill, cutting through the traffic that was queuing for the train station. She took a sip of her coffee, a final puff on her vape and then gently rapped her knuckles on the glass. The young man poked his head out from the back room, most likely a kitchen area, and looked confused. Through the property advertisements that littered the window display, she could see him taking apprehensive steps to the door, and so she lifted her police lanyard as he got closer.

He pushed open the door and looked her up and down.

'Are you the police?'

'Detective Inspector King,' she said like clockwork. 'I believe you spoke to my colleague, DS Townsend?'

'Yes. Of course.' The young man appeared flustered. 'Come in.'

'Thank you. Aidan, wasn't it?' He nodded. His face looked puffy, through a combination of lack of sleep and crying. 'First off, I want to say how sorry I am.'

'I just can't believe anyone would want to kill Natasha, you know?' He shook his head. Somewhere out of sight, a kettle stopped boiling. 'Would you like a tea?'

King waved her coffee cup.

'No, thank you, but please go ahead.'

Aidan turned and headed back to the kitchen, while King slowly took in the office. It was nondescript. Like every other estate agency she'd been in, with a few desks for the staff and little else. A few moments later, Aidan emerged with his mug, directed her to a seat opposite his desk, and then took his own.

'How are her girls?'

The young man had caught King off guard with his maturity and she shook her head.

'Her ex-husband has been informed. We have a Family

Liaison Officer with them to help them through. We are doing everything we can to find who did this.'

'Is it the same person who did that girl in over at the park?' Aidan asked, then scolded himself. 'I'm sorry. Lauren, wasn't it?'

'We don't know, in all honesty. Which is why I need to know everything about Natasha's appointment yesterday.' King placed her coffee down and took out her notepad. 'So, when did the call come in?'

'For the appointment? Erm...let me check.' The young man began moving his mouse and clicking away on his keyboard. 'Natasha had a new system implemented a few months back that logs interest to appointment times. We try to book them in as quickly as possible. Right...the call came in the day before.'

'Wow, so a quick turnaround,' King said, not wanting to betray her concern that the appointment was made after Grainger had been murdered. 'That's good service.'

'Yeah, well...Natasha prides...prided...herself on customer service.' The disbelief of the situation hit the young man again, and he lifted his cup with a shaky hand.

'I really appreciate you doing this, Aidan. It's crucial to our investigation. Are you able to give me the details of the caller?'

'You think they did it?'

'It's something we need to look at. Only a few people would have known where Natasha was going to be at that time, so we need to speak to them all.' Panic spread across the young man's face. 'Don't worry. A few police officers will be here at nine when the office opens and all members of staff are in. They will just want to take a few statements and confirm a few details.'

Her assurances didn't seem to land, and Aidan shook his head.

'I would never do anything to Natasha.'

'I appreciate that,' King said, as she scrawled the word *affair?* onto her pad. 'The name and number of the caller, please.'

'The viewing was made by Jeremy Willis.' The printer beside the desk kicked in and then swiftly shot out a sheet of paper with the information on. 'This is the number.'

'Thank you.' King took the paper, folded it, and then tucked it into her jacket. 'Finally, was there anything different about yesterday?'

'Different?'

'With Natasha. Did she seem distracted? Or worried? Were there any issues in the office or with other clients?' King asked, keeping her eyes locked on the young man.

'No. It was a pretty good day.'

'Nothing out of the ordinary? I know she was recently divorced…were there any issues with the ex-husband?'

'No. Nothing.' Aidan's voice was forceful, and King underlined her previous note.

'Okay, thank you. I know this is hard, and my team is doing everything we can to find out who did this. Like I said, a few officers will be by in an hour or so and if you need anything, please let them, or myself know.' King pulled out a business card and placed it on his desk. 'You have been really helpful, Aidan. It's much appreciated.'

As King stood and lifted her coffee cup, Aidan respectfully followed suit, and straightened his tie. She offered him a smile and then headed to the door. The sky was overcast, promising a few days of rain to erase the previous few weeks of good weather and as she marched back down to the station, King could feel the chill on the breeze that nipped at her. She stepped through the front door of the station and was greeted by a few sleepy officers, either starting or ending their shift, and then headed to the canteen.

Another coffee and a croissant for breakfast.

She took it to go, and as she made her way back to the main entrance to the stairwell, DSI Hall approached her.

'Ah, Izzy. There you are.' He looked at her. 'Christ on a cross, you look like hell.'

'Thanks, guv.'

'Have you not slept?' Her eyes told him he didn't need an answer. 'You're no good to me if you're not at a hundred percent.'

'I'm fine. Promise.'

'Walk with me.' Hall instructed and then held the door open to the stairwell. King stepped through and soon realised he was escorting her to her underground office. 'Anything so far?'

'Bits and bobs. The ex-husband has been informed. FLO should be there now to help with the kids and the ensuing days.'

'Those poor kids.'

'I know.' King sipped her coffee. 'Beyond that, I've just been to her office. One of her staff came in early to assist. Gave us the name and number of the person who booked the appointment. Uniform will get the staff's whereabouts when they get in.'

'Good work.'

'Oh, and Hannon managed to crack the accounts of the messages being sent to Lauren on Facebook. Dean Riley.'

'The ex-boyfriend?'

'Yup. She and Townsend are already bringing him in. I think he's going to want a lawyer for this one.'

'Well done, Izzy. But we need to move fast on this one.' His voice was tinged with a promise of bad news, and his face said the same as he stopped at the door to the SCU. 'The press is already running with a serial killer. I swear to God, this fucking building has more leaks than the fucking Titantic.'

'Not my team, guv. And we are on it.'

'I know. But like I said, we need to get ahead of it. DCI Lowe's team has a bit of capacity to—'

'Oh, for fuck's sake, guv,' King snapped. 'This is *my* investigation. You were there last night. He's pissed off that he's not front and centre on this.'

'Be that as it may, Izzy, he's still someone I very much trust. And finding who is killing these women is bigger than whatever issues you two still haven't resolved.' Hall spoke with an authority that deserved to be admired. 'Now, he won't be working directly with you, but he has allocated a member of CID to assist your efforts. So, please, play nice.'

King took a deep breath. She knew it was the right call, but it still felt personal. She could just imagine her ex-husband laying on the charm offensive to Hall, and the man lapping up every single drop.

'Who have I got?' she said with a sigh.

'DS Swaby,' Hall said. 'A good choice. Now, keep me posted.'

Hall left with a smile, and King stomped back into the office with her breakfast. DS Michelle Swaby was one of the few detectives in CID who hadn't fully sided with Lowe and was someone King had worked well with in the past.

It could have been worse.

And she was certain that Hall would have had a role to play in that decision.

King stepped through the confined space that comprised the SCU office and made her way to her own private room. She set her breakfast down, dropped into her chair, and fought against the craving for sleep. The sugar rich croissant was just the ticket and just as she raised it to her mouth, her team stepped in.

'Back, guv,' Townsend called out, stripping off his jacket, and draping it over the chair. Hannon did likewise, and then carefully sat down with a grimace. In her hand was a new packet of biscuits.

King put the croissant down and stepped out.

'Find him?'

'Oh yes,' Hannon said with a giggle. 'Jack had a great time at the social club, didn't you?'

King shot a glance at a sheepish-looking Townsend.

'Anything I need to know?'

'Only that I did exceptional police work.' Townsend shrugged.

'Well, colour me confident,' King said dryly. She turned to Hannon and handed her the paper from her pocket. 'Run this down. Find Jeremy Willis and get him in here.'

'Is he the guy?' Townsend asked.

'He had an appointment booked with Natasha last night and booked it after Lauren Grainger was killed.' King could feel her phone buzzing. 'So yeah, we need to speak with him now.'

'On it, guv,' Hannon said as she ripped open the Hobnobs. She crammed one into her mouth and then began hammering the keys of her keyboard. King looked at her phone and sighed as she turned to Townsend.

'Get your coat back on.'

'Where we going?'

'Hospital,' King said glumly. 'Lauren's post-mortem is done. We need to go and see what we might have missed.'

Townsend stood and grabbed his jacket, his stomach knotting slightly at the idea of the cold, butchered corpse that was awaiting him.

King's stomach was also growling, but more so for the uneaten croissant that remained on her desk.

But food would have to wait.

Someone was killing…and something told her that it wouldn't be long until they did it again.

CHAPTER TWENTY-SIX

Sitting at the bottom of the Marlow Road hill that connects High Wycombe town centre to the M40, Wycombe Hospital loomed large over the 'magic roundabout', a stone's throw from the Rye, the police station, and the overpass that leads to the Eden Shopping Centre and the rest of the high street. Built upon a steep incline, the car parks, both underspaced, and overpriced, offered yet another frustration to those visiting the hospital. The building itself had stood for over one hundred years, having being erected in 1922, thanks to the wealthy Carrington family who for over a century, not only helped to develop the town, but had also served the country and the government in a number of positions. From Viscounts to Foreign Secretaries, the Carrington name was one that was steeped in the very foundations of Buckinghamshire and although the hospital had been renovated numerous times, it still stood as one of their most generous donations.

Now, the hospital, neglected by a government who had failed to prioritise the NHS, was a gloomy, concrete structure that failed to inspire the hope that most visitors yearned for as they approached.

Despite its run-down exterior, the hospital itself had been brought in line with the newest technologies and treatments, and offered a number of specialist areas to help the public. Spread across three buildings, the hospital never felt overrun on account of not having an Accident and Emergency department, with those in need of immediate help being directed to either Wexham or Stoke Mandeville. Although there was a specialist birthing centre, the lack of an emergency operating room meant a large number of pregnancies took place outside of Wycombe Hospital, making their modern, and well-furnished centre almost redundant. Buried beneath the hospital was the morgue, where the pathology department went about their work in ensuring that all deaths were rigorously investigated and also, the bodies of the recently departed were treated with the respect and the care that they deserved. Death was an inevitable part of life, and although the consciousness may have left the mortal coil, what was left behind still meant so much to so many.

As to be expected, there was always a hint of hesitancy by those who don't frequent the morgue as they approached the doors, and King noticed the same lingering doubt in Townsend's eyes as they walked around the main block of the hospital.

'You all good?'

'Yeah, it's just never nice is it?' Townsend said with a shrug. He'd seen a few dead bodies when undercover all those years ago, but they'd usually been a result of one criminal not playing nicely with another.

This was an innocent woman. Ripped from the world by twenty-two plunges of a knife.

'You'll be fine.'

The two of them circled the main building, tackling the steep incline to the smaller building further up the hill. The birthing unit was situated somewhere within and

Townsend had a brief flashback to the night Mandy went into labour, and how everything after that became a fever dream of painful screams, unconditional love, and a constant feeling of uselessness. Somewhere inside, there was most likely another father-to-be feeling the same way, and Townsend sent his sympathies. A small car park opened up, and they marched through, pushing through the door to the Sexual Health Clinic, which was surprisingly full. Those who were waiting to be seen were all avoiding eye contact, as if their very need to be there was in some way embarrassing. Townsend found the notion of looking after their health, be it physical, mental, or sexual, was in any way shameful to be ridiculous.

'This way,' King said, having walked this path a few times in her career. They cut through a corridor and then came to a stairwell, where they took two flights down until the air felt thicker.

They were underground.

They came to a metal door that was electronically locked and King pressed the buzzer. After a few moments, a chirpy voice crackled through.

'Hello?'

'Detective Inspector King.'

'Izzy! I'll be right there.'

King turned to Townsend, who raised his eyebrows.

'Izzy, eh?'

'Dr Mitchell is one of the best, but she can be a bit friendly. She'll like you.'

'Why's that?'

The door buzzed open, and wearing a white lab coat, Dr Emma Mitchell emerged. She was in her early forties, with her mousey brown hair pulled tightly into a ponytail that was failing to disguise a few of the greys. She had the frame of a keen cyclist, and her brown eyes blazed behind the glasses that rested on her sharp nose.

'It's great to see you…' She turned to Townsend and lowered her glasses. 'And who do we have here?'

'DS Jack Townsend.'

Mitchell smiled at the accent.

'Scouse, eh?' She jolted a thumb at herself. 'Yorkshire born and bred, here.'

'That's not the same,' Townsend offered.

'I know. We're better.' She winked at him playfully. Then her face dropped. 'Right…come with me. The poor girl is through here.'

Mitchell turned on the heel of her black ankle boot and headed back into the morgue and King quickly followed. Townsend brought up the rear as the automatic door shut behind them. Instantly, the strong scent of sterilisation infiltrated his senses, and he took a few breaths to keep his eyes from watering. Mitchell turned with a smile.

'Yeah, they don't sell that at the White Company.'

Townsend chuckled. King was right. There was a real welcoming vibe to the forensic pathologist, which juxtaposed the macabre setting of her work. They stopped at a metal door ahead and Mitchell reached across for a box of gloves and drew a pair before offering the box to the detectives who duly obliged.

'Nasty one this,' Mitchell said with the seriousness it deserved. 'And I'll be honest, I'm not too sure how much I have for you.'

'Well, whatever you have could help,' King replied.

'This way.'

Pushing through the metal door, Mitchell led them both into the room, where three large metal slabs were situated in the middle of the room. Equidistant apart, all three had a large light above them and a dipped floor which led to a drainage facility for any spillage.

Only one of the tables was in use, and beneath the

white sheet, Townsend could make out the small frame of a woman.

Lauren Grainger.

'Twenty-two stab wounds,' Mitchell began as she pulled back the sheet to reveal the young woman's corpse. From the days since her death, the colour had been drained from her skin and no longer was Lauren the beacon of light that shone down on the team from her photo on the wall. Her skin was a pale grey colour. Her lips and nipples a duller shade, and her hair hung limply beside her skull.

Townsend felt himself swallow his anger.

Across the woman's body was a multitude of deep wounds, all of them now nothing more than dark openings on her skin, but would have been rich with blood as she tried to cling to life. To Townsend's surprise, King reached out with the back of her hand, and gently ran her knuckle against the girl's head.

To comfort her.

It was a genuinely touching moment, and one that Townsend could see had sent a new wave of determination through his boss.

'The poor girl,' King said. 'Anything of note?'

'Well, she didn't die of blood loss. She actually drowned as one of the first stab wounds punctured her lung and it quickly filled up with blood,' Mitchell said. Her delivery was in line with her level of experience. 'Judging by the pattern of stab wounds, there was no real skill involved.'

'How can you tell?' Townsend asked. His inexperience had led to genuine curiosity. Emma had clearly been briefed, and she offered him a warm smile.

'The angle of the wounds. The locations. Someone trained or with any knowledge would have aimed for some of the vital organs or arteries. The first stab wound...

here…' She pointed to a ragged hole in Lauren's abdomen. 'A few inches lower and it would have penetrated her stomach. But again, I don't feel this was done with any finesse or pre-planning.'

'Meaning it was spontaneous?'

'Reckless,' Mitchell continued. 'Some of the stab wounds go in deeper. Some of them at an angle.'

Mitchell carefully rolled Lauren's body onto its side, to reveal more lacerations and deep wounds on the back.

'Jesus,' Townsend uttered.

'These wounds here were the last ones,' Mitchell said confidently. 'Combined with the bruising on her knees, she was attacked from the front, and eventually, as she collapsed to die on the floor, the killer didn't stop.'

King gritted her teeth.

'Any traces?'

'Nope. Nothing,' Mitchell said. 'No skin or hair. No saliva. No semen or any signs of sexual assault, for that matter. This was a cold-blooded kill.'

'So, she didn't struggle?' Townsend asked. 'I mean, if the person stabbed her from the front, she would have seen them coming. Now I don't know about you, but if I was being approached by someone at four o'clock in the morning, I'd be a bit more on high alert.'

'Hmm.' Emma pondered. 'The killer could have snuck out. Lying in wait.'

'Not where the murder took place,' King chimed in, seemingly connecting to Townsend's way of thinking. 'Edge of the lake. Wide and open.'

'She knew who killed her,' Townsend said confidently. 'That's why she didn't struggle. Because she had her guard down.'

Both King and Mitchell looked at each other and Mitchell raised her shapely eyebrows up.

'I like him. He's good.'

King smiled and nodded.

'He's getting there.'

Townsend took the compliment as intended and graciously nodded his thanks. It wasn't something he was used to.

'I'll ping across the full report. You should have it by the time you get back,' Mitchell said as she pulled the sheet over Lauren's body once more. 'I guess I'll be seeing you again soon, right?'

'You've heard?' King said glumly.

'It's all over the news. Well, Internet news. So pinch of salt and all that.' Mitchell frowned. 'Just do right by these girls, okay?'

It was directed at both King and Townsend, and the two detectives left the morgue with a renewed sense of purpose.

Determined to catch the killer.

As they stepped back out into the brisk, overcast morning, Townsend felt his stomach rumble and knew he'd need to eat. He couldn't keep running on empty.

'Good work back there,' King said. 'You think Lauren knew who killed her?'

'I do.'

'Well then, you have a problem you need to solve,' King said as she marched ahead.

'What's that then?'

'You need to figure out who knew Natasha Stokes as well.'

CHAPTER TWENTY-SEVEN

Despite the insatiable hunger clawing at his stomach, Townsend soon found that staring at the cold, mutilated corpse of an innocent woman had abolished his appetite. He sat at his desk, picking at the chicken pasta pot he had picked up on the way back from his desk. Beside it sat an unopened packet of crisps and a bottle of water.

His body craved sleep. He'd been awake for over thirty hours and had been reliant on the boost his lunch would have provided.

But he couldn't eat.

And Hannon, who had already demolished her wrap, had noticed.

'You need to eat, Jack. Only way to get a thicker stomach.'

'I know. Think I need to sleep more than anything.'

King stormed into the office.

'Well, that can wait.' She marched over to the board where they were collating the evidence and stared at it. Without looking back, she spoke to Hannon. 'Update.'

'I called the Chinnor Wellness Spa, and they've confirmed that Mr Sykes was indeed there yesterday with his wife. Turns out, he *does* treat her to a monthly spa trip on the last Monday of every month.' Hannon shrugged. 'Who knew that a strip club owner could be such a loving husband?'

'Don't judge people,' King said sternly. 'The guy may be a bit a sleazy, but he seemed to be genuinely concerned for his girls. I take it his alibi for Lauren's death checked out?'

Hannon quickly shuffled some papers.

'Errr, yeah. Uniform came back – they've followed up with everyone working that night. All the dancers and Benny, the doorman, confirmed that Sykes stayed behind for a drink after Lauren had left.'

'Thought as much,' King said and drew a line through Sykes and 'Paradise Staff' on the board.

'Uniform say anything else?' Townsend asked, opening his packet of crisps. The thrill of the discussion had tempted him to try to eat again.

'Just that she was nice to them all. Seemed focused and spoke briefly about opening a dance studio. Was saving up for that,' Hannon said sorrowfully, knowing those dreams had been put out. 'One of them mentioned a "shitty ex-boyfriend" who hung around the place.'

'Riley,' King said with a sneer. 'He's still waiting for us, isn't he?'

Before anyone could answer, a knock echoed behind Townsend, and before they could say anything, Detective Sergeant Michelle Swaby stepped in. She was a short woman who counteracted that by powerlifting regularly, and her shoulders were impressively broad. Her blonde hair was pulled back from her head in a tight ponytail, and she looked at everyone through her thick glasses.

Her smile was infectious.

'Sorry to interrupt.' She looked to King. 'Can I have a quick word?'

'Of course. Jack, this is DS Swaby. We worked together for a few years in CID.' Townsend stood and shook her hand.

'Nice to meet you.'

'Ooo, scouse,' she said, almost unintentionally. 'Sorry, big Liverpool fan.'

'That makes two of us.' He smiled and sat back down.

'I guess now's the time to let you know Detective Superintendent Hall has ordered we work alongside CID to track down whoever is killing these women. This isn't a reflection on us as a team, more the severity of the situation and the reality of our resources. Michelle, grab a seat or a desk…' Swaby shuffled in and perched herself on the edge of Townsend's desk. King continued. 'Hannon will get you up to speed shortly, but before we go speak to Riley, anything else?'

'One more from me.' Hannon held her hand up, her eyes locked on her screen. 'I did some further digging into the charity payment from Lauren's account. I had to run it through a few databases, but the payment was made to a Bucks Home Space, which is a Christian charity created to protect vulnerable men, women, and children. It doesn't have much of an online presence, which makes sense, and I'd imagine it's more of a need-to-know basis – referrals from police, hospitals, schools, and the like. You said that Lauren was taken into care, right?'

'Yes. Her mother said that Lauren was taken from her in her teens.' King turned to Swaby. 'The mother had substance abuse issues.'

Swaby was making scrupulous notes. Townsend watched, impressed.

'Like I said, not much in a way of an online presence, but I did find the name of a Father Gordon Baycroft as a contact. I've pulled up his information and have a contact number. Again, he doesn't have much of a social media presence, but he is in his late sixties so…'

'My father is on TikTok…' Swaby blurted out, drawing a few chuckles. 'I'm just saying, some oldies are good with computers.'

'That's true,' King said. 'But I doubt they have technology courses in the church. Great work, Nic. Let's speak to Father Baycroft and see if he can give us a little background on Lauren. If her mother's past is as shifty as she made out, there may be someone who has a grudge or another reason to maybe target Lauren. Jack, give him a call will you?'

'On it, guv.'

'And try to find anything that connects Natasha Stokes to Lauren Grainger. If our theory that Lauren knew the person who killed her is correct, then that same person knew Natasha.'

'Why do you think that?' Swaby asked. A reasonable question, considering she'd just joined the case.

'Because the person who killed Natasha Stokes booked an appointment with her in an empty house a few hours after Lauren Grainger was killed. They knew she was an estate agent and where she worked. It's a theory, but it's our best one. Right, Nic, get Michelle up to speed and, Jack, call a priest.'

'Amen,' Townsend said with a smirk. 'Where are you going?'

'I'm going to ask that little shit, Dean Riley, if he knows Natasha Stokes'.

King strode out of the room like a woman on a mission, and Townsend felt a ping of disappointment that he wouldn't be there to watch it. It was probably sensible, considering their altercation that morning that he be kept away from Riley, but he would have loved to have seen the fear in the young man's eyes when King let loose on him.

Something told him that when she had the bit between her teeth, Detective Inspector Isabella King was a terrifying prospect.

Across the small office from him, Swaby was leaning to peer at Hannon's screen, as the motormouth raced through the past few days and the evidence they'd been collating. It wasn't so much as finding out what had happened, but confirming what hadn't happened. By trimming the fat off the lives of these victims, they would be able to narrow down on the people who had the motives, and then eventually, dig out the truth of what happened.

The truth was that two women had been targeted and brutally killed in cold blood.

They just needed to find out who did it.

Swaby was scribbling away into her notebook, making key notes and points to ensure the necessary information had filtered through. It was only Townsend's third day on the team, but he was pretty clear on the tension that existed between the SCU and CID.

More specifically, between DI King and DCI Lowe.

But egos and feelings needed to be parked, especially when a killer was striking down the innocent, and considering the genuine friendship that seemed to exist between King and Swaby, it wouldn't help to have another capable set of eyes and ears on this.

Stomaching the last forkful of chicken, Townsend then opened the email that contained the information around Bucks Home Space, and then lifted his phone. His lunch was threatening to repeat on him, but he swallowed it down with a swig of his water and then went about calling a priest, knowing it would take every bit of his resolve not to ask why, if there was a god, he would allow something like this to happen.

CHAPTER TWENTY-EIGHT

DI King was expecting a frosty reception when she finally arrived at the interview room, and Riley delivered.

'Fucking took your time.' The young man spat at her before his appointed Duty Solicitor whispered into his ear and Riley rolled his eyes. When he had been taken in by Townsend, Riley had requested representation, and the uniformed officers who booked Riley had already contacted the Defence Solicitor Call Centre to arrange it for him. Rupa Patel was a known figure at High Wycombe Police Station, as she was often the one who was sent to offer free legal advice for those on Riley's side of the table. Never too antagonistic, King had often found her to be a smart and reasonable solicitor, even if she could often provide a bump in the road. Patel and King shared a respectful nod before King began the recording, introducing herself and everyone in the room.

'Mr Riley, I'm sure you're aware as my colleague's told you that as of now you are not under arrest, but we do want to question you regarding the murder of Lauren Grainger at four o'clock on Monday morning.'

'I didn't fucking do anything.'

King ignored him, allowing Patel to do her best to control his outbursts. King opened her laptop onto the desk and then set her eyes on him.

'When we last spoke, Dean…can I call you Dean?'

'You can call me a cab…'

King ignored him.

'Dean, when we last spoke, you said that after you got out of prison, you and Lauren split up.'

'Yeah, when she started taking her clothes off for money,' Riley said angrily. 'Like I said, I didn't want to be with a whore.'

Next to him, Patel shuffled uncomfortably in her seat. It drew a small echo of sympathy from King, who wondered how difficult it was to try to look after people like Riley.

'Now, I asked you if you had any contact with her or saw her again and you said, and I quote, "Nope".'

'Sounds about right.'

King tried to hide her smile, especially as she was leading him down the path she wanted.

'Dean, do you know a woman called Natasha Stokes?'

'Who?'

'Natasha Stokes,' King repeated firmly. 'She owned an estate agency just up the road. Blonde hair. Pretty. Divorced.'

'She sounds great.' Riley smiled at his solicitor. 'But I don't know who ya talking about. Why would I know her?'

'Because she was killed yesterday evening in the same way that Lauren Grainger was.' King could see the colour drain from the young man's gaunt face. She turned her screen around to show the smiling face of Natasha. 'This is her.'

'I don't know her,' Riley said, his voice trembling. 'Look, I haven't done anything.'

'No?'

'He has said so.' Patel cut in, clearly annoyed by King.

'Okay.' King turned the laptop back and tried to navigate the sensitive mouse pad. 'It's just, I'm finding your answers hard to believe, Dean.'

'Well, that's your problem.'

'Actually, it's yours. You said to me on Monday, and earlier in this chat, that you never saw or contacted Lauren. Right?'

'Again,' Patel interjected. 'My client has already answered that question.'

'I appreciate that, I do.' King turned the laptop to face Dean once again. 'Over the past six months, Lauren had been receiving numerous offensive and threatening messages on social media from no less than six different accounts.'

Riley squirmed a little.

'She dances for a lot of perverts.' He shrugged. 'Comes with the job I guess.'

'Let's have a read of some shall we?' King turned the laptop back to herself. 'You dirty slut. You're nothing but a whore. And this one here is the one that really interested me – I should kill you for what you've done to me.'

King fixed Riley with a cold, unblinking stare. He shuffled in his seat and tried to look nonplussed.

'They weren't from me.'

'Funny. See, my team is pretty good with computers and all these accounts were set up and the messages sent from the same IP address. Do you want me to tell you the IP address?'

Riley snapped.

'I didn't mean it.' Riley slammed his hands on the table. 'I just wanted to let that bitch know how much she hurt me.'

'And by bitch, you mean Lauren Grainger?'

'Yes.'

'So after stating to both myself and DS Townsend that you hadn't spoken to, or made contact with her, you are admitting that you harassed her with these messages which included threatening to kill her?'

Patel leant across to whisper something in Riley's ear, but he shrugged her away.

'I was high. Drunk. Whatever. She hurt me so I…'

'What? You wanted to hurt her?'

Riley dropped back in his seat, his eyes watering as the realisation of the situation began to set in. As Patel leant across once more to offer some professional advice, King drew up another image on her screen and turned it to face the two of them. It was a grainy CCTV image of a man in a black hoodie.

'Nice hoodie.' King nodded at Riley's top. 'Quite similar to the one in this image, don't you think?'

'It's a black hoodie.' Riley sighed. 'I'm sure lots of people have them.'

'Yes, but check the date and time of this image. It was less than half an hour before Lauren Grainger was killed, taken up the street where she left work.' King's confidence turned to something more terrifying. 'Where this man, wearing a hoodie such as yours, waited for her and most likely followed her to end her life. Is this man you?'

'No.'

'Then where were you at three forty-two on Monday morning?'

'I told you, I don't know.'

'Dean Riley, I'm arresting you on the suspicion of the murder of Lauren Grainger. You do not need to say anything…'

'What the fuck?'

'…but it may harm your defence if you do not mention when questioned something which you later rely on in court. Anything you do say may be given in evidence.'

King looked to Patel, who seemed resigned to the arrest happening. 'I'll give you two some time, and someone will be back soon.'

Riley stared vacantly at the table as King slammed her laptop shut, nodded to Patel and then marched out of the interview room, knowing that whatever she had on Riley wasn't bulletproof enough to make the charges stick. But there were too many coincidences, too many links to Riley that meant she couldn't afford to let him run away.

Not when they were close.

King marched back through the station, oblivious to any passing officer or colleague who may have offered her a greeting and by the time she'd stormed back into the SCU office, her stomach was growling.

'Guv?' Townsend looked up, the phone held to his ear. She ignored him, bypassed Hannon and Swaby too, and retrieved her croissant from her desk.

It was delicious.

Townsend shot a glance to Hannon, who just smiled and shrugged, and Townsend stood and approached her door.

'How did it go?'

'I arrested him,' King said with a mouth full of pastry. 'He lied, on record, about never contacting her and he also can't account for his whereabouts.'

'Is that enough?' Townsend asked with concern.

'No. It's not. But he is wearing a black hoodie—'

'Not to piss on your chips, but I have a black hoodie at home. They're pretty common.'

'Shall I arrest you then?' King said, trying to inject some levity. 'But we can't let him go just yet. He'll vanish because he knows the finger is pointing his way.'

'So, what do we do?'

King paused for a moment of clarity and then marched out to the rest of the team. Hannon and Swaby lifted their heads from the desk. King approached the board and slapped her hand against it.

'We need to connect Dean Riley to Natasha Stokes. He's under arrest for the murder of Lauren Grainger, and we need to find a connection between him and our second victim. We also need to find out where the fuck he was on Monday morning.' King turned to Hannon. 'Any headway on that burner phone?'

'Not yet, guv. I've been getting Michelle up to speed.'

'Park it. Michelle, start working on where Riley was on Monday morning. Nic, get that burner phone tracked. If we can pinpoint the call or the find what store it was brought in, we can start working back from there.'

'Do you think he's smart enough to get a burner phone?' Townsend mused. 'I mean, he fucked up with the IP address.'

'We have to eliminate it if so,' King said. 'But good point.'

Before Townsend could respond, his phone buzzed. It was the front desk, and he thanked them.

'Guv, Father Baycroft is here.'

'Go.' King nodded encouragingly. 'And see if he knows anything about Dean Riley. If Lauren was donating to the Home Space, there is a chance her and Baycroft still talk.'

'Will do.'

Townsend set off in a brisk stride, knowing that the stakes were being raised with every passing minute.

CHAPTER TWENTY-NINE

Walking into the waiting room at the police station, Townsend wasn't too sure what to expect. His mind had immediately painted a picture of Father Baycroft as a slight and elderly man who ambled about in a black tunic. When the officer behind the desk pointed out Baycroft, he was happy to be surprised.

Baycroft lifted himself from his chair with relative ease and stood possibly an inch or two taller than Townsend himself. He looked trim, an elderly man who looked after himself, but the almost white, thin hair that seemingly hovered around his skull and the wrinkled eyes behind his glasses betrayed his physical fitness. He offered Townsend a warm smile and extended a slightly shaking hand in his direction.

'Detective Townsend?' His voice was calm. A voice of authority. Townsend took his hand and shook firmly, impressed by the man's grip.

'Father Baycroft.'

'Please, call me Gordon,' he said politely. 'I don't expect people to bend to my faith. You can't presume these days.'

'I know. Thanks for making time for us, we really appreciate it. This way.'

Townsend motioned for Baycroft to follow and slowed his own pace to allow him to comfortably keep up. Townsend took a guess the man was in his late sixties and didn't want to rush him. Baycroft followed with little issue and Townsend opened the door to the first available interview room.

'Thank you.'

'Can I get you drink?' Townsend asked. 'Tea? Water?'

'No, no. Thank you. It's very kind but I feel I won't be here too long I'm afraid.' Townsend followed Baycroft into the room and motioned to one of the chairs. Opposite to how briskly he stood, Baycroft lowered himself slowly, his joints clicking. 'You're not from around here are you, son?'

'What gave it away?' Townsend said with a smile as he took the seat next to him, turning it to face the amiable priest.

'I have a nephew who went to university in Liverpool,' Baycroft said aimlessly.

'Poor lad. Right…sorry to cut to this, but as I said on the phone, this is a matter of urgency.'

'Yes, of course.' Baycroft sighed and swallowed his sadness. 'Poor Lauren. She was such a lovely girl.'

'I understand she came to you at Bucks Work Space when she was fifteen?'

'Fourteen. But yes, that's right.' Baycroft nodded to himself. 'Poor girl. Her mother was beyond saving – drink, drugs, men. It was an horrendous environment she came from. I always hoped we'd helped her off that dark path and onto a better one.'

'Is that what Work Space does?' Townsend asked, making a few notes. 'Is it a religious place, I mean?'

'Oh no, not at all. My church, the one in Hazelmere, we had a number of charity programs many years ago when there was more money in this town, and we got involved with a shelter that evolved into a secret safe home for vulnerable people. Men, women, kids. All sorts. It was a place for them to find a corner of safety in the world.'

'When did Lauren leave the home?'

Baycroft sat back and blew out his lips, deep in thought. Townsend liked the man and could see why he was perfect for helping those in need.

'Not long after her eighteenth birthday, I would say. There were on-site carers and nurses. So, while it was hoped that most people's stay would be temporary, there were some who were with us for a few years. But we are going back nearly a decade, so I'm not one hundred per cent sure on that.'

'Do you have records?'

'We do, but I'm not involved with the home as much anymore.'

'Oh, you were the name that my colleague came across when looking online.'

'Well, given my age, I've taken a bit of a backseat. Also…' He lifted the hand that Townsend had noticed was shaking. 'Father Time seems to be catching up with me.'

'I'm sorry to hear that.'

'Don't be. God's will may be mysterious, but we can only accept it and learn from it. But it taught me to step back from my duties a little. Now, I just help out at my church and try to enjoy some of the wonderful countryside we have.'

'Well, I'm new to the area so any recommendations would be welcome.' Townsend scribbled down a few last notes. 'Who would be best to talk to about residency records?'

'Oh, it's all gone digital now. But I can put in a word. I understand this is a serious police matter, but our compliance team is very strong on the privacy of our residents. Which I agree with.'

'Understood.'

'But I'll speak with them and see about getting the records released. Anything to help you find who did this to that poor girl.' The emotion of Lauren's death was beginning to show in Baycroft's eyes, despite his attempts to hide it. Townsend closed his notebook, not wanting to drag the man's heartache out any longer.

'Did anyone from Lauren's past ever cause any problems when she was with you? Any ex-partners from her mum or—'

'No. The home was very secretive. Doctors, social workers, police. They would bring people to us, so it was never a case of people just showing up.' Baycroft smiled. 'I'm sorry I can't be more helpful.'

Townsend stood and extended his hand.

'You've been a big help. Thank you. I know this is hard for you to hear.'

'Just catch this person. Please,' Baycroft said firmly. 'I'll call you when I have access to those records.'

'Appreciate it.' Townsend opened the door for Baycroft, who, under the emotional strain of Lauren's death, seemed less stable. The man hadn't said it was Parkinsons, but the shake in his hand seemed worse and his once confident stride a little laboured. Townsend walked him back through the station to the front door, where a light drizzle had begun to fall upon the town. 'Finally, does the name Dean Riley mean anything to you?'

'Riley? Riley?' Baycroft frowned as he searched his memories. 'Oh yes. He took quite a shine to Lauren when he stayed with us.'

'He stayed at Home Space too?'

'Only for a few months,' Baycroft said. He then looked

around for anyone and then spoke quietly. 'between you and me, I was happy when he went back home.'

'Thank you, Gordon. You've been a big help.'

The old priest said his farewells and shuffled out into the light rain, drawing his collar up as he disappeared around the corner. But by then, Townsend was already bounding down the stairs two at a time back to the SCU. As he burst through the door, all three women looked up at him.

'Riley stayed with Lauren at the Home Space,' Townsend said excitedly. 'That's how they met.'

'Okay,' King said flatly, drawing a frown from Townsend. 'But that's not enough to add to our theory. Based on what you and Nic have told me, his mum doesn't seem too bothered about him, so I don't think it's beyond the realms of possibility that he was taken into care, too. Was there anything about past partners or anything about Natasha?'

'No.' Townsend seemed disappointed. 'The people who ended up at Home Space were usually brought in by social workers or police. They didn't disclose the location to many people, and we might have to wait on the records. Father Baycroft said he'll get them for us as soon as possible.'

'How was he?' King asked.

'Heartbroken. But he was helpful enough. Hopefully, we get those records soon.'

'Good work, Jack,' King said, picking up on his deflation. 'Anything and everything can be important right now.'

Townsend took a moment to reflect on his own inexperience. King was right. Everything was important, but not everything was relevant, and the last thing he wanted was to start chasing his own tail.

'I just wanted something big that we can shake this case

up with, you know?' he said as he dropped into his chair. Before King could respond, Swaby, who had perched on the end of Hannon's desk, clapped her hands together.

'I might just have it,' she said gleefully.

'What's that?' King said, leaning over her shoulder. Townsend stood as Hannon scooted round on her chair.

'You asked me to look at the CCTV images. Well, I can't give you an identification of the man in the hood, but I can give you confirmation of who's phone was pinpointed to within a few metres of that area at that time.'

With a triumphant press of the enter key, window opened up on her screen, with the number of the phone being tracked and the person it was registered to.

'Dean Riley,' King said as she squeezed Swaby on the shoulder. 'Good work, Michelle.'

Swaby beamed at the rest of the team as King headed to the door.

'Guv?' Townsend called after her. 'Where are you going?'

'To speak to Hall. Then you and I are going to drop this bombshell on that little shit's head.'

King disappeared through the doorway, and as her footsteps echoed into the distance, Townsend turned, and looked up at the board. They now had legitimate death threats from a jilted ex-partner and could now place him at the scene.

All the dots were connecting.

Except one, and it was the one that sat heavy in the pit of Townsend's stomach and made him question the path they were treading.

Natasha Stokes.

Why on earth would someone like Dean Riley kill someone he didn't know?

CHAPTER THIRTY

'I loved her.'

Riley's words were heavy with heartache and as the tears poured down his cheeks, he shook. Townsend and King sat across from him, allowing him a moment of grief. Rupa Patel was once again sitting by his side, and she offered her client a tissue. He took it, but the floodgates weren't closing anytime soon.

'So why did you send those messages?' King asked, refusing to budge.

'I was mad. Angry,' Riley said through sobs. 'I came outta prison and she'd moved on. I didn't…you know… know how to handle it.'

Townsend clasped his hands together and rested them on the table of the interview room.

'Threatening to kill her is a bit extreme,' he said firmly. 'Now, I've been married a long time, and trust me, we've had our ups, and downs. But I've never said anything like that.'

'I drink. I take drugs.' Riley admitted freely. 'Sometimes I'm not quite in control, you know?'

'Like on Monday morning?' King asked.

'We've been over this,' Patel said with exasperation.

'I know, but your client said he had no recollection of where he was. Well, perhaps I can help him.'

As King was updating DCI Hall of their progress, Townsend had requested the printouts of the GPS location of Riley's phone. Swaby had printed it out for him, and now King placed the damning evidence on the table.

'What's this?' Riley sniffed.

'This, Dean, is proof that you were there on Monday morning.'

'What?'

'We were able to track your mobile phone to within a few metres of the exact location the man from our CCTV was, at the same time of the morning.' King looked at him. 'So, what were you doing there?'

Riley looked to his Duty Solicitor in panic. Her despondent sigh told him there was no way out of it.

'Dean.' Townsend cut in. 'It's important you answer that question.'

Silence hung in the air of the interview room, and Riley lifted his cup of water with a shaking hand. As he managed to swallow some, he wiped his mouth, and took a breath.

'Look, I was trying to pluck up the courage to speak to her. That's all.'

'At four in the morning?' King said with a raised eyebrow.

'She won't speak to me. I've done it loads of times… waited outside and thought about approaching her, but I never do.' Riley shook his head. 'I was too fucking scared of being rejected again.'

Townsend looked at the young man. The false bravado of the man who had confronted him in the social club had evaporated. Deep down, he was just a young man with a broken heart, who was lashing out because he couldn't deal with the pain.

Did that make him a killer?

'Tell me what you know about Natasha Stokes.' Townsend changed the subject. The name sparked a recognition from Riley.

'That name again. She's already asked me that and like I said, I don't know who the fuck you're talking about.'

King took control of the situation.

'Dean, we have you making death threats to a woman who was found dead a few days later. You have now confessed that you just so happened to be outside her place of work, in the early hours of the morning, minutes before she was murdered.' King stacked up the papers and stood and turned to Patel. 'You need to have a talk with him. He needs to understand what's happening. This is serious.'

As King turned to the door, she glanced at her watch. It was past six, and Hannon, and Swaby would most likely be gone. Townsend offered Riley a firm nod and then followed his boss out of the room.

'I didn't do this,' yelled Riley, as Townsend closed the door, shutting off the sound of the young man slamming his fists onto the table.

'Good job in there.' King offered. 'Why don't you get yourself home?'

'Cheers, guv,' Townsend said, flicking an anxious glance back at the door of the interview room.

'Everything okay?' King asked, her arms folded.

'I just…I don't think he did it,' Townsend replied.

'Well, be that as it may, right now, the evidence we've got puts him at the scene and with the motive. You said this was a crime of passion, right?' King shrugged. 'Nothing drives pain more than a broken heart.'

'I just think we're missing something,' Townsend said, shaking his head with annoyance.

'Well then. Go home. Get a good night's sleep and get back here bright and early to figure out what.'

'Night, guv,' Townsend called after King as she walked back down the corridor towards the canteen, telling Townsend she wasn't planning on heading home anytime soon. Part of him wanted to stay, to trawl through the evidence word by word until something leapt out at him. But the lure of another evening with his daughter was too strong, and after popping back to the office to retrieve his jacket and a few files of the case, he headed to his car. A few uniformed officers offered him a wave, which he returned in kind, before pulling out of the station towards his nemesis of a roundabout. With the drizzle turning into a summer storm, the roads were a little slow, with the traffic backed all the way up the Marlow Hill towards the motorway. Thankfully for Townsend, he was able to turn off halfway up, noticing the single lane traffic due to a traffic collision further ahead. Once he was on the country roads back to Flackwell Heath, he flew back, and was pulling up to his house in no time at all.

He couldn't wait to get inside.

To see his girls.

As he stepped through the door, he wasn't greeted by the recently-regular smell of a home-cooked meal, and as he stepped through into the kitchen, he found both Mandy and Eve sitting at the dining table.

'Hello, ladies.'

'Hey, babe.' Mandy leant back and puckered her lips for a kiss, which he eagerly took. 'Good day?'

'Busy,' he said, sliding off his jacket before leaning over Eve's chair and burying his face in her hair to kiss her. 'Hey, pickle.'

'Look at my new pencil case, Daddy,' she said without looking up. 'I got lots of new bits.'

'Wow.' Townsend faked enthusiasm. 'All ready for school, huh?'

'Yup.'

'Do you like school?'

'Yup.'

Townsend rolled his eyes as Mandy giggled. It was like getting blood out of a stone.

'Are you excited about meeting new friends?' he asked, and Eve sat back, and contemplated.

'Hmm. Only if they're nice.'

'Well, yeah. You don't want to spend time with not nice people, do you?'

'No. But you do.' Eve looked at him. 'Mummy says we need to be extra nice to you because you don't spend time with nice people.'

'Well, your mummy is very smart isn't she?' He winked at his wife. 'Good day?'

'Yeah, we went to the Eden. It's massive in there,' Mandy said as she stood. 'I got some outfits for work…'

'Your job from home…'

'Look, mister,' she said with a smile. 'I want to feel the part, so I'm going to dress the part. I also got little-un here some school bits.'

'Yeah, I got a new dress.'

'Oh wow. Can I see?' Townsend said, walking to the fridge, and retrieving a beer. 'Pizza tonight?'

Mandy nodded, and then she suggested a fashion show for Daddy, which Eve got overexcited for. As they charged upstairs to get changed, Townsend took a quiet few minutes to decompress. A moment where most people would unknowingly reach for their phone and scroll mindlessly was something he never understood. His phone was still in his jacket.

All he wanted was a few minutes to enjoy his beer, and

appreciate what could come home to every night. The past week had shown him to not take any of it for granted. The rest of the evening passed with a constant laugh-track, as Eve, and Mandy did an over-the-top routine in showing him their new clothes, with Mandy selecting a different song on her playlist for the catwalk. Eve strutted through the kitchen like a model, and she giggled loudly as her mum did the same.

The house was starting to fill with happiness.

Starting to feel like home.

They tucked into the takeaway pizza that soon arrived at their door, with Eve rationing the garlic bread unevenly in her favour.

Soon, Townsend found himself helping her into her shorts and T-shirt, emblazoned with Disney Princesses, as she scrambled up onto the bed they'd recently bought for her new room. It had a small compartment underneath which she'd turned into a crafts desk, and she clambered up the ladder until she was laying down at Townsend's chest height.

'Night, pickle,' he said, leaning over the wooden frame that kept her secured up high, and kissing her forehead. 'Thanks for being a good girl.'

'Daddy…' Eve said, looking up at him with her big blue eyes. 'When you were gone, weren't you with nice people?'

Townsend was stopped in his tracks. Eve was so young when he first went undercover, and over the years, they'd kept as much of it from her as possible. She didn't need to know any more than that he was working, but as she'd got older, and too smart for her own good, she'd begun to understand the job he did.

The reason the police were needed.

He rested his arms on the wooden barrier and then his chin on them and smiled.

'No. I wasn't.' He couldn't lie to her. 'But I had you and Mummy to make up for it.'

'Were you stopping the bad people?'

'Yes, angel.' He stroked her hair with the back of his fingers. 'That's what Daddy does.'

'Are there still bad people outside?'

The inner thought process of a young child was something that would cause Townsend constant bafflement, and he looked at his daughter with nothing other than immense pride.

An incredible kid.

His kid.

'Yup,' he said with a nod. 'Sadly, there are always bad people. That's why we need to be good.'

'Oh yes, we need to be good.' She agreed. 'And those people shouldn't be bad all the time.'

She turned over onto her pillow, her eyes closing as sleep began to call her.

'Why's that then?'

Eve yawned as the final words filtered from her lips.

'Because my daddy will catch them.'

And she was asleep.

Townsend's heart slammed against his ribs, his daughter's words, and innocence filling him with love and pride in equal measure. He stood for five minutes, watching his little girl sleep peacefully until he was disturbed by his wife who had come to find him. They embraced for a few minutes before she said she was going to have a nice, long bath, and read her latest book.

While his wife was enjoying the pleasures of relaxation, Townsend sat himself down at the kitchen table. He popped the cap off another cold bottle of beer and then opened the first folder he'd brought back from work.

As much as he wanted to lose himself in the tranquility of his home life, the morbid thought of Lauren and

Natasha's grieving families clung to the forefront of his mind like a parasite.

His eyes scanned over the words before him, and he knew he needed to find something – anything – that he'd missed.

He needed to find the killer.

Before they killed again.

CHAPTER THIRTY-ONE

Regret.

That was the overwhelming feeling that coursed through Michaela Woods's veins every waking minute of the day. It clung to her like a leech, and she knew that for the rest of her life, it was a feeling she would constantly battle. Regret that she ever dabbled with drugs and the regret that it tore away everything she'd ever loved.

She knew, as a recovering addict, that it was a harsh disease that would follow her around until her dying day, but now, a few weeks shy of her fortieth birthday, she realised that she needed to shoulder some of the blame. It wouldn't make up for the things she'd done, but it would at least go some way to laying a smoother path back to her daughter.

Dominique was fourteen.

And Michaela hadn't spent a full day with her in over a decade.

Just the thought of missing out on all the little things – the idle chit-chats over breakfast, the irrational teenage meltdowns, the snuggles on the sofa watching whatever reality show she'd become obsessed with – broke her heart, but she knew it was deserved.

Jonathan, her ex-husband, was as loyal and as loving as a man could be, and his dedication to Dominique was obvious for the world to see. He was the one, when Michaela's addiction began to worsen, who stuffed her into rehab, pleading and begging with her to get better.

But she'd let him down.

Let them both down.

When Michaela had met Jonathan, they were both studying law at Manchester University, and they fell madly in love and headed for London together to begin their careers in law firms and live a comfortable life. They married young, perhaps too young, and when Michaela had fallen pregnant with Dominique, she did her best to hide her disappointment. She loved her daughter, deeply and truly, but at twenty-six, she felt like she was giving up a few years of really understanding who she was in life.

She went from student to trainee solicitor to mum in a blink of an eye, while Jonathan, with his good looks and raw charisma, became a prolific and well-respected solicitor for one of the capital's top firms. Not only that but considering the lack of black men in the profession, he became a vocal figure in the impoverished parts of the city, driving charity and educational initiatives to help young black children pursue careers often seen as beyond them.

He was a hero.

All she felt like was a mum.

She had unhealthily hidden her post-natal depression, which never really subsided, even when Dominique started school. She went back to work, but felt behind the curve, so when she was invited on a work night out, and someone invited her into the toilet cubicle for a 'booster', she accepted. She'd never done cocaine before, but as soon as she drew it into her system, she'd felt a levity that had been lost for years.

It was a high she continued to chase, and soon, her mind was consumed with her next fix.

It decimated her marriage.

Alienated her child.

Ruined her life.

A whole decade gone as quickly as a line up her nostril.

Multiple trips to rehab. Countless 'Day Ones'.

But she never really made it back.

Estranged from her daughter, Michaela's mental health had spiralled, and she focused more on her addiction than getting her life back on track, which made her an easy target for the many dealers who were more than happy to take advantage. Although the drugs hadn't helped, Michaela was a beautiful woman. Her dark skin had become rougher due to the drug abuse, but she was still a stunning woman.

To the dealers, it was easy to exchange a bag of cocaine for a blow job and in her most desperate times, combined with her isolation from the family she'd pushed away, she'd willingly debased herself.

But no more.

The last eight months had been the most positive in years, and although she'd fallen off the wagon a few times, she'd ensured that she climbed back on once the binge was over. A few lost days here and there were to be expected, but now, life wasn't just about her next bag of white.

It was about being a functioning human.

Being a mum.

An old friend from university, Marcus, had a small law firm in Beaconsfield and had offered her a chance to start afresh. It was an admin role, but it paid okay, and allowed her to once again dabble in the world of law. It put a roof over her head, food in her fridge, and she even offered to pay for Dominique's next school trip. Jonathan, who hadn't remarried but was in a committed long-term relationship with a woman named Jennifer, had been reluctant to let her back in. But Dom had a curiosity about who her mother was, and there had even been a few meet-ups in a local coffee shop.

Baby steps.

That's what she clung to now.

Baby steps that could potentially grow into leaps.

She pulled her car over onto the side of the road and stepped out, looking up at the large, four-bedroom house that Jonathan had bought two years ago. It was in Chesham, a small town on the other side of the Chilterns and a fifteen-minute drive from her small flat in Beaconsfield. His Range Rover was on the driveway, alongside Jennifer's more modest Ford Fiesta, although Michaela noted the very recent license plate. They did well for themselves, and she knew beyond the door, her daughter lived a life of perceived privilege that was a testament to the hard work and dedication of her father.

Michaela had nothing to do with it.

But she wanted to.

She looked up at the window above the door, where the light was peeking through the drawn curtains. She knew it was Dominique's room, she'd seen her on one of her other numerous drive-bys, and for the next five minutes, Michaela stared up and let the tears fall down her cheeks. It might not have been the healthiest way to spend her evenings, but they were necessary.

A reminder of why she didn't go back to her ex-boyfriend, a man who had been loving enough, but had sold cocaine throughout High Wycombe and the surrounding areas.

A reminder of why she needed to keep herself clean.

To have a chance at being the mother she'd never been.

She noticed a curtain twitch on a neighbouring house, and Michaela swiftly got back into her car, wiped her tears, and pulled away, cutting back through the heavily wooded Chesham Bois towards Amersham, where she would then ascend Goor Hill up to Amersham Road, which would lead her on a pleasant drive back to Beaconsfield. It was a journey she could do on autopilot, and while her body safely navigated the car all the way home, her mind was focused solely on her daughter.

She would stay better.

Stay clean.

Reach out to Jonathan and show him as many times as it took to convince him that she could spend time with Dom again. Build a relationship and have a reason to keep away from the life she'd been able to climb out from. As she parked the car on the road outside the block of small flats she called home, she stepped with purpose from her car towards the gated garden outside. As she did, she heard footsteps behind her and turned.

It was half ten, and the road wasn't exactly a hub of activity beyond the residents.

Her eyes widened with shock and a smile spread across her face.

'Oh my god.' She approached the man with a smile. 'What are you doing here?'

The pain of the knife was instant, a burning sensation that filled her neck as the blade buried into the side of her throat. With eyes bulging with panic, Michaela looked up at her killer and with the face of her daughter flashing in her mind, clawed at him with the remaining strength in her arms. Her nails made contact with his face, but as he yanked the knife from her neck, the wound began to pump blood and she stumbled backwards into the shrubbery. He drove the knife into her stomach, pushing her down into the weeds, and as the vision of her killer lifting the knife once more began to fade, she saw Dominique's beautiful face and smiled, before everything went to black.

CHAPTER THIRTY-TWO

It was a common occurrence for DI King to startle awake and realise she was asleep on her sofa. It was even more common that when she did, the thumping headache of a full bottle of wine was the usual cause of it. It wasn't something she was proud of at all, and every night, as she drove back from the Thames Valley Police Station to her spacious two-bedroom flat in Cookham, she would tell herself that she would have a clean night.

That tonight was the night that she would stop drinking.

It was a twenty-minute drive from the station, one that took her through the affluent town of Marlow. The quaint high street, filled with luxury boutique clothes shops and independent art galleries, was a magnet for local celebrities, with a number of well-known TV and radio personalities often visiting the outlets, or taking their children to the vast park along the River Thames that cut through the town on its way towards the country's capital. Most nights, as she passed over the narrow bridge, she looked out at the boats gliding down the Thames and wondered how nice it would be to just sail away.

Away from the grind and grit of her job.

Away from the chaos of her social life.

After her marriage to DCI Lowe had broken down, King had walked the well-trodden path of most people who had been devastated by the ending of a long-term relationship. It hadn't been her decision, and for the first few months, her denial had seen her seeking comfort in the arms of random strangers. The immediate pleasure quickly turned to a deep dissatisfaction, and it wasn't long before King realised that she needed to make peace with herself before she could move on.

It didn't help that her ex-husband was on her doorstep, thriving in an environment that catered to the male ego and when she found out about his new relationship, that was the trigger for the reliance on wine.

Her life became a sequence of two things.

Throwing herself into her work and throwing herself into the bottle.

She did her best to hide it, although the rest of CID knew what was going on. It's hard to conceal a drinking problem in an office full of detectives, and when Hall offered her the opportunity of running the Specialists Crime Unit, she jumped at the chance to be separated from the rest of the team. As much as she hated the disrespect of being dumped in a basement to do busy work with a team of inexperienced or troubled detectives, it meant she could hide her shame in a dark corner of the building. But then that sorrowful, pathetic drunk would clash with her own inner-detective, who despised that she was hindering her ability to do her job.

She was a damn good detective.

One of the best in the county.

But she was stuck in a loop of self-destruction. She'd leave the office every night, vilifying herself for not being strong enough, but then that same self-loathing would see her stop at the same off-licence every night to pick up a bottle, served by the same shop keeper who offered her a regretful smile. He knew she was an alcoholic, but it wasn't his responsibility to get her to stop.

Every night would see her collapse on the sofa, half a bottle already gone, and then, when the final glass was knocked back, she'd black out until the hangover wrestled her awake.

Rinse and repeat.

Except, this time, it wasn't the buzzing of her headache that summoned her to consciousness, although it was lingering dangerously in the background.

It was the buzz of her phone, rumbling on the glass top of her coffee table.

With a grunt, she sat up, her work shirt creased against her lean body and her hair, usually brushed straight, was a wild, ragged mess. She yawned, then scowled at the stale smell of her breath, and then her eyes scanned the room.

The phone rattled the glass once more and clarity snapped in, and, ignoring the headache, she lifted the phone.

DSI Hall.

'Fuck,' King uttered and then lifted the phone to her ear. 'Guv?'

She could hear the background noise. Enough to tell her he was outside, and enough to tell her he was at a crime scene. Her heart dropped before he even spoke.

'It's happened again, Izzy,' Hall said solemnly.

He told her where and within two minutes she was brushing her teeth and picking out a new shirt as quickly as she could. On the way out of the door, she swallowed two paracetamol in a lame attempt to stem the hangover. It didn't work, and as she sped down the M40 that connected High Wycombe to Beaconsfield, her head rocked with a vengeance.

She needed to quit drinking.

She just had to.

The motorway at half midnight was completely clear, and she put her foot down, eating up the miles between the two towns as quickly as she could. As she turned off to head to Beaconsfield, she could feel her knuckles tightening over the steering wheel as the fury of another murder began to overwhelm the hangover.

Another woman dead.

It meant that whoever was doing this had a serious reason to, and a compulsion to kill.

It meant it would happen again until they stopped him.

And it also meant that all the work done to prove Dean Riley was the killer had been in vain. As grotesque as the young man was, he was currently locked in the holding cells at High Wycombe Police Station.

Dean Riley wasn't their man, and as she approached the flashing blue lights and the growing crowd of morbidly curious spectators, she couldn't think of a more sobering thought. King pulled her car up onto a nearby curb and killed the engine, then threw open her door and welcomed the drizzle that had begun to fall upon the muggy, summer evening. As she marched towards the crime scene, she ordered the leering crowd out of her way, before demanding the nearest uniform officer on the cordon to move them further away. What turned her stomach most was the number of people who were holding up their phones, trying to record the murder scene as some sort of exclusive.

They'd post it to social media in the hunt for likes and recognition, when all they were doing was impeding the hunt for the killer.

King showed her ID to a few more officers en route to the crowd of overall-wearing SOCOs, who were already going to work, despite the conditions, to salvage the crime scene. Hall had told her the victim's name, Michaela Woods, and as King approached Michaela's body, she felt her stomach flip.

She could have been looking into the mirror.

A middle-aged Black woman, slender build, but with her hair braided, the woman was splayed out across the concrete, her neck open from a deep stab wound. Her white top had been soaked red, and instantly, King could see another six or seven violent stab wounds.

The woman had been butchered.

Just like Lauren Grainger.

Just like Natasha Stokes.

With her eyes locked on the latest victim, King didn't notice DSI Hall approach from her right.

'Michaela Woods. Forty-one years old. She lived in one of these flats,' Hall said, pointing to the overarching building. 'Her car's parked just down the road and…'

'She was killed on her way home,' King said, not taking her eye off the body. 'Which meant he was waiting for her.'

'Which also means whatever path you were going down with Riley is the wrong one.' Hall's voice sounded regretful.

'We need to eliminate everyone, sir. Riley has now been eliminated,' King said through gritted teeth.

'Look, Izzy.' Hall's tone had already shifted to apologetic. 'I know how much this case means to you, and I know you have a loyalty to find these women's killers, but…well…you look like crap.'

'Excuse me?' King spun to her boss, feeling the weight of the bags under her eyes. 'You called me in the middle of the night. I'm hardly going to be dressed to the fucking nines, am I?'

Hall squinted as he stared at her. Searching.

She knew he could see her shame.

'Is that all it is?' he asked as if he knew the truth. 'Because I need you at your best. *These women* need you at your best.'

'Yes, guv.'

'Uniform are already going door to door. We've already got a search out for anyone in the area within a few miles radius and the CID night shift is already trawling through CCTV,' Hall stated, impressively already commanding the crime scene.

'What do you need me to do?'

Hall turned to her, his jaw set straight and his eyes radiating with the authority he had commanded from his years of service. He was firm, but he was fair.

He nodded to her, as if it was one final throw of the ball for her to run with.

'I need you to find the sick bastard doing this.'

With a nod of understanding, King strode back to her car with determination pumping through her veins, and a promise to herself and the victims that she'd break her vicious cycle of self-destruction.

There were more important things than her own misery.

Someone was killing.

And she had no idea who.

CHAPTER THIRTY-THREE

It was a little after 5 a.m. when Townsend's phone had buzzed, and the moment he saw King's name on the screen, he rolled out of bed and knew exactly what had happened. The call lasted ten seconds, but Townsend didn't need the request from King to get himself into the office.

He was already getting dressed.

Mandy stirred from her side of the bed, and he quickly kissed her on the top of her head, told her he loved her, and dashed out of the room, ducking his head into Evie's room to see her still sound asleep. He whispered his goodbye to her before dashing to his car, and within minutes, he was racing down the empty country roads towards the town centre. Within half hour of King's call, Townsend was bursting through the side entrance of the station, his lanyard flapping around his neck, and as he took the stairs two at a time down to their office, his phone buzzed.

King again.

'CID Office. Soon as you can.'

He turned on his heels and darted up through the near

empty station, with the night shift officers woozily winding down the final hour of their shift. Townsend had little time to speak with them, and he bounded up the stairs and made his way to CID which was a hub of activity. Most of the team were sitting at their desks, and at the front of the room, Townsend could see that a replica board had been constructed that mimicked the one they had on the wall of their office. Copies of the victims' photos were pinned to it, along with all the other information they'd procured over the past week, but most notably, with a big cross through the picture of Dean Riley. He hadn't even given the young man a second of consideration, but seeing it swiftly brought to reality that they'd been chasing the wrong lead.

That all their efforts had been for nothing.

He could feel his stubbled cheeks turning red and Townsend tried to bury his embarrassment. His 'imposter syndrome' had been something that had been almost eradicated by the apparent progress they'd been making, but now, with all their work focused in the wrong direction, he felt like a fraud among the rest of CID. As his eyes scanned the room, he caught DS Swaby looking at him from across the office, and she motioned to the empty seat beside her. As he sat down, the rest of the team turned their attention to the board at the front, where DI King stood, arms folded, and a solemn look on her face. She nodded to Townsend, seemingly grateful of an ally in the room, and then she cleared her throat. Behind her, the seniority of DCI Lowe and DSI Hall loomed large.

'Right. Here're the facts,' King started, her voice a little wavering. She began to move to the board. 'Lauren Grainger. Natasha Stokes. Michaela Woods. All three murdered brutally by a killer showing a distinct pattern of panicked knife attacks. We don't believe these to be random, especially as the killer lured Natasha to one of her properties through her work and based on the location of the other killings, had been lying in wait for Lauren and Michaela. Now, we've been working on the assumption that our victims knew their killer and—'

'Wasn't Dean Riley here last night?' One of the detectives interrupted. 'He was the person you arrested?'

King drew her lips into a tight line and gritted her teeth. Townsend looked beyond her to Lowe, who seemed to offer a nod of appreciation at the interruption.

'We had established means, motive, and opportunity for Riley, as he *was* at Paradise the night of Lauren's murder and had sent her death threats. My team had been working diligently to establish a connection between him and Natasha, but as of last night, that line of enquiry is now over. We'll be releasing Riley this morning.'

'The work done so far has been great,' Swaby chipped in, clearly a well-liked voice of authority among her peers. 'We've got some incredible detail on both Lauren and Natasha and have been working with their respective FLOs to build a clear picture.'

She looked to King, who mouthed 'thank you'. Before she could continue, DSI Hall stepped forward, a small action that seemingly sent a shockwave of attention through the room. Usually a picture of composure, the Detective Superintendent looked tired and agitated.

'Bottom line, we need to pick our game up. Specialist Crimes has done a great job so far, but this is now a priority for every single person in this room. Three women have been killed in a week. The town is terrified, and I've got the mayor and every one of my superiors so far up my arse on this, I could floss with their shoelaces. Now, I know there are some issues among some people in this office.' A few detectives shuffled uncomfortably in their seats. Townsend looked to King and Lowe, but their seniority shone through. 'But I want that shit shut down. Understand? We've got lots of information on this board, and we have a load more coming. Uniform are writing up the statements they've got, a FLO has been assigned to Michaela Wood's ex-husband and we've already confirmed his alibi as well as his new partner. But we need to widen the net. We need to establish what links these three women, why they were targeted, and who by. We cannot, and I can't stress this enough, allow this man to do this again. Do we understand?'

A collective 'Yes, sir' echoed from the room and Hall gave them all a curt nod before he turned to King and Lowe, lowering his voice for their ears only.

'Now, you two, play nice. These women deserve our everything.'

'Yes, sir,' Lowe responded, ensuring he spoke first.

'Yes, guv,' King said with a sigh.

'Right. Get to it.'

Hall marched through the office and off into the corridor, and instantly, the volume rose as all the detectives began to discuss the case. Townsend stood and approached King and Lowe, who were already in what looked like a strained conversation.

'Fine,' King snapped.

'Look, I'm just saying fresh eyes could help.' Lowe had a slightly patronising tone. 'Your team has collated an awful lot of information, but you've been focused on the wrong bit. So we can investigate the Woods murder, and you go through what you have so far to try to establish a link.' Lowe glanced at the approaching Townsend. 'Can I help you?'

'No, sir.' He turned to King. 'You okay, guv?'

'Long night.'

'It looks like it,' Lowe snarled. 'You look very tired, Izzy. As for you, DS Townsend, maybe you could go back to your office and make yourself useful? I've already got a team of competent DSs so—'

'Leave it,' King said sternly. 'Let's just find out who is doing this, shall we?'

'Absolutely.' Lowe held up his hands. 'Remember, Jack...whenever you fancy it.'

Lowe made a small, shadow boxing motion, extending another invitation for Townsend to meet him in the ring. Townsend chuckled and shook his head.

'Sorry, sir. But I've got a murderer to find. But have fun.'

Before Lowe could respond, King took Townsend by the arm and the two of them headed back through the CID office. Swaby swiftly lifted her notepads and laptop and followed. The noise of the office disappeared behind them and once they were in the stairwell, King pulled out her vape and took a long puff. Her hand was shaking with anger.

'You know you can't do that in here, right?' Townsend observed. King shot him a glance, and he shrugged, just as Swaby stepped past.

'See you down there,' she said, the tension of the case doing nothing to dim her bubbly personality.

'Thanks, Michelle,' King said, then took another puff. The tropical fruit smelling vapour filled the stairwell, and she turned to Townsend.

'I just...I just can't stand how much he gets to me.'

King sighed and Townsend was slightly taken aback by the rare moment of vulnerability. It had been nearly a week, and having worked together tirelessly, a respect had been forged within the ranks of their respective positions.

But this was an extension of friendship.

Townsend looked back over his shoulder to the corridor beyond the stairwell door, and then shrugged.

'Then don't let it.' King frowned at him. 'Look, he might be a senior officer, but that doesn't mean he can't be a prick as well. Best way to beat someone like that is show them that they can't get to you.'

'Yeah, I know. It's tricky. He is a prick.'

'Oh god, yeah. A royal one at that.' The two chuckled. 'So what now?'

Townsend looked to his boss, who took one final puff and then pocketed her vape.

'We go back through Lauren and Natasha's files. Everything. We look for some other connection beyond Dean Riley or being blonde women. Then we find this guy before Lowe does.' King stopped on the stairs. 'But first, how much shit are you able to swallow?'

'Excuse me?' Townsend raised his eyebrows.

'We've got to tell Dean Riley he's free to go.'

King set off back down the steps, and Townsend took a second to compose himself, readying him for the nailed-on onslaught of abuse the two of them would be receiving. As he fell in step behind King, he at least made her smile with his response.

'Oh, goodie.'

CHAPTER THIRTY-FOUR

'Well done. Seriously. Great work.'

Riley's sarcasm matched the sneer across his face as he was marched from the holding cell to the custody desk where he'd been booked in the day before. King and Townsend had to take their medicine, knowing that despite the litany of issues the young man had, they did in fact have the wrong guy. As the officer behind the counter passed across the transparent bag containing Riley's possessions, Rupa Patel attended to the necessary paperwork. King stood, arms folded, while Townsend leant against the wall behind her.

'You're not out of the woods yet,' King said, not believing it herself.

'Oh yeah…I must have snuck out of this cell and killed that woman.' Riley laughed. 'Why don't you try some actual police work next time?'

Townsend pushed himself off the wall.

'And next time you find some unlucky woman who's thick enough to give you a try, maybe don't stalk them like a jealous prick and send them death threats.'

'Right, enough of that,' Patel said sternly. The Duty Solicitor shot a glance to his superior officer.

'She's right, Jack,' King said with a roll of the eyes.

'Yeah, Jack.' Riley chuckled, then threw a couple of mock jabs. 'Next time, I won't give you a free shot.'

'The only thing you'll give me, mate, is a headache,' Townsend spat back.

'Are we done here?' King said to Patel, who signed the final sheet.

'Yep. Mr Riley, you're free to go. Officer Bentley will show you out.'

Riley had already pulled a cigarette from the box he had retrieved from the bag and tucked it over his ear. With a cocky grin that revealed stained teeth, he waved to both detectives, not even acknowledging Patel. He took a few steps before he turned back, the arrogant façade dropped.

'I hope you find who killed Lauren,' he said with a shrug. 'I know what you think of me, but she probably isn't the only one with an ex-partner.'

King masked her surprise by the man's contrition, pushed out her lip in contemplation, and then nodded to him.

'That's fair. Look after yourself, Dean.' Her voice took on an extra layer of authority. 'Let's hope we don't see each other again.'

Riley nodded, flashed one more glance at Townsend who stared him down, and he then disappeared around the corner behind PC Bentley. Rupa Patel raised her eyebrows to them both before making her own exit, clearly dissatisfied in her client. Left alone, King turned to Townsend.

'Tell me, how satisfying was it when you hit him?'

Townsend grinned.

'Greatly.'

'Jealous.' King blew out her cheeks. 'Right, let's get back to it.'

The two of them set off back through the station, where it seemed like someone had pressed double speed. With the news of a third murder flooding through the building, there was an extra hop in every officer's step, a sense of urgency in every move. King was of the opinion that every crime or case should channel the same feeling, but the monotony of the paperwork and the excessive red tape often crushed even the keenest of spirit.

Within a few minutes, King and Townsend stepped through the door to the SCU where Swaby had now crammed another desk next to Hannon, and the two women were absorbed by their screens. Townsend's desk was cluttered with a few files and a computer he had yet to turn on since he'd arrived that morning. In fact, it was a desk he'd barely sat at since he'd meandered through hours of CCTV footage.

He had a horrible knot in his stomach that a similar fate awaited him.

The tedious task of building a new theory.

'You okay, guv?' Hannon asked, turning in her seat. She had her hand clutched around a cup of coffee from her favourite shop, and only then did Townsend realise she'd popped one on his desk, too. As he reached for it and flashed her a smile, she handed one to King.

'Thanks, Nic.' King took a sip. 'I take it Swaby has caught you up to speed?'

'Yeah. Fucking awful,' Hannon said with a solemn shake of the head. 'These poor women.'

'Well, it won't do them any good for us to be moping about.' King put her cup down and clapped her hands together. 'Right, we need a new avenue. All the work you guys did in getting us to Riley, it was good work. Don't let the fact he's the wrong man dissuade you from that. It was good, solid detective work, and instead of sitting here feeling sorry for ourselves, we need to go again. So…any ideas?'

King clicked her fingers a few times, as if fishing for ideas. Swaby sat back in her chair while Townsend leant against his desk, sipped his coffee and scanned the room.

'I have something,' Hannon offered. 'I spoke with DS Ramsey first thing, and…'

'DS Ramsey?' Townsend cut in.

'Oh, she's been assigned to Michaela Woods' next-of-kin as their Family Liaison Officer. The murder has hit the daughter, Dominique, pretty hard, as well as her ex, Jonathan. She's been talking with them, fleshing out who Michaela was and the sole reason for her separation from the family was that Michaela was a serious drug addict.'

'Really?' King was clearly surprised. She turned and looked at the picture of Michaela that Swaby had already pinned on the board.

'Apparently it began not long after she went back to work after having Dominique. It got pretty bad by the sounds of it. Numerous stints in rehab. Even more relapses. The reason Dominique was living with him was because it wasn't safe for her to be around that sort of environment.'

'Heartbreaking. But makes sense,' Swaby added. She was a proud mother of two boys, both in school. 'Must have been hard for all of them.'

'Apparently she'd been ten months clean,' Hannon continued. 'However, Jonathan did say that she's had an on-and-off-again relationship with one of her dealers, which was what he believed caused all the relapses. He didn't give a name, but said he was a big guy who often worked as a bouncer. So…being the unsung hero of the team that I am, I've been doing some digging and guess who's had a couple of dropped charges for possession with intent to supply?'

Townsend stepped forward as Hannon turned her screen. King leant down and her eyes widened.

'Benny,' King said with venom. The man's instantly recognisable face filling half the screen.

'Yup. Benny Hughes. The door man at Paradise.' Hannon began scrolling through the file. 'Apparently, he's had numerous run-ins with our guys. They've done a few raids on his flat, but we've never been able to get anything to stick.'

'This is great work, Nic,' Townsend interjected, causing Hannon to mockingly do a small bow. She winced as she did.

'He's right. Great work,' King said, as she sent the picture to print. She quickly rushed to the printer and then stuck the photo of Benny's face next to Dean's.

'So we know it couldn't have been Dean, as he was here last night…'

'Well, he couldn't have killed Michaela.' Townsend observed. 'He was still there the night Lauren was murdered, and he did threaten to do so.'

'You said all along, you didn't think he did it,' King replied. 'But you're right, we can't take him down off this board. Not yet, anyway.'

'Riley's a low-level drug dealer,' Swaby interjected. 'Could be a link?'

'Could be,' King said, and drew a line between the photos of the two men and then took a step back. 'But what are we not seeing here?'

'We need a connection to Natasha,' Townsend said. 'Right now, we have one man with a link to Lauren, and another with a link to Lauren and Michaela.'

'Hold up…' Swaby said excitedly, her eyes glued to the screen as her fingers danced across the keys. 'Holy shit.'

'What?' King said, hands on hips.

'I've just pulled up all of Benny Hughes' personal

records, and eighteen months ago he moved into a flat on a nice road in Downley.' She turned to Townsend and smiled. 'Up near Sands.'

'Oh, right.' Townsend nodded his thanks. He recalled cutting through Sands on his way to Lane End, and it helped for him to have a mental map of the vast town of High Wycombe.

'Guess who holds the lease?' Swaby said with an excited grin.

'You're fucking kidding me?' King stepped round to confirm it with her own eyes. 'Stokes Homes.'

'Yup.'

'Jesus,' Townsend said. 'Well, let's go, and get him shall we?'

'I was thinking the same thing.' King patted Swaby on the shoulder. 'Great work, ladies. Seriously.'

Hannon threw up a thumb.

'Feel free to reward us with biscuits,' she added.

'We'll see,' King said with a wry smile. She turned to Townsend as she headed to the door. 'Shall we?'

'You betcha.'

Townsend fell in behind King as she left the room, and as they made their way up the stairs towards the car park, she called into Hall to update him and to request uniform support. Seemingly pleased with the response, she made her way to the passenger side of Townsend's car, and then moments later, Townsend pulled out of the station car park, off on the hunt for another suspect, and hopefully, another step closer to stopping another woman being brutally murdered.

CHAPTER THIRTY-FIVE

'Ah, fuck it.'

Benny chuckled to himself as popped the cap off the bottle of beer and then closed his fridge. He stepped back across the small, modern kitchen of his flat, bypassing a row of dirty plates and unwashed glasses that lined the countertop. The living room wasn't much better, with the furniture covered in unwashed clothes, empty takeaway boxes, and random scatterings of newspaper. He wasn't due at Paradise until later that evening, and a few late-morning bottles of beer, along with a few lines of coke, would set him up for the rest of the day. He still needed to hit the gym, where he would lift the heaviest weights he possibly could to maintain the hulking frame. He wasn't particularly muscular, with his flabby gut sagging over the hem of his boxer shorts, but he was a bulky man and was more than happy to throw his weight around.

When the odd idiot got out of line with one of the girls, Sykes was pretty supportive of Benny's methods, which usually included a few hard digs, as well as a fair old kicking once he had manhandled the perpetrator out of the club.

Sykes was a good man, and Benny enjoyed working for him. The man even looked the other way as Benny sold his supply to eager customers, and there wasn't an evening where Benny didn't at least make a few hundred pounds from his side hustle.

Drugs were easier to get a hold of than most people realised, and instead of asking around, Benny went right to the source. Darnell Jessop was a notorious drug dealer, but when presented with the brutish bouncer who demanded to become a sales channel, Jessop did the smart thing and took Benny on-board. Now, Benny had a constant supply of cocaine, which he charged extortionate prices for. If anyone baulked at the price, it only took a knowing look from Benny and the promise of pain to get them to cough up the cash.

Plus, having access to the drugs made it easy to lure in the women, especially those so dependent on their next hit, they were willing to do anything to get it.

Anything.

Casually decked out in his boxer shorts and a white vest which exposed the intricate ink work that covered his thick arms, Benny tapped out a line of cocaine onto his cluttered coffee table, neatened it with a bank card, leant forward, and sniffed it vigorously.

The shot hit the back of his skull like a sledgehammer, and he fell backwards, gasping with ecstasy as the effects began to rush through his body. He felt great.

Invincible.

He lit a cigarette, picked up his beer, and then meandered to the patio door, which opened up onto a courtyard he called a garden. His flat was on the ground floor, and while the courtyard was technically communal, the other residents seemed too intimidated to use it as much as he did. Whether it was his incredibly intimidating stature or his flagrant drug use, he didn't care.

As he took in the nicotine of the cigarette and the greenery of the garden, his thoughts were rocked by a thumping against his front door.

Thud. Thud. Thud.

'Benny Hughes.' The vaguely familiar woman's voice echoed from beyond. 'This is Detective Inspector King. Please open the door.'

'Fuck.'

The cigarette dropped from Benny's mouth, and without even stopping to get dressed, he threw open the door fully and burst through into the courtyard. There was a side path that ran along the side of the block of flats, but that would lead him directly to what he would imagine would be a number of police officers waiting for him. On the far side of the courtyard, there was a low fence, which separated the property from a wooded area that had a roughly beaten footpath that would lead back towards town.

He set off as fast as he could; the door slamming against the brick wall behind him, shattering a pane of glass. That had clearly been enough to notify the cops that he was making a break for it, as by the time he'd made it to the far end of the courtyard, he could hear the thumping footsteps crunching the stones of the side path. He glanced back, recognising the detective that was chasing him, and as Benny tumbled over the fence and onto the muddy path beneath, he heard the scouse accent as he approached the fence himself.

'Benny, stop running!'

'Fuck you,' Benny spat back, scrambling to his feet, and he began to run through the trees, his knees scratched from his fall.

It was no use.

DS Jack Townsend scaled the fence with little problem, and as Benny heard the footsteps gaining on him, he abruptly stopped, spun, and clobbered Townsend with a hard right hook that sent the detective spiralling towards the nearest tree.

'Bad day to be a copper.' Benny snarled. The cocaine pumping through his veins was just feeding his feelings of invincibility. He stomped towards Townsend, who pushed himself up off the tree trunk, blood trickling from the cut that now dominated his left eyebrow. Townsend rolled his shoulders, and he approached Benny, who charged once again, only this time, Townsend saw it coming.

Swiftly, he stepped to the side, hooked the errant punch that the big man had thrown and then stomped forward into the man's shin, knocking his leg back, and sending him falling. Using the man's own arm to guide him, Townsend slammed Benny face down onto the ground, before burying his knee into the man's spine and wrenching his arm up behind him until the tendons of his shoulder threatened to snap.

A mixture of fury and embarrassment exploded from Benny in a venomous roar, but Townsend dug his knee further into the man's spine, pulled the other arm back and managed to slap the cuffs around his meaty wrists. As he stood back up, Townsend put a little extra pressure on his knee, a final parting shot to the big man.

'Bad day to be a bad guy.'

As Benny shuffled uselessly on his belly, Townsend took a step back, keeping his eyes on his prisoner at all times. He let out a deep breath, as his adrenaline began to subside and then turned to see King lowering herself over the fence. Down the far end of the woodland path, he could see the two uniform officers rushing towards them.

'Jesus, are you okay?' King asked, looking at the gash above his left eye.

'I'm fine.' Townsend shrugged. 'I've been hit harder by a lot tougher.'

'Fuck you,' barked Benny. 'Take these cuffs off and I'll show you tough.'

The uniform hit the scene and between the two of them, they managed to pull Benny to his feet, despite his attempts to shrug them off. King stepped towards him, even though his eyes were burning a hole through Townsend.

'Benny Hughes, I'm arresting you on suspicion of the murders of Lauren Grainger, Natasha Stokes, and Michaela Woods. You do not have—'

'Michaela? Michaela's dead?' Benny's tough guy act slipped.

'—to say anything. But it may harm your defence if you do not mention when questioned something which you later rely on in court. Anything you do say may be given in evidence. Understood?'

'I didn't kill those girls,' Benny angrily snarled. 'This is a fucking stitch up.'

'Get him back to the station,' King ordered, and the two uniforms began the long, protracted struggle of shifting a twenty-stone man against his will. King watched them for a few moments before turning back to Townsend.

'You need to get that looked at.'

'Guv, seriously. I'm fine.' Townsend waved her off.

'Well, it's an order,' King said firmly. 'Give me your keys. I'll drop you off at the hospital on the way back to the station.'

'Fine.' Townsend relented, and the two of them began to follow in the same direction as the ongoing struggle. 'He seemed genuinely surprised.'

'Who? Benny?'

'Yeah. When you mentioned Michaela. He seemed almost hurt by it.'

'Doesn't mean he didn't do it,' King said. 'Remember...everything is something until it isn't. Right, let me make a call.'

As they walked, Townsend wiped away some of the blood from his eyebrow with the back of his hand. The wound hurt, more than he was letting on, but considering the horrendous beatings he'd taken when undercover, one punch to the face wasn't going to put a stop to his day. As he wondered how much time he'd need to spend at the hospital, King's call to Hannon connected.

'Nic, it's me. Yeah, we got him.' She paused to let Hannon speak. 'We're heading back now. Jack's okay, but he got a little whack. He'll be with us later, but I need you to go through every statement made by Sykes and the girls who work at Paradise.'

There was another pause, and before King made it clear, Townsend already knew her train of thought.

'Yeah, all of them. I want to see if any of them mentioned Benny being with them when they closed that night.'

CHAPTER THIRTY-SIX

As the day went on, a thumping headache had begun to dominate Townsend's skull. The blow he'd taken from Benny had been struck with such venom, that he'd need five stitches to pull it back together, and now he was sitting on a hospital bed, waiting for a doctor to give him the go ahead to get back to work. His phone pinged with another worried message from Mandy, and he felt a surge of guilt at sending her a blood covered selfie with the simple sentence of:

Busy day at work.

The humour had obviously been lost in translation, and it had taken fifteen minutes to calm her down and explain that it was just a little cut from a brief scrap with a suspect. Although he had lighthearted intentions, Townsend knew it had been insensitive, as Mandy had witnessed him take a savage beating during his time undercover.

Almost to the point of death.

He sent her another text just to make sure she was okay.

Don't worry about me. I'm all good. Just a little bump, is all. Xx

She'd probably give him both barrels when he got home, but it was just part of his job. Benny was their lead suspect behind the murders of three women, and Townsend wasn't just going to let him get away. Besides, swiftly taking the big man down had done wonders for his own self-confidence, as well as his reputation. The two young officers who had the arduous task of hauling the behemoth to their car would no doubt be spreading the word of what he'd done.

His mind also pushed through the pounding headache to wonder what was happening in the interview room. There was no doubt that King would have had Benny sitting on the other side of the table, a duty solicitor beside him, while she grilled him alongside DS Swaby. He'd already witnessed firsthand how effective King was at picking apart a suspect and he wondered how far down the rabbit hole Benny had spiralled.

If he had killed Lauren, Natasha, and Michaela, had he admitted it?

Could all of this be over?

But a sickening thud hit the bottom of Townsend's stomach, and he knew what it was.

Doubt.

All the evidence now pointed towards the burly doorman, but Townsend couldn't shake the horrible, nagging feeling in the pit of his gut that it didn't fully add up. King, who he'd developed an immediate respect for, would point to all the red flags surrounding Benny. It was their duty to follow up on them.

But similar to Dean Riley, Townsend had a nagging sense of dread that while they were looking left, their killer was running right.

The buzz of his phone shook him from his thoughts.

Just stay safe. Idiot. Xx

He chuckled. Mandy had a way of bringing him back

from a dark or troubled place, and just the simplest of affectionate insult brought a beaming smile across his face. He wanted to rush home, hold his girls, and spend the rest of the day with them, but he knew that was a pipe dream. Until they got a confession or could prove beyond any measure of doubt that Benny was the killer, he'd be strapped to his desk, trawling through information, and working with the team to find that silver bullet.

With a sigh, he responded.

Don't wait up. Busy afternoon ahead. Xx

A 'sad face' emoji came back, and Townsend sighed with disappointment. Mandy was proud of him, the job he did, and how dedicated he was to the cause. She'd understand, but with the in-roads he was making with rebuilding his relationship with his daughter, Townsend knew an absent evening could derail it. The curtain to his bed was peeled back, and a young, fresh-faced doctor stood, holding his clipboard in his arms. The white coat looked way too big for him.

'Right, detective…let's have a look at you once more.'

The man popped the clipboard on the bed beside Townsend, then clicked on his little pen light and checked both his eyes. Townsend sat still and obedient, and the doctor then did a quick check of the stitches.

'There doesn't seem to be any signs of a concussion,' the doctor said confidently. 'I'd say you're good to go. Just try to take it easy out there, yeah?'

'You betcha.' Townsend lied.

None of it was easy.

As he stepped out of the main door of High Wycombe Hospital, he was greeted by a summer shower, with the recent sunshine making way for some dark clouds and a torrential downpour. It was a five-minute walk back to the station, so Townsend zipped up his bomber jacket, tucked his hands into his pockets and marched on with his head down. The 'magic roundabout', which sat between the hospital and the station, was easier to navigate on foot, and it took only three minutes for him to push open the door of the station and step through. The desk sergeant gave him a nod as he stepped in, and Townsend returned in kind, before unzipping his sodden jacket. As he slid it off, he turned and saw Father Baycroft rising from one of the seats. A tatty old box sat on the one next to him.

'Ah, DS Townsend,' he said with elation.

'Father.' Townsend extended a hand. Baycroft took it with one that shook unintentionally. 'What brings you here?'

'Please, call me Gordon. I have those files and…' Baycroft noticed the fresh cut across Townsend's eyebrow. 'Good heavens, are you all right?'

'Oh what? This? It's nothing.' Townsend smiled. 'You should see the other guy.'

'Violence is never the solution,' Baycroft said with a sigh. 'But needs must in times like this I suppose. I brought you those files you asked for.'

'Thank you. That's very kind.' Townsend looked at the man. Despite his height and the broadness of his shoulders, he looked like he was fighting a losing battle. The tremors of his Parkinson's disease were relentless, and his face looked gaunt.

'I hope they help and they can bring some justice for poor Lauren.' He shook his head once more. 'But I must go. There's a church fête for me to attend and…'

'It's chucking it down out there,' Townsend warned. 'Wait here, and I'll grab my keys and give you a lift. It's the least I can do.'

'Oh, I don't want to be a bother.'

'Nonsense.' Townsend gave a dismissive wave. 'Give me a minute.'

Townsend scooped up the box and then headed to the

stairwell. As he stepped into the SCU office, neither Swaby nor King were there. No doubt they were still grilling Benny. Townsend was gutted he'd missed out on it, but thankfully, King had left his keys on his desk. He swapped them out with the box of files, and then headed back upstairs, where Baycroft smiled warmly as he approached. Townsend pulled his car up to the front of the station, and Baycroft carefully lowered himself into the passenger seat. They raced up the hill, past the train station, and before long, they saw the signs for Hazlemere, where Father Baycroft's church was located. Stuck in a little traffic, Townsend turned to Baycroft, who was contently looking out of the window.

'Question for you, Gordon. Were there any incidents at Work Space that you can remember?'

'Incidents?' Baycroft turned to look at him, his wrinkled brow furrowed in confusion.

'The people who came to you. Who stayed at the home. They were all there for their own safety. Were there any incidents where people showed up unannounced or did something they shouldn't?'

'Not that I can think of. I mean, we did have a direct line to the police for a while, so when some of the more unfortunate souls lost their way, there might have been need to call them…'

'Lost their way how?'

Baycroft paused for thought. Townsend flashed a glance at the older gentleman and could see him battling against a fading memory and a cruel disease that exacerbated the process.

'You have to understand, for a lot of the young men and women who came through our home, they were escaping some dark places. Places where it can get into your skin and then become part of the fabric of who you are. Drugs. Violence. These things stay with people.'

'There were issues with drugs there?' Townsend asked.

'Sometimes. Sadly. Yes.' Baycroft pointed to the church on the road ahead. 'Just there, please.'

Townsend turned back to the road, indicated, and then pulled the car up to the gate of the church. Beyond the gate, there was a large gazebo with a number of stalls set up beneath it. Behind each one, an elderly member of the community stood or sat, glumly looking out at the terrible weather that had put a dampener on the fête. The tables, covered with freshly baked cakes or the usual bric-à-brac, were devoid of any customers, and Townsend felt a small ache of pity for them.

'Did you ever come across the name Benny Hughes?' Townsend asked as Baycroft reached for the door handle.

'Benny Hughes?' Baycroft repeated, deep in thought. 'It doesn't ring a bell. But my mind isn't what it was...'

'No worries.' Townsend offered him a smile. 'I'll dig up the reports of those incidents from the archives and check them myself.'

'Is he the man who did it?' Baycroft asked as he opened the door. 'The man who killed that sweet Lauren?'

'I don't know,' Townsend said truthfully. 'But I'll find out. Thank you for your help.'

'Anytime.' Baycroft eased himself out of the car with some trouble and then ambled around to duck his head in. 'Look after yourself, detective.'

Townsend gave him a thumbs up, and then the elderly priest closed the door and shuffled as quickly as he could through the gate towards the gazebo. Blowing out his cheeks, Townsend caught a quick glance of himself in the mirror, and admired the impressive cut that sliced through his eyebrow.

It would leave a scar.

A reminder.

As he brought the engine to life, and waited for the

passing traffic to subside, Townsend caught a brief glimpse of Baycroft under the gazebo, seemingly at odds with a younger priest, who seemed pretty upset by something.

The politics of a church fête.

Townsend smirked as he pulled away.

If only his own troubles were so quaint.

CHAPTER THIRTY-SEVEN

Townsend stepped back into the SCU office and was greeted by the beaming smile of DC Nic Hannon.

'Christ,' she said with a grimace. 'You look like hell.'

'Thanks.' Townsend chuckled. The walk from the car to the station through the downpour had soaked him through. Combined with the stitches and bruising that dominated his eyebrow, he knew he was a sight for sore eyes.

'You okay?' Hannon asked with genuine concern. Beside the coffee on her desk was an open packet of biscuits.

'I'll be fine.' Townsend collapsed in his chair and then arched his head towards King's office. 'Where's the boss?'

Hannon finished the remnants of the biscuit she'd just stuffed into her mouth before answering.

'In with Benny.'

'Still?' Townsend sat forward. 'You think it's going well?'

'Well, I don't think he's admitted to anything as of yet.' Hannon turned back to her screen. 'If he has, then all this will be for nothing.'

'What you working on?'

'I'm going through the statements from the dancers at Paradise. Sykes' too.' Hannon shook her head. 'I tell you what, some of these write-ups aren't worth the digital paper they're written on.'

'That bad, huh?' Townsend felt his stomach grumble and reached for a biscuit. Hannon slapped his wrist.

'Hands off, scouse.'

'You greedy cow.' The two of them chuckled, and then Townsend took one of the biscuits.

'They're just so devoid of any real information. Although, boss was right. None of them mention that Benny was with them for their after-work drinks.' Hannon scanned her eyes across her dual screens. 'All pretty much the same. Sykes opens the bar up to them after the club closes. A few of them took him up on the offer. No funny business, or anything like that.'

'Well, no. Sykes is husband of the year.' Townsend drew a confused glare. 'He took his wife to the spa earlier this week. Apparently, it's a monthly tradition.'

'Huh. Who knew a man who paid women to take their clothes off for other lecherous men to stare at would be such an old romantic?'

'Doesn't do us any good to pre-judge people.'

'Is that why you didn't think Riley did it?' Hannon asked, sipping her coffee. Townsend sat back in his chair and sighed.

'I just didn't feel it.' He shook his head. 'I haven't been doing this long enough to have a "hunch" per se, but I've spent my life around some pretty bad people. I mean, *put-you-in-the-ground* bad. Riley's a mouthy little bastard, but he isn't a killer.'

'And Benny? What's your gut telling you?'

'Well, my eyebrow's telling me he hits like a sledgehammer. But I don't know…there doesn't seem to be anything concrete.'

'He has a tangible link to all the victims,' Hannon offered. 'You'd be hard pressed to find someone else in the town who happened to have a link to all three women who were killed within five days of each other.'

Townsend leant forward in his chair.

'But is that enough?'

'It better be.'

The voice caught them both by surprise, and as they spun to the door, DSI Hall stepped in, a smile on his face. Townsend stood, and as Hannon struggled to get to her feet, Hall waved her back down.

'Hello, sir.' Townsend greeted him.

'Townsend.' He took a closer look at the cut on Townsend's eyebrow and tutted. 'I see you're settling in well.'

'Well enough, sir.'

'I mean, there's being thrown in at the deep end and then there's having someone hold you under water.' He pointed to the injury. 'You had that looked at I see?'

'Yes, sir. All good to go.'

'Good to hear.' He turned to Hannon. 'How about you? How are you holding up?'

'Oh, I'm just fine, sir. Women being brutally murdered in my hometown. You know…the usual.'

A wry smile crept across Hall's face, and Townsend appreciated the sentiment. The man was respected throughout the Thames Valley Police Service, and on the few occasions he'd been in his company during his first week, Townsend could see why. Hall carried himself with the authority his experience commanded, but what made him so well respected was his treatment of his subordinates.

He cared.

Footsteps closed in outside the door, and King and Swaby stepped through, both looking a little rattled from their experience. King, quite noticeably, looked tired.

'Welcome back,' Hannon said dryly, as Swaby dropped down into the seat by her cramped desk and stole a biscuit.

'I trust our man didn't confess to it,' Hall stated, his arms folding across his chest. King sighed and shook her head.

'If I hear the phrase 'no comment' one more time today, you'll be locking me up.'

'It's his right not to answer any questions,' Hall said. 'It's up to us to answer them for him. Anything we can use? Anything at all useful?'

'He did admit to selling drugs from his position at Paradise,' Swaby offered. 'Said he used burner phones, which was why we wouldn't be able to trace his actual mobile phone to any of the locations.'

'The call made to Natasha to book the house viewing was made from a burner phone,' King added. 'So there's that. Oh, and he said he stayed behind at the club for a drink the night of Lauren's murder. Nic, how are we getting on with those statements?'

'Well, he's lying,' Hannon replied. 'None of the statements mention Benny being present. But, to be honest, there isn't much to them. Very few have lists of names who were actually in the room. Others mention some. Others don't. Quality stuff.'

'Figures.' King sighed. She had a lot of respect for uniform, knowing the heavy workload and copious amounts of red tape they had to cut through to do it. But sometimes, the results spoke for themselves. She turned to Hall. 'We'll find something concrete, sir. But he's offering us nothing right now.'

'Well, make sure that you do. The clock's ticking and

unless you find something of substance that we can pin on him, you'll have to let him go. Now, DCI Lowe and his team have been working on tracing the killer the night of Michaela Woods' murder. I'm sure they'd appreciate an update.'

'Yes, sir.' King nodded, and then gently waved her vape stick. 'Give me five minutes.'

'Three,' Hall countered, then turned to the rest of the team. 'Keep up the good work, everyone. Everything...and I mean everything, could be crucial.'

'Thanks, sir,' Townsend responded on their behalf, and Hall took his leave, and Townsend sat down again. King took a moment, looking up at the board and blowing out her cheeks.

'Michelle, try to work your magic again and see if you can pinpoint any burner phones to any of the murder locations. I know it's a long shot, but if we can find even a shred of a signal nearby, we can try to run back through the serial numbers to see when it was bought and where.'

'I'm on it,' Michelle said, spinning round in her chair and opening up another window on her screen. King leant over Hannon's desk.

'Call Sykes. Tell him that Benny has been arrested and we need him in here. *Now.*'

'Yes, guv.'

'Tell him if he doesn't come in willingly, I'll come down there, and cause a problem,' King said firmly. Her eyes were shrouded with dark bags. 'We need to know where Benny Hughes was in the earlier hours of Monday morning.'

'Leave it with me. Now go, your three minutes are running low,' Hannon said with a nod to the door. King smiled and then, with her vape in hand, stormed towards the door. Townsend spun in his chair.

'What do you need from me, guv?' He asked eagerly.

King stopped, leant across his desk, and then tapped the tatty box of files Gordon Baycroft had given him.

'Time to dig in,' she said with a grin. Townsend's face fell, clearly enough for her to notice. 'Sometimes we need to search through the weeds. Besides, you could probably do with a calmer afternoon.'

'Oh yeah, this will *definitely* help my headache.'

King chuckled at Townsend's dry remark, before disappearing through the door. Townsend sighed and looked around the room. Swaby was already lost in the programs on her laptop screen, whereas Hannon had the phone lodged between her ear and her shoulder, trying to connect the call.

This was all part of the job.

Unfortunately, detective work didn't play out like it did on the television or within books, where the murder victim just so happened to be the only person that still kept a diary which was full of valuable clues. Or a killer who had an elaborate tattoo or facial disfigurement.

Detective work was long, it was arduous, and it was unglamorous.

But it was necessary.

Everything was necessary.

Townsend pulled out the paracetamol from his pocket, threw two into his mouth and then tipped them back with the lukewarm bottle of water on his desk. Then, he stepped out of the office to the run-down coffee machine in the corridor and returned with a sludgy, bitter coffee that clung to the back of his throat with a stale aftertaste.

With a sigh, he dropped down into his chair, lifted the lid off the box of files, and pulled the first stack of papers out. There was no discernible order to the paperwork, nothing that would make the task any easier.

As he began to read through its contents, he just hoped

beyond hope that everything they were doing would be worth it.

CHAPTER THIRTY-EIGHT

Sykes sat across the table in the interview room with his arms folded across his chest. His wrinkled face was scrunched in a frown and as the door opened, he glared at both King and Townsend as they entered. It was clearly not how he was supposed to be spending his evening.

'You better have a real good explanation for this,' he snapped.

'Likewise, when it comes to that shirt,' Townsend responded, taking his seat. Sykes looked down at the colourful Hawaiian shirt with offence.

'Mr Sykes, thank you for coming in voluntarily,' King said, starting the interview. 'It's much appreciated.'

'Well, you didn't give me much of a choice, did you? Also, how long is this going to take? I'm supposed to be at the club right now.' Neither of the detectives answered him. Sykes huffed. 'Look, whatever you think Benny's done, he hasn't done it. He might be a bit rough around the edges, but he's a softy when you get to know him.'

'Oh, I did.' Townsend pointed to the gash on his eyebrow. 'Real sweetheart.'

'Assaulting a police officer is the least of his problems,'

King said. 'We're pretty sure Benny is using his position at your club to sell cocaine. A lot of cocaine.'

'Absolutely not,' Sykes said, seemingly oblivious. 'Not on my premises.'

'Well, he does it at the door,' Townsend said. 'But the reason we called you in, Sykes, isn't to see if you've been turning a blind eye. No, we need to know if Benny was with you on Monday morning.'

'Excuse me?' Sykes raised his eyebrows in surprise.

'When Lauren was murdered,' King said solemnly. 'If you recall, you and a number of your dancers stayed behind for a drink after the club closed.'

'Yeah, we do that most nights.' Sykes looked offended. 'Hey, it's hard work for them. Least I can do is give them a few drinks on the house.'

'We're not questioning your intentions. From what we can see and what we've heard, you run a pretty safe environment for those women,' King said with a hint of a compliment. 'But Benny said in his statement that he also stayed behind for a drink, but none of the other girls' statements seem to corroborate that fact.'

'Probably.' Sykes shrugged. 'Benny's always ducking in and out…'

A penny seemed to drop, and Sykes took a moment of contemplation. Townsend leant forward slightly, taking charge of the interview.

'Graham…it's *very* important that you remember.'

'No…he couldn't…' Sykes said to himself.

'Was Benny there that morning?' Townsend asked again, his voice firmer.

'I mean…I think…' Sykes was flailing. The realisation beginning to take over. King leant forward, a calmer presence than Townsend.

'Graham, we've arrested Benny for the murder of Lauren, as well as the two other women who've been killed this week.' Sykes went to interrupt, but she held up her hand. 'We have very strong evidence that suggests he knew all the victims.'

'That doesn't mean he killed them.' Sykes raised his hands in irritation. 'For Christ's sake, I knew Lauren.'

'Yes, but your alibi checks out,' Townsend answered. 'Nobody is able to place Benny with you when Lauren was murdered. We're not asking for a character reference, or for you to try to defend him. Nor are we accusing you of anything. We haven't been able to establish any alibis for him for each murder. But right now, if you want to do what's right by that poor girl, and the two other women victims, then I'm asking you to really think. Was he there?'

Sykes finally seemed to grasp the severity of the situation and sat back in his chair, deep in thought. After a few moments, the worry across his face became evident, and he looked up at both of them.

They already knew the answer.

'No,' Sykes said quietly. 'He wasn't.'

'Right…' King said, already getting from her chair. 'Thank you, Graham. You've been a big help.'

'Tell him…' Sykes looked crestfallen. 'Tell him I'm sorry.'

'For what?' Townsend shrugged. 'If he did do this… then you've just helped us get a step closer to gaining those victims and their families a little bit of justice. Let's go.'

Townsend ushered Sykes to the door, and the confident swagger of the man had been replaced by guilt-laden steps. Although not a criminal himself, Sykes clearly lived by the code of trust and looking out for his employees, and dropping a man he considered a friend in it had clearly been difficult. Townsend had seen similar during his years undercover. People who were just trying to get by and make ends meet. They'd forge a loyalty for those in the same ship as them, even if some of their actions weren't strictly legal.

As he stopped by the door to the station, he extended his hand to Sykes, drawing a line under any animosity between them.

'Thanks for your help, Graham,' Townsend said firmly. Sykes looked him up and down and then reluctantly shook it.

'Just...do right by that girl.'

'Will do.'

Sykes took a step closer and lowered his voice.

'Did he do it? Benny?'

Townsend couldn't answer. Not just because it was an ongoing investigation, but once again, it was due to the nagging feeling in his gut. He offered Sykes a smile instead of an answer.

'We're doing all we can.'

With that, he turned, and headed back to the interview room, where King was standing outside waiting, her arms folded, and a look of agitation. Townsend approached tentatively.

'Everything all right, guv?'

'You think we're on the wrong track, don't you?'

'Excuse me.'

King wasn't grilling him, but more...confronting his opinion.

'You said in there "if he did do this".' King raised her eyebrows. 'Remember what I said about facts over theory?'

'I know, guv. But I can't say for sure until—'

'We prove it beyond doubt. That's what we are trying to do, Jack,' King assured him. 'But we *have* to follow every lead and we *have* to be guided by the facts of the matter. Not the theory.'

'It's called being a good detective.' King and Townsend

spun to see the smug grin of DCI Lowe behind them, his hands on his hips. 'You'll understand it one day, newbie.'

Townsend went to respond, but King held up a hand to stop him.

'Head back to Swaby and Hannon. I'll be down in a minute.'

'Yes, guv.'

'Atta boy,' Lowe said as Townsend walked by, and then threw up two fists and weaved slightly. 'Remember, newbie, anytime.'

Townsend ignored the threat and disappeared around the corner, leaving Lowe to face the thunderous frown of King.

'What happened to working together?'

'Ah, it's a light ribbing.' Lowe shrugged. 'If he can't take it, then maybe he's not as tough as he thinks he is.'

'Well, if this is just another pissing contest, I have a lot of work to be getting on with—'

'Actually, I just wanted to catch you before I left for the afternoon. I'm due in court shortly, but I spoke with DS Ramsey earlier. She gave us a bit more information about Michaela Woods, and my team has done some digging.'

'And?'

'It's not great. I mean, we're talking a serious drug addiction. We've dug into what she told us and we've established a decade of drug abuse, rehab, and relapse. Pretty nasty stuff. A couple of hospital visits which were due to domestic abuse. Temporary housing. Then another relapse. It seemed like no matter how hard she tried to get back to her daughter, something was always pulling her back in.'

'It's heartbreaking,' King said, to herself more than anything.

'Well, her friend offered her a steady job at his law firm. Apparently, she's been ten months clean and had to abide by regular and random drug testing. We've spoken with the team there, and they all have alibis. But they confirmed that Benny was her off-and-on-again lover.'

'Really? He denied that when we spoke to him.'

Lowe shrugged.

'Look, I'm just keeping you updated. This is your case, Izzy. Do I think it should be mine? Yes. I'm not going to lie. But right now, *we* are not important.'

'Agreed,' King said. 'Thank you.'

'We'll keep digging more into her life, see if there's anything that can make this make a little more sense. Let's see what else Benny is keeping from us. Keep your phone on.'

King nodded, and Lowe took his leave. As he left, she had a small flicker of passion shake her heart, before she immediately quashed it with memories of how selfish the man was. He was being a team player now, but she was certain it was because Hall was watching over the investigation.

An investigation that she needed to get right.

With an extra urgency in her step, she headed back down to the SCU office, ready to wade into the avalanche of information of paperwork with the rest of her team, looking desperately for breadcrumbs.

It was going to be a long night.

CHAPTER THIRTY-NINE

By the time Townsend pulled onto his street that night, it was past eleven o'clock. Every house was dark, with his neighbours already tucked up in bed. Beyond the brief glimpse of a fox scurrying across the road and disappearing into the surrounding trees, there were no other signs of life. He pulled his Honda Civic up onto the driveway and killed the engine and sighed. The toll of his first week as part of the Specialist Crimes Unit was beginning to show, and his body ached and his head thumped. He glanced up at the rear-view mirror, the bruising around his cut eyebrow was now a nasty yellow colour.

In a way, he was glad that Mandy would be asleep.

As much as he wanted to wrap his arms around his wife and just hold her for a while, he could do without the lecture of being careful or for her retreading old ground of what had happened when he'd been undercover.

This was supposed to be different.

It was supposed to be safer, and while she loved and admired him for his dedication to police work, she'd made it clear that she just wanted him home safely every night.

He wasn't even sure what Eve would say.

She'd probably conjure up some wild story of him fighting a monster, but there was every chance that seeing her father with such an injury would rock their recently rebuilt relationship. If she began to worry about his job, then she could grow to resent it and the last thing Townsend needed was another hurdle to scale just to spend time with her.

With his body aching and yearning for sleep, he stepped out of the car and made his way into the house.

It was immaculate, as always. It was a ritual that he and Mandy had got into early on during their introduction to parenthood, that as soon as Eve went down for the night, they 'de-childed' the house. Even through the crippling exhaustion of the first few months, one of them, usually Townsend himself, would have a quick whip round the house and tidy up any toys or mess that their little whirlwind had left in her wake. It became part of their daily routine, and in the eight years since, when Eve had gone down to rest, the cleanup would begin.

Mandy even did it solo during his three years spent undercover, such was their dedication to the cause.

Tiptoeing through to the kitchen, Townsend felt his heart melt at the state of the kitchen table.

Mandy's laptop was still open, although the screen had long since shut down. Sprawled around the machine were a few Post-it notes, along with a notepad full of notes and ideas. With her interview fast approaching, Townsend had been blown away by her preparation. It was a process that had been alien to him, as he'd known since a young age that he'd wanted to follow in his father's footsteps and join the police. There were rules and procedures, along with specific fitness and mental requirements, all of which he'd passed with flying colours.

There were no idle questions such as '*What skills can you*

bring to the team?' or *'What ambitions do you have over the next five years?'*.

It was very black and white.

He wanted to serve and protect his community and uphold the law.

It had been so long since he'd seen Mandy really throw herself into a job, a side effect of his time away, that he stood for a moment and envisaged just how good she would be in her new job. Although the world had changed post COVID to shift the working world to a more remote normality, he was certain she would light up any meeting room, whether digital, or physical, with her charm. As striking as she was to look at, it was her infectious smile, genuine interest, and dirty laugh that would cause people to gravitate towards her.

The woman was one in a million.

Townsend had no idea what a 'Virtual Assistant' for the CEO of a 'Tech Start-Up' actually did, but as he looked at the sterling preparation his wife had done, combined with who she was at her core, he knew she would thrive.

He pulled open the 'man drawer' of the kitchen and gently rummaged through the hodge-podge of batteries, instruction manuals, and takeaway menus until he retrieved a box of paracetamol. With his head lightly throbbing, he knocked two back with a gulp of water and then crept up the stairs as quietly as he could. He peered into his own bedroom, where Mandy was lying peacefully, facing away from the door and her hand stretched out across his pillow.

With a magnetic pull, he found himself leaning over her and kissing her gently on the forehead. She stirred slightly, a brief smile, before the sleep reclaimed her.

Then he went to Eve's door, and with a gentle nudge of his shoulder, he eased it open. The room was bathed in a soft, orange glow from the nightlight plugged into the far corner, illuminating the neat rows of her teddy bears and dolls that she spent hours hosting parties for. A bookcase, affixed to the wall, was filled with a new collection of books. She was a keen reader, and having graduated from the usual children's books about Gruffalos and dragons, she was now very much entrenched in the world of Roald Dahl. So much so in fact, that Townsend had been looking at booking a trip to the Roald Dahl Museum and Story Centre that was less than fifteen miles away in another part of the county.

She'd love it.

Eve was sprawled across her bed, one leg flopping over the unicorn duvet cover and her arms wrapped around her favourite stuffed animal.

She was his world.

Townsend stood for a minute, appreciating the silence of the night and sheer peace with which his daughter slept. He'd spent too long away from her to ever fully forgive himself, but after a week spent dealing with the deaths of other people's daughters, all he wanted to do was scoop her up into his arms and hold her until morning.

Instead, he lowered himself down onto the mattress beside her, popped a little kiss on the top of her blonde head, and then gently draped an arm across her. He breathed her in and closed his eyes.

When he opened them again, Mandy was standing over him, a loving smile across her face and a finger pressed to her lips. In her other hand was a mug of freshly made coffee, and she beckoned Townsend to follow her.

Carefully, he lifted his arm from Eve, rolled off the bed onto the floor, and then stepped out onto the landing to greet his wife with a kiss.

'What time is it?'

'A little after six,' she said in a hushed tone. She handed him the coffee. 'Figured you'd need this.'

'Thanks.' He took it gratefully and drank half of it in one go. 'Sorry, I meant to come to bed last night but—'

'Don't apologise.' She beamed. 'It's amazing to see you two together.'

Townsend smiled in agreement. It had been a long, and often painful road back to his daughter, but their new surroundings, and new home and seemed to have given birth to a new start.

For all of them.

After finishing his coffee, Townsend stripped off yesterday's clothes and hopped into the shower, before brushing his teeth and washing the cut that now ran through his eyebrow. He then threw on a new shirt and a black pair of jeans, and by the time he made it downstairs, Eve was already sitting at the kitchen table, an episode of some Disney cartoon playing on her tablet and a bowl of cereal in front of her.

'Daddy, what happened to your eye?' she asked with concern. Townsend flashed a glance at Mandy before answering.

'Your silly daddy only walked into a door at work on his way home.' He shook his head and blew out his lips, drawing a smile from his girl. 'That's why I was late home. I had to go and see a doctor about it.'

'Clumsy boy!' Eve said through her giggle.

Townsend turned to his wife, who threw her arms around him as he buried his face into her neck. As they pulled apart, she pushed onto her tiptoes to reach his ear.

'Be careful out there.' Her voice was as serious as he'd ever heard it. He pulled back, smiled, and then kissed her.

'Always,' he replied. She frowned. They both knew that was a lie. Townsend then clasped his hands together.

'Right, ladies, have a great day. Daddy's going to go catch some bad guys!'

As he strode to the front door, he couldn't help but smile at the *WHOOP WHOOP* that came from his daughter.

It was a happy home. Filled with love and laughter.

Which made it even more jarring when he arrived at work, knowing they were hot on the heels of a man who had devastated three others.

CHAPTER FORTY

Benny had already been taken to the interview room on the ground floor, where Rupa Patel had once again been assigned as the duty solicitor. Townsend had arrived earlier than usual but wasn't surprised to find DI King already seated at her desk, wading through a stack of files. After a couple of pleasantries, Townsend offered to go on a coffee run, and King gave him five minutes to get up the hill and back. Thankfully, Hannon's recommendation not only sold the best coffee he'd tasted in a long time, but the owner rushed anyone with a police lanyard to the front of the queue.

One of the very limited perks of the job.

When Townsend returned with a piping hot coffee in each hand, King was waiting for him outside the station with her vape in her hand.

'Thanks, Jack.'

'No worries.' He smiled. She looked tired. Struggling. 'You all good, guv?'

'Just been a long week,' she said, as she pulled a few paracetamol out of her pocket and washed them down with the coffee. She motioned to his eyebrow. 'How's the head?'

'It's fine. It looks worse than it is.'

'Wanna go and see the guy who did it?' King turned to the station door.

'After you.'

King led the way, and Townsend followed her to the interview room. A few days before, they'd dragged Dean Riley over the coals, and judging by the bored expression on Rupa Patel's face, she believed they were making the same mistake again. Before Townsend had even closed the door, Benny stood, his hands still shackled by his cuffs.

'Look, mate, I just want to apologise for yesterday.'

Townsend waved away the apology, and Patel advised Benny to sit still and be quiet. King went through the usual rigmarole of the interview introduction, stating everyone's names for the recording before she fixed Benny with a cold, hard stare.

'I hope, for your sake, Mr Hughes, you've found a few other words other than 'No Comment' today.'

Patel cleared her throat by way of interruption.

'My client is well within his rights to offer that answer.'

'He is,' King snapped back, her eyes still fixed on the large man before her. 'But it would probably do him more good to start telling us the truth.'

'I didn't kill these women,' Benny stated firmly. 'Why the fuck would I want to do that?'

'That's what we are trying to figure out,' King said. She was in complete control and despite being half the man's size, she clearly made Benny feel a little uncomfortable. She turned to Townsend. 'Do you want to run him through it?'

'Sure.' Townsend leant forward. 'So in the early hours of Monday morning, Lauren Grainger was murdered in

Wycombe Rye. Stabbed to death multiple times. Tuesday early evening, Natasha Stokes, owner of Stokes Homes estate agents just up the hill there, was lured to an empty house she had on the market and again, like Lauren, was brutally murdered. And Thursday night, just shy of midnight, Michaela Woods was found murdered outside her block of flats in Beaconsfield. You knew these women, yes?'

'Well, knew is a strong word…'

'Yes or no?' Townsend cut in. Benny seemed to stiffen with anger. 'Did you personally know these women?'

'Yes.' Benny's voice was laced with anger. 'But that doesn't mean I killed them.'

'Maybe. Maybe not.' King mused. 'But I'd say three women, from three very different walks of life, living in very different places, with no discernible connection, probably don't all know many of the same people.'

'That's a pretty speculative assumption,' Patel interjected. King clearly wasn't having any of it.

'Is it? Because to me, if we did a Venn Diagram of our three victims, I'd say that the intersection where they meet will be pretty small.' She turned back to Townsend. 'As you were.'

Townsend sipped his coffee and continued.

'Early hours of Monday morning…Lauren leaves work…then what?'

'I don't know.' Benny shrugged. 'I said goodbye, and she headed home.'

'And you stayed behind for a drink, right?' King asked. Benny nodded.

'Sykes opens the bar up after a shift. It's not illegal.'

'But it is a crime to lie to the police,' Townsend said. 'See, Benny, we've spoken to everyone who *was* there when Sykes opened up the bar, and no one can place you there.'

'That's their problem then.' Benny's defiance seemed to agitate Patel beside him.

'Well, actually, it's your problem. Sykes himself said you weren't there. So if you weren't where you said you were, where were you?'

Benny looked at Patel, who nodded her permission.

'No comment.'

'Come on, Benny.' King slapped her hand on the table. 'We've already established you lied. What about Michaela Woods? She was *just* a customer, right?'

'So I shift a little bit of gear on the side? Surely you guys have bigger problems right now than a few bags of coke?'

'True.' Townsend agreed. 'One of them being that Michaela Woods was an ex-girlfriend of yours. For quite a while. But, she'd been clean for ten months, so I'll ask you when did you last see her?'

'Who told you that?' Benny exclaimed, struggling to mask his worry.

'Detectives, eh?' King said. 'Always bloody finding things out, aren't we? Listen, Mr Hughes. You've lied to us twice, one about your whereabouts, and one about your relationship with one of the victims. You can listen to your solicitor and 'No Comment' us till the cows come home, that's your right. But right now, I'd say the only card you have to play is the truth.'

Townsend looked at Benny, who looked defeated. Watching King work, the way she could unnerve a suspect but also gain their trust in a heartbeat, was one of the most impressive things he'd seen.

'Can I have a cup of tea, please?' Benny eventually stammered. Whatever tough-guy façade he lived behind had been shattered, and despite his hulking frame and granite-like fist, he looked like a scared little boy. Townsend obliged, left the room, and a few moments later, returned with a polystyrene cup of tea. Benny took it, had a few sips, and then took a deep breath.

Once he got started, he didn't stop. Patel tried a few times to remind him of his rights, but the barrier had been broken. The terror of the finger being pointed in his direction had caused a course correction from the stubborn brute, to a man who offered up as much information as he could to try to clear his name.

He wasn't at Paradise when Lauren was murdered, because he was picking up a kilo of cocaine from someone he wouldn't name.

He knew of Natasha Stokes, but he never dealt with her directly. Every drug dealer he dealt with used a burner phone.

And finally, he did have a long and toxic relationship with Michaela Woods, but he hadn't seen spoken to her since her last stint in rehab.

By the end of his monologue, Benny's voice was cracking, and a few tears of panic ran down his face.

'Look, I know the drugs and shit are going to get me into trouble. But I'm not a killer. I'm not.' He looked down at the table and shook his head. 'I didn't do this.'

King, who had made a number of notes in her notepad as he had spilled his truth, slammed it shut, and looked up at him.

'We'll see, won't we?' She stood up, pocketed her notepad, and then straightened her jacket. 'That's it for now. I'll have uniform stop by and take you back to your cell.'

King terminated the interview and headed to the door, closely followed by Townsend, who stopped and looked back at the whimpering giant in the chair.

It was that feeling again.

Something didn't feel right.

As they stepped into the hallway, they were greeted by DSI Hall.

'Izzy, a word?' He beckoned her with a finger. 'How's the eye, Jack?'

'Still working, sir.' Townsend nodded respectfully. He turned to King. 'See you down there, guv.'

Townsend made his exit, disappearing round the corner towards the stairwell.

'Any progress?' Hall asked, gesturing towards the door of the interview room.

'Perhaps. Few things we can look into. A few things we can't.' King looked back at the door. 'But there is enough here to keep him.'

'But not enough to charge him.'

'Sir?'

'It's all circumstantial, Izzy. You know that,' Hall said firmly. 'Take Townsend and a team to his flat and turn it upside down. You need a murder weapon, or something that puts him at one of these murders. Right now, his only crimes are knowing the individual women who have been murdered.'

'Three completely different women, with no connection to each other. Besides him.'

'Like you said. Enough to make him a person of interest. But you need to find me something within the next twenty-four hours, otherwise that man walks out of here.'

'Yes, guv.' King sighed. She knew he was right. But something on his face told her that wasn't all. 'Anything else, guv?'

Hesitantly, he pulled out his mobile phone, scrolled through the screen, and then handed her the phone. At first, she frowned. She wasn't a big fan of Twitter, or any social media for that matter, but once she read the first post, her eyes widen in horror.

'What the hell? When was this posted?'

'This morning,' Hall said sadly. 'They must have seen you in some of the photos that had been published on the

Buckingham Presses account. Judging by your reaction, I take it you understand how bad this is, optics wise.'

She absolutely did.

The post was as sensationalist as one of the red top tabloid papers.

DRUNK DETECTIVE HUNTING SERIAL KILLER. DON'T WE ALL FEEL SO SAFE!?

Worse, there was three photos, taken candidly on someone's phone, of Detective Inspector Isabella King buying two bottles of wine. Each one was dated, hammering home the message that she was hitting the bottle and hard.

The number of likes, retweets and comments made her hand shake, and as she scrolled through the first few, she had to fight back the sudden urge to vomit.

'What a disgrace.'

'These poor girls deserve better.'

'DI Drunk on the case.'

She pushed the phone back to Hall and pressed her hands to cover her face.

Cover her shame.

'Sir, I can explain…' She began fruitlessly. Hall lifted his hand.

'Don't worry. We're going to bury it. We've got people working on it right away. For now, I need you to keep a low profile. You might not like it, but myself and DCI Lowe will handle any press duties for this case.' He took a step towards her. 'But I need you take care of yourself, Izzy. Not as your superior, but as a friend. You're not the first detective to hit the bottle. You won't be the last. But you're no good to me, to your team or to those poor girls and their families if you're not at one hundred percent.'

King took a few deep breaths. She could feel her hands still shaking, and her anger threatened to explode in a flood of tears that she didn't want to share with anyone. Hall reached out, put a hand on her shoulder and squeezed.

'Head in the game, Izzy.' He offered with a smile, before turning, and walking off up the corridor. King stood on the spot for a few moments, her head spinning at not only the intrusion into her private life, but for the very hard slap of reality it had delivered.

She was letting everyone down.

Lauren Grainger. Natasha Stokes. Michaela Woods.

They all deserved justice and hunting their killer through the blurriness of a hangover meant King might have overlooked or missed something. Taking a deep breath, King scolded herself one more time and then looked back at the door to the interview room, and made a silent promise to prove that the man sitting at that table was a cold-blooded killer.

And she had to do it in less than twenty-four hours or he'd walk free.

The clock was ticking.

CHAPTER FORTY-ONE

As expected, Benny's flat was a complete tip. After the man had made a break from it the day before, King had assigned uniform to keep a watch on the place, but without Hall's permission, they hadn't gone inside. Townsend had led the chase around the building and through the courtyard, but now, with the permission granted, King and Townsend had the authority to turn the man's flat upside down.

Not that he'd notice.

The kitchen was stacked with dirty dishes and empty takeaway cartons, and enough empty beer bottles to start a dangerous bowling alley. The remnants of cocaine were easily identifiable on the edge of the kitchen counter, as well as on the similarly untidy coffee table in the living room. The open-plan kitchen backed onto the unkempt living area, which was nothing more than a leather sofa, coffee table, and a TV unit, which held a large, flatscreen television as well as a PlayStation. The place severely lacked not only a woman's touch, but any sense of care or attention. There was nothing on the walls, no decoration of any description, and the wooden floor was littered with empty packets and carrier bags.

'This place would give Mandy a heart attack,' Townsend said with a chuckle, as the two of them stuffed their hands into latex gloves. His wife was a neat freak, and her constant 'upgrading' of the 'decorative bits' in their house had been a source of Townsend's amusement for some time.

As Townsend pulled apart the front room, King found herself in the bedroom, which was heavy with the stale smell of sweat. A large, unmade double bed filled most of the room, opposite a built-in wardrobe that was filled with dirty clothes. The one bedside table, like most surfaces in the house, was sprinkled with white powder, and a few used condoms were stuffed in the bin. With considerable force, she lifted the mattress from the bed, and stuffed between the planks, she found two large, tightly wrapped bricks of cocaine.

Enough to put the man away for a long time.

With her phone, she took a few pictures of them, before turning her attention to the wardrobe. Rifling through the man's dirty laundry wasn't the most pleasant of tasks, but she was adamant they needed to search every single centimetre of the flat.

They needed to find a murder weapon.

Unfortunately, the knife block that sat atop the kitchen counter was fully stocked, and none of them had any traces of blood on them. They'd get them lab tested as a priority, but King was already certain they'd come back clean.

If Benny *was* the killer, then the knife would be somewhere else.

The search of the wardrobe revealed a few smaller bags of cocaine and a few sizable rolls of fifty-pound notes, but nothing murderous.

Nothing that confirmed Benny was the killer.

With a deep sigh, she rocked back onto her knees and then searched through the drawers. The only surprising find was a couple of pairs of women's underwear, trophies perhaps, but considering that none of the murdered women had been sexually assaulted, King didn't draw from them other than Benny was a man who kept a trophy or two.

A drug dealer.

But as of that moment, an unproven murderer.

King stood and marched back out into the tiny hallway, and peered into the bathroom, where Townsend was busy rattling through the cabinet.

'Anything?' she asked.

'Beyond the fact the man hasn't seen a toilet brush in his life? Afraid not, guv.' Townsend pulled a small bottle out of the cabinet and shook it. 'Antidepressants.'

'Well, pumping class A drugs into the streets of your hometown probably weighs down on your conscience.' King put her hands on her hips. 'Fuck.'

'What do you want to do?' Townsend asked as he closed the cabinet.

'We'll get SOCO in here to sweep the place. Who knows...maybe they'll find something we didn't.' King shrugged. 'We'll nail him for the drugs, see if that shakes him up a bit. But it's not enough.'

'You think he did it?' Townsend asked, knowing he would draw the incoming scowl.

'Right now…he's our best lead, Jack. We need to follow the facts through until they're disproven.' King offered him a smile. 'But if you have another theory, save it for when we get back.'

The duo left the flat, leaving the uniformed officer to wait for the SOCO team to arrive. On the drive back to the station, Townsend pulled into a small side street, where they picked up a quick lunch to have back at the station where, upon their arrival, Hannon, and Swaby were hard at work.

'How did it go?' Hannon asked.

'It was a shithole,' Townsend said, collapsing into his chair. 'Lots of drugs.'

'Drug dealer has lots of drugs in his house,' Hannon replied dryly. 'I'll phone the paper and let them know.'

The office erupted into a chuckle and Townsend rolled up a Post-it note on his desk and jokingly threw it at her. King, perched on the edge of Townsend's desk, took a bite of her chicken wrap before steering the conversation back on topic.

'Michelle. Any luck with those phones?'

'Afraid not,' Swaby said with a sigh. 'The whole point of those phones is to be discreet. I'm running through serial numbers that have been bought in the area, but we don't even know if the person who made that call was even nearby when they made it.'

'Any luck with the signals?' King asked hopefully. Swaby shook her head. 'Damn it.'

'I did some digging,' Hannon offered. 'But there doesn't seem to be any links between Riley and Benny. I figured maybe they were in the same circles, but whoever Riley is selling for, it isn't Benny.'

'Who knew High Wycombe was such a hotbed of drugs?' Townsend said. 'What about Sykes? Do you think there's more to him?'

King took a moment of consideration and then shook her head.

'Everything he's offered us so far is the truth. Alibis. Reasons. To be fair, despite running a seedy business, he seems like a fairly stand-up guy.'

'Then what are we missing?' Hannon said to no one in particular.

Townsend leant back in his seat, staring at the board. Plastered across the top were the three faces of innocence, all struck from the world by a brutal hand. Beneath it, a myriad of information, drawn arrows, and pictures of murder scenes and potential suspects. Everything they knew was on the board, yet the answer wasn't there.

Finally, he spoke.

'Motive.' All eyes turned to him, and he suddenly felt slightly exposed. 'We had motive for Riley, but we know he didn't kill Natasha Stokes for certain. Considering the pattern of kills, it's unlikely he killed Lauren or Micheala, too.'

'Look, Jack, I know it's frustrating, but we can only work on what we've discovered so far,' King said with a sigh. 'I know it's frustrating, but right now, all signs point to Benny.'

'Because he knew them all? I get that. But I'm not asking *if* he killed them. I'm asking *why* he would kill them?' Townsend looked at the three women in the room, who looked at him with intrigue. 'All I'm saying is, we're spending all our efforts hunting for a murder weapon to tie this man to these killings. But why would he have done them in the first place? If we look at it logically, killing Lauren doesn't make a shit tonne of sense, as she was the main money maker at Paradise, and according to the other girls who worked there, got on pretty well with Benny. Killing Natasha Stokes puts his lease in the hands of someone else and could cause him issues, especially as he keeps all his drug supply in his home. And if Michaela Woods was a customer and off and on again lover, then that impacts him in a couple of ways. It just doesn't make sense to me.'

A silence hung uncomfortably in the room for a few seconds, and all eyes fell on King, who was rubbing her chin with careful consideration.

'So, you think we're wrong?' she asked. King didn't seem angry, but she was certainly testing him.

'Not wrong. Maybe just blinkered.' Townsend shrugged. 'We're all looking at what *has* been done. But not *why* it was done. Couldn't hurt to look at it from a different angle.'

King stood and walked to the board, casting her eyes over the diligent and painstaking work of her and her team.

'Okay, Jack,' she said without turning back to look at him. 'Find me a different angle. Find me some hard proof that we're looking in the wrong place, and we'll put another board together. But let's make it very clear, we can only keep Benny in here for the rest of the day otherwise DSI Hall *will* order him to be released. And if he is the monster killing these poor women, I don't want to be the one to let him go. So, Jack...you've got a few hours. Let's see what you can find.'

'Yes, guv.' Townsend stood eagerly, taking his lunch to go. King turned to the rest of the team.

'Find me something. Anything,' King stated firmly. She called out to Townsend just before he left the office. 'Oh, and Jack. Don't take this personally, but I really hope you're wrong on this.'

Townsend nodded with a smile.

'Me too, guv. Me too.'

CHAPTER FORTY-TWO

Something just didn't seem right.

Townsend stood, casting his eye out over the lake that was the epicentre of Wycombe Rye, and pulled his bomber jacket tight. The warmth of the summer was swiftly fading, and another wave of drizzle had begun to descend from the clouds above. The vast fields were empty, save for a few dedicated dog walkers, and the small kiosk to his left hadn't even bothered to open today. The pedalo and row boats they offered were all tied up against the side of the lake, and the coffee shop shutter was firmly shut.

Beneath his feet, the faded stain of blood still peeked through a few cracks in the concrete.

This was where Lauren Grainger had been murdered, and Townsend thought that by bringing himself back to the crime scene, he might find inspiration from something.

Anything.

DI King had given him a few hours to develop another angle, and the clock was ticking.

And something just didn't seem right.

It was the same feeling he'd felt in his gut when they dragged that delinquent, Dean Riley, over the coals. Benny, who had split Townsend's eyebrow with a violent strike and was clearly a serious drug dealer, was someone that demanded the police's interest.

He belonged in prison.

But Townsend didn't think the man was a killer.

It was a testament to King's leadership that she'd afforded him the opportunity to look elsewhere. All the evidence was pointing towards the Paradise bouncer, but without the glue they needed to make it stick, King's focus was quite rightly on finding the damning piece of evidence that meant the book could be thrown at the man.

Hannon and Swaby were onboard.

But instead of chastising him for theorising that they had the wrong man, King was pushing Townsend to prove his theory.

And in doing so, prove himself.

Townsend knew there were eyes on him. His road to becoming a detective sergeant reeked of an apology, with the Merseyside Police trying to make up for the horror he'd faced during his three years undercover. There were those who dismissed him as a fake detective, and when one of those people was the head of CID, it meant Townsend couldn't afford any mistakes.

He couldn't prove them right.

But as he stood, looking at the looping concrete path that ran around the lake and up through the trees, he couldn't connect the dots. It was fact that Benny had been on the door when Lauren had left the club early on Monday morning. Townsend had done the walk himself before he'd arrived at the Rye, detouring from the station to the strip club, which hadn't opened for business yet.

Seven minutes.

That's how long it had taken him to follow the quickest path to the Rye, which cut underneath the overpass and across the magic roundabout, thankfully, at a designated zebra crossing. Considering the attack on Lauren came from the front, it meant he had to have arrived at the park before she did, which would have been near impossible without her seeing. Townsend had done the necessary checks and confirmed that Benny didn't have a registered vehicle. He'd sent a police constable off on the errand of looking for any stolen cars in the area on Monday morning, but even then, the chances were slim.

It was a seven-minute window.

With his hands stuffed in his pockets, Townsend marched down the pathway that separated the lake from the playing fields parallel and followed it all the way down to the car park that sat in the heart of the Rye.

Six minutes.

He timed it.

Even if he'd jumped in a car the second Lauren had turned away from him, he would still have been cutting it fine. The pathway that looped up from the car park and into the woods before bending back round to the kiosk took a further thirteen minutes to walk.

From either oncoming angle, there was no way Benny could have been in front of Lauren when she was murdered. Unless she got held up? It was a possibility, but from the last image of her on CCTV as she passed from overpass to the magic roundabout, it looked like she walked at a brisk pace.

Townsend sighed.

It didn't seem right.

He turned and marched back to the station car park, hopped into his car, and pulled out, cutting through the traffic and onto London Road, cruising past the main road that overlooked the Rye itself. Even from there, the only entrance in was a ten-minute walk to the spot that Lauren was killed, and with no car, would have been an easy fifteen-minute walk from the high street.

He got back in his car and carried on, crawling through the traffic as he approached the end of the long road that led to the M40.

Townsend pulled the car up onto the curb outside of the house that Natasha Stokes died in. Police tape still clung to the door frame, battered and beaten by the sudden yet not unsurprising turn of the British weather. The overgrown garden had been downtrodden by the number of police boots across it, with the SOCO team going through every blade of grass with a fine-tooth comb, doing exactly what he was doing right now.

Looking for something.

Anything.

Despite the overgrowth, there weren't a multitude of places to hide. The front of the house arched out in an impressive bay window, but the small gap between the window and the overgrown bush was narrow. A hulking frame like Benny's had no chance of being shielded by it, and although some of the bushes were beginning to tip due to their neglect, when Natasha arrived at her appointment, it would have been daylight. She would have seen him.

So where did he hide?

Again, it wasn't improbable that Natasha had been distracted by her phone or something else, not to notice him, but a man of Benny's size would stick out like a sore thumb, even in the periphery.

With a grimace, Townsend turned, and left the garden, got back into his car and then turned at the next roundabout, following his satnav as it guided him through a maze of pleasant country roads towards Beaconsfield. As he sped down one country lane, he passed a sign for Odds Farm, a charming-looking place that he earmarked for a future family day out. Spread across acres of land, the farm offered everything from feeding the animals, informative talks, and tractor rides, as well as an enormous playground and indoor soft play.

Townsend turned onto Old Beaconsfield high street, which did little to hide its affluence. The quaint cobble streets were lined with expensive boutique outlet stores and non-chain restaurants. The cars that were parked sporadically in the designated spaces were all high-end, making his rather modest Honda Civic stand out. Eventually, he pulled up to the block of flats where Michaela Woods had been murdered.

He stepped out of his car and walked to the spot where her body had been found, and he squatted down by the dried blood that had yet to be fully cleansed from the pavement. Retrieving his phone from his pocket, Townsend tapped in the address for Paradise into the map app on his phone.

Just under eight miles.

He then replaced Paradise with the name of Benny's street in Downley.

Again, just under eight miles.

If Benny did kill her, then he would have needed to have either stolen a car, booked a cab, or taken the train. All three of them were easily checkable, and as he made his way back to the car, Townsend called the young police constable who was checking the previous car theft and asked her to check for the night Michaela was murdered.

She quickly confirmed that both days were a dead end.

He thanked her and then swiftly drove to Beaconsfield Train Station, which was slap bang in the middle of Beaconfield High Street, a good mile or two away from where Michaela Wood had been murdered. With the rough time of death being between eleven and midnight, it meant there would have only have been two trains Benny could have realistically caught.

A quick flash of his badge allowed Townsend into the

station manager's office, and the manager was more than happy to allow Townsend a look at the platform CCTV from two nights ago. There were no train delays that evening, so pinpointing the arrival of the Chiltern Mainline run train was easy.

A few people got off.

A few people got on.

None of them was Benny Hughes.

Townsend thanked the station manager for his help and then headed to the taxi rank situated at the front of the station. It took two minutes for them to confirm that they didn't have any bookings that would have matched Benny's journey either to or from the station. They also confirmed that nobody matching Benny's description had been in there. As Townsend headed back to his car, he called Hannon.

'Hello, Sherlock,' she said with a giggle.

'Haha. Very good. Did Benny have an actual phone?' Townsend asked. 'Besides a burner?'

'What, like a smartphone?' Hannon tapped on her keyboard. 'Nope. Nothing on him when you guys brought him in.'

'Okay. So we can rule out an Uber account?'

'Yeah. I mean, I can check, but I'd say it's a safe bet. Why?'

Townsend sighed as he looked back at the station.

'Because unless a man of that size can run faster than Usain Bolt, or he has an unknown friend with a set of wheels we don't know about, I don't think he killed Michaela Woods.'

The statement seemed to catch Hannon off guard.

'Really?'

'Yeah.' Townsend looked out across the train station car park. A worried frown furrowed his brow. 'In fact, I don't think he's killed any of them.'

CHAPTER FORTY-THREE

The rush hour traffic was already in full swing as Townsend crawled down the hill past High Wycombe train station, with the one-way system causing a minor log jam as people raced to get home. Eventually, he coasted down through the traffic lights and pulled into the car park of the police station, offering a quick wave to a few officers who were heading out in a patrol car. The drizzle had morphed into a summer shower, indicating the beginning of the summer's end.

He was already soaked through by the time he stepped into the SCU office, where Hannon was shutting down her station.

'You off?' he asked, wriggled free from his jacket.

'Yeah. I've got a date with a dentist.'

'Fun.' Townsend smiled. 'Tell him how many biscuits you eat per day.'

'It's a her actually. Sexist.' Hannon stuck her tongue out at him as she left, and he looked around the rest of the small, cramped office. Swaby was nowhere to be seen, and King was on the phone in her own office. He took a seat at his desk, nearly knocking over the box of files that Baycroft had kindly delivered for him, and he made a note to return them soon. They'd provided no help, but it wouldn't hurt Townsend to at least make the old man feel like he'd been of use.

'So?' King's words interrupted his train of thought, and he spun in his chair. 'How did you get on? Have a new theory for me?'

'Umm…I have something. You got a map of this town?'

'No. We have the Internet, Jack,' King said with a chuckle. 'Why?'

Townsend stood, and he picked up one of the pens for the whiteboard and crudely drew an oval on the empty bottom half of the board. He then drew an 'X' on one side.

'So this here, is where Lauren Grainger was murdered, right?' He then drew two arrows curving around the lake and pointed them at the spot. 'We know that she was attacked from the front, as the first stab wounds were in her stomach and chest.'

'Correct.' King folded her arms and perched on the edge of Townsend's desk. She was interested.

'We also know that Benny *was* on the door when Lauren left Paradise over here.' He drew a 'P' on the other side of the board. 'Now, to get from Paradise to the lake, it takes seven minutes. I timed it and based on the CCTV footage of her last steps, Lauren was on course to do the same.'

'Go on.'

'Well, that means Benny had to get from Paradise to this side of the lake to approach Lauren in the way we believe she was murdered. The only other entrances he could have taken that would have allowed him to overtake her are here and here.' He marked them on the board. 'It's a six-minute walk from the car park of the

Rye to the spot where Lauren was killed. Now Benny would have to have driven a five-minute drive around the one-way system and the side road to get to this car park, which means there is no way he could have got there in time.'

'Unless he ran?' King offered. She wasn't goading, just suggesting.

'We've both seen him run. He's hardly Linford fucking Christie,' Townsend said. He then tapped the other side of the lake. 'Now, if he came through the woods, again, he would have had to have parked in the car park, and then that's an even longer walk. Thirteen minutes to be precise, and I walk pretty quickly.'

'And there are no other possible entrances to the woods?'

'None that are of public access. You have the Carrington estate on the other side of the fencing, but no walk through.'

'Right, we'll get uniform to search the woods, see if there are any cut-throughs, or any damage to the fencing.' King shrugged. 'See if there is any possibility of a way through.'

'That's not all.' Townsend then tapped the photo of the garden pinned to the wall. It was from Natasha Stokes' murder. 'I thought I'd check out the house on London Road. See it in the daylight and with fresher eyes. There's no way a man of Benny's size could have hidden in that garden.'

'It was overgrown.' King gestured with her hand.

'I know, but not to that extent. There is a small nook to the side of the bay window, where the overgrowth hides the wall, but I barely fit into it and I'm half his size.' Townsend stood with his hands on his hips. 'Plus, she was murdered in the early evening. Plenty of sunlight. She would have seen him.'

'Distracted maybe?' King mused. 'She did die with her phone in her hand.'

'Possible. But you said we need to make this bullet-proof. No way we can pin this on him if we are saying 'maybe she was distracted'.

'Fair point,' King said, nodding her acceptance.

'Then we come to Michaela Woods. Did you know that Benny Hughes doesn't have a registered vehicle?'

'I did.'

'So I checked the train times in and around Michaela's murder, and there were two potential trains Benny could have got on that would have taken him home. I've already reviewed the CCTV of the station for both arrivals, and he didn't get on either one of them.'

'Could have taken a cab?'

Townsend raised his finger as if he'd thought of that. King smiled, clearly impressed.

'I checked with the local cab office by the station. There were no walk-ins or bookings for a cab to or from High Wycombe for a man matching Benny's description.'

'Uber?'

'He had a burner phone. No apps. No way to log in.' Townsend tapped the board. 'So unless he has an acquaintance ferrying him around to kill these women, I can't find a logical way he could have been there.'

Townsend feared the worst. King had sent him off on a mission to find an alternative theory to the one they had circumstantial evidence for, and all he'd done was debunk most of their case. She looked up at the board with authority, running her tongue on the inside of her lip. She pulled out her vape and flagrantly disregarded the no smoking rule of the station. Finally, she turned to Townsend.

'Good work, Jack.'

'Really?'

She nodded purposefully.

'It's what we do. We detect. We hunt down leads, but we also need to process the facts that are put in front of us.' She blew out the fruity vapour and stuffed the stick back into her pocket. 'I'll get some of Lowe's guys to look into an accomplice, any known acquaintances of Benny's who have access to a vehicle. It might be nothing, but we'll see if they can provide their whereabouts the night Michaela and Lauren were killed.'

'You still think he did it?'

'I can't rule him out. As good as all this is, Jack, and you have picked up some glaring holes in our case against him, they can all be explained. Our job now is to rule out those explanations, and if we can…then we might have to hold our hands up and say we've got the wrong guy again.'

'Hall won't like that.' Townsend sighed. 'Lowe will love it.'

'Forget about Lowe. He's not worth your brain space. And leave DSI Hall to me. He wants this cleared up as quickly as we do, and if I ask him for a little more time, he'll handle whatever push back we get from Benny's solicitor.'

'Right. What do you need from me?' Townsend asked, the adrenaline pumping.

'It's been another long day. So go home. Get some rest.' King ordered, and then pointed to the box of files. 'And get those out of here, will you?'

'First thing, guv.' Townsend lifted his sodden jacket from his chair and then turned to King. 'If it's not Benny…what do we do?'

'What do you mean?'

'We don't have any other leads and there's a killer out there.'

'We go again,' King said firmly. 'We look back at what we know hasn't happened and determine another possibility of what has happened. There are connections we haven't made yet. We can tie both Lauren and Michaela to known drug dealers, so that might be an avenue worth looking into. But how Natasha fits in, I don't know.'

King looked up at the board. At the faces of the three women who had been brutally wiped from the earth.

Her fists clenched.

'We'll catch them, guv,' Townsend said with unwavering belief.

'I know. We just better make it quick.' King turned and nodded to him. 'Good work, Jack. We'll make a detective out of you yet.'

Townsend made his way back through the station, past a few colleagues who bid him good night, and it was only as he dropped into the driver's seat of his car and caught a glimpse of himself in the mirror, that he realised he had a massive smile across his face.

CHAPTER FORTY-FOUR

The night shift was perfect for Irena Rosolska.

Very few people came through during her shift, and although it fell upon her more than her co-workers to ensure the shelves were replenished and the tiny stockroom was neat as a pin, it wasn't difficult work. Those who did stop by were usually friendly enough, and the station was equipped with enough safety precautions to ensure if anything did go wrong, she'd be safe. The till was behind a perplex screen, and had an instant lock mechanism, as well as the door to the station.

Besides, there was nothing that scared her.

Not anymore.

Irena often wondered what life would have been like if she'd never met Tomasz. It was a lifetime ago, when she was a bright-eyed student in Warsaw, in her native Poland, and had been swept up by his good looks and matching charm. She'd only ever had one boyfriend, but like most teenagers, they'd never fully understood what passion was.

Tomasz did, and for a few months, he had thrown her into a world of ecstasy and fulfilment, and the two of them would skip classes at the University of Warsaw and would lose day after day between the sheets. It was eye opening and thrilling, and when the day came that Tomasz revealed his true self, her entire reality was shattered. Claiming to have arranged a secret trip for them, she was driven to an abandoned warehouse where, along with four other women, she was accosted by masked men who snatched her from her life and forced her into the world of sex slavery.

She tried to fight back at the beginning, but the operation was as cunning as it was cruel, and by forcing her into a drug addiction, her dependence on her next fix soon outweighed her desire to be free. For eight years, Irena was lost in a hazy nightmare, semi-aware of what was happening to her but also too hooked on heroin to truly care. At some point along her harrowing journey, she ended up being smuggled across to the United Kingdom where she was placed in a home in North London under the brutal and abusive watch of a man named Adam.

Every three months, Adam would shift the women to new houses, where other grotesque men would watch over them, teasing them with drugs, and forcing them to degrade themselves for their next fix. It had been over six years since her day of freedom. She'd been in the cramped, two-bedroom home on the outskirts of High Wycombe when the police arrived, part of a calculated and widespread operation across multiple police services. The men were duly arrested, and Irena and the other women were given all the love and care they needed to get through their ordeal.

Until they weren't.

After a successful spell in rehab, Irena found herself alone, and abandoned in a foreign country. The temporary accommodation they'd provided had always been exactly that; temporary. She had too much shame and anguish to ever return home, and with little skill or experience, she fell back into the world of prostitution. It lasted a little over eight months before she was arrested for the first time, and within a year, she wound up facing a nine-month prison sentence.

It was during her time in prison that she'd found solace in the library, her once capable and logical mind finding stimulation from the books about financial management and trading and upon her release, Irena had vowed to follow a career in financial trading.

That was why the job at the petrol station was perfect.

Her ten-hour shift paid reasonably well, and it meant that for at least half of it, she could work through the online courses she'd signed up for through government grants for further education. It gave her the peace and quiet she craved, all while putting enough money in her bank account to cover the cost of her studio flat, which was a five-minute walk away in West Wycombe.

The station itself was set on the very edge of the town, looming over a roundabout that connected Wycombe with the long and windy country roads towards Saunderton or Stokenchurch. Across the road, the gothically-named Hell-fire Caves sat beyond a large hill, as well as other nearby National Trust locations that offered the natural beauty of the Chilterns.

For the first time in over a decade, Irena had found herself feeling not only hopeful, but happy, and while the scars of her traumatic past were deep and permanent, she was working to put them behind her.

As with all her shifts, it passed without incident, beyond a crude comment from one of the customers who made a crass proposition that she ignored. Irena had always been pretty, with her high cheekbones and long, blonde hair, and despite the years of abuse, that beauty still shone through. She had ignored the comment and sent the customer on his way and then lost herself in her laptop when Gus had arrived to take over.

Five a.m. already.

They exchanged a few pleasantries. Nothing more than small talk, which was how Irena liked it. Her life was hers now, and she didn't want to fill it with friendships or build bridges to people who could betray her. She often wondered about finally reaching out to her parents, who must have been shattered with grief at losing their daughter. It would give them some peace of mind to know she was alive, but Irena often wondered if the truth was worse.

Would they rather believe her dead than to know that for nearly a decade, she was lost in a world of drugs and prostitution? That she'd done unspeakable things to worse people?

The summer months were slowly coming to an end, and Irena could sense the change in the air when she left the station. It was still dark outside, and the humid mornings had been replaced with a sharp chill that necessitated a jacket. She said her goodbyes to Gus, helped herself to a coffee from the dispenser, and then headed out the door onto the station forecourt. It was empty, with all six pumps waiting standing idle. On the main road ahead of her, a few early risers approached the roundabout and then sped off on whatever journey they were on.

All she could think about was her next exam, which was only two weeks away.

Soon, she'd be qualified enough to apply for junior positions in financial management firms, but she was also keen to get into online trading. She'd always had a penchant for numbers and patterns and was certain she could make a good career out of it.

For the first time in her life, it seemed like she had possibilities. That finally, she could move on.

As she cut across the forecourt, she looked back to the

window of the kiosk. Her eyes were instantly drawn to the figure that was standing down the side of the station itself, hands stuffed in the pockets of his jacket. It startled her, but before the panic kicked in, she breathed a sigh of relief.

Then a smile spread across her face as she approached, and as she threw her arms open, her eyes bulged with shock as the knife plunged into her stomach. The pain was instant, and her body shook as she looked up in fear. The gloved hand pulled the knife back, wrenching it free from her flesh, and as she stumbled to her knees, she could feel the blood rushing through her fingers. She collapsed onto her back in the shadows, shielded from the forecourt, and as she looked up in horror, the knife was driven down into her chest.

Then again.

And again.

And with her hopes and dreams spilling out of her body in a bloody puddle, she finally closed her eyes and everything went black.

CHAPTER FORTY-FIVE

Townsend didn't even say goodbye to his family that morning. When his phone buzzed, it stirred him from his sleep, and he had pushed himself away from Mandy, lifting the arm that was draped across her and he lifted it to view the screen.

DI King.

He sat bolt upright.

He knew what the call was for. She didn't need to confirm it for him.

Within minutes, he was creeping down the stairs, buttoning up his shirt, having dropped a kiss on both Mandy and Eve's foreheads while they slept. With his stomach turning, he got into his car, racing through the streets that had yet to fully wake up. The call had come in a little after six that morning, and by quarter to seven, he was pulling into the station. King had told him to head there instead of the crime scene, and as he stepped into the SCU office, he was surprised to see Hannon already at her desk.

The look on her face said it all.

Fear.

She nodded to the coffee she'd put on his desk, and he sat down, and faced her.

'You okay?' he asked. She shook her head.

'No. Not one bit.'

'Me neither.'

DI King strode into the room, her face like thunder, and the bags under her eyes indicating another restless night. Townsend offered her a good morning and instantly regretted it. She stomped to the whiteboard and drew a big cross over the picture of Benny Hughes. She then put the cap back on the pen and slammed it on the desk.

'Right.' She addressed them both. 'I don't need to tell you what's happened, do I? The woman's name is Irena Rosolska. Thirty-two years old. Polish. She worked at the petrol station on the roundabout at the West Wycombe turn off. Multiple stab wounds. Out in the fucking open.'

King sighed, her hands on her hips.

'Family notified?' Townsend asked, leaning forward in his chair.

'Not yet.' King shook her head. 'The woman was smuggled here years ago as part of a human trafficking organisation. She was one of the women liberated by Project Downturn.' She saw the blank expression on both their faces. 'It was a huge operation across multiple counties to crack down on prostitution. They found poor Irena locked up in a house on the outskirts of town. She'd never given any next-of-kin and in the years since then, she's had a few run ins with us. I guess, a life like that's hard to get away from.'

Hannon looked pale.

'That poor woman.' Her voice was shaking. 'How much horrible can one person take?'

'Hey, I need you to park it,' King said firmly. 'I know this is shit. It's terrifying, and it feels like we're chasing our fucking tails, but these women, they *need* us right now. And right now, poor Irena can't be just another number on this bastard's list.'

Hannon took a breath and straightened up with a slight wince. She nodded to King.

'Any witnesses?' Townsend asked. 'If it was out in the open—'

'None.' King cut him off. 'It happened not long after five. She had just finished her shift, and her colleague was in the back of the garage, putting his lunch in the fridge. Plus, there were no cars on the forecourt either. We checked the CCTV.'

'Any leads from that?' Hannon chimed in, back in the room.

'The killer knew where to stand. The sick bastard was lying in wait by the side of the garage where the CCTV doesn't reach. All we have is Irena leaving the shop with a coffee in hand, stopping for a few moments and then walking until she disappears off the screen.'

'So he didn't jump her?' Townsend said. 'She saw who it was and like the others—'

'She knew who did it.' King finished it for him and nodded. 'That's the most likely scenario. A woman with her past, the things she's been through…there's no way she would approach a creepy guy loitering outside a petrol garage in the dark. Whoever killed Irena was someone she knew.'

'Well, it ain't Benny,' Hannon said in disappointment. 'You were right, Jack.'

'Forgive me if I don't take a victory lap.'

'Look, we did what we should have done.' King leant against Hannon's desk, her arms folded. 'We followed every lead we could that brought us to Benny. Now, we don't know if he knows Irena, and even if he did, we know he didn't kill her because like Dean Riley, he was downstairs when another woman died. Uniform are knocking on doors in the surrounding areas, Swaby is upstairs in CID running through CCTV to check any vehicles that passed near the area. But you speculated yesterday, Jack, that maybe he had help?'

'I mean, that's just a theory, guv…'

'Well, we don't have much else right now, do we?'

'Well, you better find something soon.'

The authoritative voice of DSI Hall drew all the attention to the door, as the Detective Superintendent strode into the room. His police tunic was smartly pressed, and he carried his hat proudly under his arm. His thinning, grey hair was neatly combed and sat above his thick, grey eyebrows that were furrowed into a scowl.

Townsend and Hannon stood, but Hall waved them down.

'We are looking into a few—'

'What? Theories?' Hall snapped. 'This situation is getting out of control. Four women dead in one week. Four! And for the second time, we have the wrong person sitting in our cells. So tell me, what is this theory?'

Hannon shot a glance to Townsend, almost a shake of the head. Townsend could see King squirming slightly and stood up again.

'That maybe Benny Hughes has an accomplice.'

'An accomplice?' Hall repeated. 'That's what we are going with? So when I get grilled by the press in an hour, who are knocking our fucking door down in fear, I should tell them that our best theory is that the person we spent hours of work on but clearly didn't kill Irena, *might* have an accomplice. I've got an entire town that's terrified and I have two major roads currently closed. So this *theory* is based on what?'

Townsend went to respond, but King stepped forward.

'DS Townsend did some exceptional work in eliminating Benny's possible attendance at Michaela's murder unless he had someone who was helping him.'

'So you proved that the man you were holding overnight for these murders wasn't at one of the crime scenes?' Hall was furious. 'So why were we not looking elsewhere?'

'We had reason to believe that it was a strong possibility and—'

'Do you believe it now? Why don't you go and ask him? No offence, but DS Townsend isn't the best placed person to be entering theories into the investigation. Especially when all resources should be spent on what evidence we *do* have.'

'May I speak, sir?' Townsend asked. Hall's head snapped to the side, his eyes wide with his answer.

'No. Sit down.' Hall waited, and Townsend did. 'I have no choice, Izzy, but to hand the control of this investigation over to DCI Lowe and—'

'Oh, fuck off...'

'And...I expect you to work as hard as you have been. I'll forgive that outburst. I know this was more than just a case for you, and the work done so far will be recognised as such.'

'I don't give a shit about the credit, sir.' King protested. 'But this team has given everything to try to find this bastard and we are still in the best position to do so.'

Hall looked at both Hannon and Townsend apologetically, and then looked back to King. He adjusted his stance, reimposing his authority.

'Bring whatever you need to up to CID. Lowe and I will be in his office.' Hall turned on his heels. 'I am sorry, DI King.'

With that, he stepped through door and disappeared up the corridor. King stood on the spot, her arms by her side, and he fingers twitching. Both Townsend and

Hannon shared a glance before Townsend stood and approached her.

'Guv, I'm sorry.'

She forced a smile as she composed herself.

'Don't be. Either of you.' She seemed to be pushing her anger down. 'This doesn't reflect on the work either of you has done.'

They knew what she meant. The buck stopped with her and although Hall's promise that the Specialist Crimes Unit would be credited with their help into the investigation, the bottom line would read that the decision was made that DI King was no longer fit to lead the investigation.

Once again, DCI Lowe had won.

After a few awkward moments of silence, King slapped her hands together, as if snapping herself back into the room.

'Give me five minutes. I need some air.'

'Sure,' Townsend said, returning to his seat. 'Need me to do anything?'

She nodded to the box of files on his desk.

'Yeah, take those files back will you?' She stopped at the door. 'And send Benny Hughes home.'

King disappeared and Townsend looked at Hannon, whose face told him that she was feeling the same way he was.

The same way King was.

The feeling that seemed to match the decision the rest of CID had made.

The Specialist Crimes Unit had failed.

CHAPTER FORTY-SIX

The next hour was one of the worst of Detective Inspector Isabella King's career.

After a quick vape, she thought she'd calmed herself down enough to face whatever was awaiting her when she went to meet with DSI Hall and DCI Lowe, but what had seemed like a meeting between the senior figures swiftly became a public execution. She knew that she and her team had done everything within their power to find the killer, but the moment she walked into her ex-husband's office, she knew it didn't matter.

The smug look of victory across his handsome face told her what was about to happen.

Throughout her tenure with the Thames Valley Police, through the good times and bad, DSI Hall had always been a fair boss. As much as it pained her to be in the process of handing over the investigation to CID, she knew it wasn't personal. Hall had pressures, both internal and external that meant he needed the case resolved as soon as possible. The man was firm but fair, and if there was any regret that things had come to this, he was using his wealth of experience to keep it well hidden.

Lowe, on the other hand, was revelling in it.

As she began to discuss their lack of progress in the office, Lowe made the decision that his entire team needed to hear it, to save time in him relaying the information second hand once she'd gone. King tried to protest, but Hall had given control of the case to Lowe and his team.

It was his to manage how he deemed fit, and despite the reasoning being complete bullshit, the team needed to know exactly where they were picking it up from.

'Shall we?' Lowe had said with an arrogant smirk, holding the door open for King to trudge out, defeated, to the rest of her former team. Lowe had followed her out and then clapped her hands loudly. 'Everyone, all ears. DI King is going to run through the investigation up to this point.'

All eyes turned to her. Swaby's were full of apology.

For the next thirty minutes, King walked them all through the work that had been done. The pursuit of Dean Riley and his links to Lauren Grainger. The death threats he had sent to her, as well as being present on the night of the death. It was all completely undone when Lowe pointed out there was no link from Riley to Natasha Stokes and that another woman died with Riley in custody.

The rest of the team exchanged glances.

King wanted the room to open up and swallow her.

But she pushed on.

She relayed the investigation into Paradise, with the collaboration with uniform to flesh out what working life was like there and how, through the hard work of the team, they were able to connect the door man, Benny Hughes, to all three victims. Benny Hughes, who was also a prolific drug dealer and, as proof of his assault on DS Jack Townsend, a man capable of violence.

Once again, Lowe had cut her off at the knees.

'But again, a man who was in custody when the fourth

victim was killed, right?' Lowe shrugged, performing to the team. 'Perhaps DS Townsend should think before he goes charging into action.'

'Actually, DS Townsend has been a key part of this investigation. In fact, yesterday, he did some fine detective work in establishing a solid theory that Benny Hughes may not have been working alone.'

A smile fell across Lowe's face. The loyalty he commanded from his team gave him a captivated audience, all of whom saw him as the alpha of their pack. It was a constant struggle for someone like DI King, who would always be fighting back against the macho bullshit that came inbuilt with a patriarchy.

'So your detective spent a day working on a theory that counteracted the one you were working on?' Lowe looked confused. 'Yet we didn't release Hughes until another kill came in?'

King knew what he was doing.

He was discrediting everything her and the SCU had done, and she looked to Hall who quickly shut Lowe down and stepped forward.

'This is a *team* effort,' Hall stated. 'The reason this investigation is now under the control of CID is simply a matter of resources. DI King and the rest of the SCU will be working alongside you all, sharing resources and information until this is over.'

'Yes, sir.' Lowe nodded. 'Of course.'

'Someone is killing,' Hall said, looking across the room, and ensuring he had everyone's attention. 'And people want answers. We *need* answers. So whatever opinions people might have, bin them. I want all focus on finding who's doing this and I want that bastard brought in. Understood?'

A resounding 'yes, sir' echoed through the CID office, and Hall then motioned for Lowe and King to step back into Lowe's office. Once he'd closed the door, he turned to them both.

'You two. Work it out.'

'I'm fine.' Lowe shrugged.

'There is nothing to work out.' King agreed.

'Fine. But this isn't a pissing contest. This is a necessary move to bring this killer in. Now, Marcus, we have the press coming in today and I need you to know this case like the back of your fucking hand. So whatever you need to know, get it from King. Otherwise, let's get back to work.'

'Yes, sir,' Lowe said and turned to his ex-wife. 'I think we're done here, aren't we?'

King didn't respond. She simply threw open his door and stormed out, heading straight through the open office of CID, knowing that every pair of eyes, besides DS Swaby's, were judging her.

Seeing her as a failure.

As fast as she could, she marched to the car park, ignoring any pleasantries from colleagues. She just needed some air, and as she tucked herself away in the corner of the car park, she clung to her vape and contemplated the idea of smoking an actual cigarette again.

Maybe it would help?

What had started out as the biggest opportunity of her career was transforming into a nightmare, and with her professional reputation hanging by a thread, she knew her personal one was being damaged also. The Thames Valley Police had acted swiftly to remove the posts painting her as a drunk, but the word had already got out and there would no doubt be a number of her colleagues wondering if she was even capable of being handed the case in the first place.

Hall had put his faith in her, but he hadn't handed her the case.

She had been available when the call came in, and her boss had seen it fit to give her the chance.

A chance that clearly, by the fact that she'd been ordered to hand it back to the first choice, she'd wasted.

With a dull ache in the back of her skull, she trudged back to the SCU office, her mind wrapped up in the embarrassment she'd just endured and the idea that she hadn't been good enough.

They hadn't done enough.

Townsend turned in his chair as she walked in.

'All good, guv?'

'What do you think?' She snapped. Hannon looked up from her desk.

'Well, we can still do what we can to—' Townsend responded, but King held up her hand.

'What we are going to do, Jack, is what we've been told to do. And that's hand everything over to CID and then support them going forward.'

'Come on, guv. We've done so much work,' Townsend protested. King's eyes bulged.

'Just listen to me, Jack. Please. Instead of racing around, disproving the work we are doing or trying to find other theories, just listen.' King was clearly annoyed, but she could see the hurt in Townsend's eyes. 'I know you're just trying to help, but right now, I just need you to listen.'

King turned around, and her elbow caught the box of useless files that Townsend had rested on the side of his desk. They crashed to the floor and spilled across the room. The final piece of straw onto the camel's back.

'And get rid of these fucking files like I told you to!' King yelled and then stormed off to her office, slamming the door so hard the entire SCU shook. Townsend watched her go. His confidence shattered, and wearily, he lowered himself down to the floor and began to collect the loose sheets of paper. Hannon handed him one, and with some difficulty, she lowered herself down to help.

'Don't take it personally, Jack.' She offered. 'She just needs to blow off some steam.'

'She's right, though.' Townsend sighed. 'All this work, and where the hell has it got us?'

Hannon looked him in the eye and smiled.

'It gets us closer to whoever is doing this.'

Townsend accepted the bunch of papers from Hannon, combined them with his own and then stood. He offered his colleague a hand up, before straightening them out on his desk and putting them in the box.

He turned to Hannon with dejection.

'That's the problem, though, isn't it? We don't have anyone for this.' Townsend put the lid back on the box. 'Whatever we did, it wasn't enough.'

Hannon went to respond but stopped herself. Townsend wasn't looking for pity, and she didn't have any for him. He was a good man and a good detective, but he'd just taken a hell of a knock. All the situation needed was a little time and it would be water under the bridge.

But time wasn't a commodity they had.

And right at that moment, the only water Townsend could comprehend was the thought that he was drowning.

CHAPTER FORTY-SEVEN

'I understand that this is a worrying time for the good people of this town and this county. But I want to assure every person that the Thames Valley Police has placed every resource possible to bringing this to a swift conclusion and to provide justice to the victims and their families.'

As DCI Lowe let his natural charm crash across the press room like an unstoppable wave, DI King stood at the back of the room with her arms folded. Numerous members of the press were there, all of them from their own local imprints or websites, all wanting information about the story that had shaken the quiet suburbs to its core.

Four women dead in a week.

A serial killer on the loose.

Sensationalist headline after headline had dominated the local news sites, and with national interest now being taken, DSI Hall, and DCI Lowe had taken it upon themselves to get out in front of it. Hall's reasoning for having Lowe join him was twofold. As much as King couldn't stand the man's arrogance, he had the charisma and authority to command most rooms. Secondly, he needed to take King out of the firing line.

She knew she'd let herself down.

The drinking had become such a formality that she hadn't realised it had become a problem, but Hall had already made it clear that it had to stop. She had told herself for years that she didn't want to become a cliché of a detective, but now with a failed marriage and a drinking problem, she'd done exactly that. The internet had allowed invasions of her privacy to become accepted as a 'scoop', and had she been sitting at the front of that room fielding questions as to why she hadn't caught the killer yet, she knew someone would bring it up.

This case wasn't about her and her issues.

It was about the four women who had been stricken from the world by the hand of a monster.

Hall could handle the blowback from the public. He was too long in the tooth to take it personally, and behind the scenes, he had already taken the necessary steps to speed up the investigation. Any queries from senior people in the town, as well as within the Thames Valley Police would fall on him, and by positioning himself front and centre, Hall was essentially taking any heat off the team.

It was admirable, but it didn't make King feel any better.

As the press conference began to wind down, King made her exit, pushing through the doors and making her way back through the station to the stairwell and down the well-trodden path to the SCU office. It felt deathly quiet, especially since DS Swaby had been moved back up to CID for the duration of the case, and most likely permanently once Hall and Lowe determined the future of the Specialist Crimes Unit. It would be back to cold cases and admin.

Busy work to allow the failures to justify their pay packets.

Hannon was, as always, glued to her screen, her hand reaching to half eaten packet of Oreo's beside her keyboard. Her monitors were filled with CCTV footage, and when King asked her how she was getting on, she did so already knowing the answer.

'Not much, guv.' Hannon grunted. 'Nothing we can really go on.'

'Keep going,' King said half-heartedly. The feeling of failure hung heavy in the office, and as King dropped down behind her own desk, she looked back out into the office.

Townsend wasn't there.

Neither was the box of files.

A twinge of guilt spasmed in her side and King regretted how their last interaction had played out. For all his inexperience, Townsend had proven himself to be an exceptional detective. Sure, his constant questioning and looking at different angles was annoying, but it was needed. It never hurt to have a different view, even when all the evidence was pointing in one direction.

He was smart.

He was brave.

He was, in fact, an asset to the team already, and her feeling of failure extended to him. His immediate loyalty to her had already seen him clash with Lowe, and she worried for his future within the Thames Valley Police once the inevitable happened and Lowe decided to 'make changes' to the way the team operated. It would be a shame, as Townsend's tenacity, and inquisitive nature were traits that the force needed.

She needed to make it right with him, and although it probably wasn't advisable for herself, she decided she'd invite him out for a drink that evening to clear the air.

Feeling like a spare part, she made up an excuse to Hannon and left the station, wandering down the high street of Wycombe and letting her mind wander.

What had they missed?

What connected all these women? Or were these attacks just as random as they appeared?

Without realising it, she turned into the alleyway that led to Paradise, where a different man stood at the door. As tall as Benny but without the bulk, King flashed her badge, and much to his displeasure, he let her in. The late afternoon crowd wasn't nearly as large nor as rowdy as what was to come later that night, but King made her way to the bar where Sykes did his best to hide his concern.

She made it clear she wasn't there for him.

Or was she?

With considerable willpower, she turned down his offer of a drink, and instead, asked him some basic questions to see if his story was still straight. Sykes saw right through it, chastising her for playing games and after an apology, she asked him if he knew the other women. If the names Natasha Stokes, Michaela Woods, and Irena Roslova meant anything to him.

They didn't, and as she left, he offered her a parting comment that cut her to the core.

'Why don't you go and focus on who actually killed these women?'

With those words stinging her heart, she made her way back out into the town and walked in any direction away from the station, trying as hard as she could to clear her head.

She was a good detective.

She knew that.

But this had been her opportunity to prove it, and to forge a life outside of Marcus Lowe's shadow and rebuild up the self-worth that had been shattered by his betrayal.

Not only that, but four innocent women had been brutally murdered in cold blood, and although she'd spent every sober moment of the last week thinking about them, she'd let them down.

She had failed.

After an hour's walk, King found herself on a small field among a housing estate near Cressex, where a few park benches lined the pathway that led to a small park that was surrounded by trees. With numerous rows of houses running down one side, and a secondary school the other, it felt as closed in as she did, and she dropped down onto the bench and took out her vape.

She sat, and she puffed, contemplating the next move.

For over an hour, she wrestled with the idea of swallowing her pride, falling in line, and just following DCI Lowe as he led the case forward. It would be for the best and as long as she got Hannon and Townsend out the other side, she would absorb any of the backlash and humiliation that came with it.

Her team had done her proud.

That was enough for her.

But it wouldn't be enough for those poor women.

Only as the sun began to fade behind darkened clouds, did she glance at her phone. She had a few messages from Hannon, but nothing urgent enough for her to panic.

She also only had two per cent of battery left and with a mile-long walk back to the station, King sighed, pocketed her vape, and began the walk back. As she did, she told herself over and over that there would be no drinking that night.

But truthfully, she knew that would just be another failure to add to the long list that would lead her to the bottle, anyway.

CHAPTER FORTY-EIGHT

With her feet aching from the long walk, King finally turned onto the street of the station, and the building loomed large at the bottom of the hill. As she walked, she checked her phone once more, and the battery had completely died. She had wanted to call both Hannon and Townsend and apologise for her outburst, but she was hopeful she would catch both of them before they went home. The streets of High Wycombe were at a standstill, with the ongoing police investigation at the petrol station in West Wycombe causing two major road closures. The alternative routes had meant that every way in and out of the town were mayhem and King knew it would be just another stick to beat her with.

The outrage over the murders was genuine, but now that the ripple effects would be reaching people just trying to get home to their families, the uproar would be even louder.

People only truly cared about tragedies if it impacted them directly.

With the clouds darkening above, threatening to treat the town to another summer shower, King put on her game face and stepped through the door of the station. It was time to step up, fall in line, and work as hard as she could to help CID bring this killer in.

She would face the repercussions later. Right now, the only importance was the justice for those poor women.

As she stepped past the front desk, the officer behind stood, and rapped his knuckles on the glass to get her attention. He was young, less than a year out of training, and he waved to her.

'DI King.'

'Yep?' She forced a smile. She just wanted to get back to her office.

'Errr…someone stopped by to see you. He's over there. He's been here a while.'

King turned and her eyebrows raised with surprise at the old gentleman who was sitting on the plastic seats that ran along the wall of the waiting room. He was holding a neighbourhood safety leaflet in a shaking hand, and he only looked up as she approached.

'I'm Detective Inspector King,' she said in her well-rehearsed voice. 'Is everything okay, sir?'

A warm smile spread across the man's face as he eased himself out of the chair.

'Please. Call me Gordon.'

'Oh, Father Baycroft.' The penny dropped and King extended her hand. 'How are you?'

He took it with his own, the uncontrollable tremors noticeable.

'I'm very well. And please, just Gordon.'

King took a swift glance at her watch.

'Have none of my colleagues been to see you?' she said with a slight frustration. She didn't have time for this.

'I did come to collect my box of files but actually, I wanted to see you, too.' His voice was soft. 'I know it's been a difficult time. Lord knows, these deaths have shaken many of us. But I just wanted to say that I saw what was written about you online and I wanted to offer my support to you.'

King shuffled uncomfortably on the spot.

'Thank you, Gordon, but you didn't have to.'

'The internet is a spiteful place. I've witnessed firsthand the dedication of your team to find out who killed those poor women.'

'You knew Lauren Grainger, didn't you?' King said with a smile. 'I did,' Baycroft said with a sigh. 'She was a sweet girl. Troubled mind you, but she came from trouble. By the time she left us, she seemed destined for great things.'

'I'm sure my colleague, DS Townsend asked, but do you remember anything from her time at Home Space that could help? We know her mother was lost in drugs…did anyone come looking for her?'

Baycroft shook his head.

'How about the name Benny Hughes?' King asked quietly. 'Does that name ring any bells?'

The name seemed to register with the priest, and he looked at her with fear.

'It rings a bell. But…things are a little misty for me nowadays.' He held up his quivering hand, putting his Parkinsons on display. Just then, the door opened, and Hannon walked through, zipping up her jacket. She stopped as she saw them both and approached.

'Guv. I'm heading out.'

'DC Hannon, this is Father Baycroft.' King introduced them and Hannon took the elderly gentleman's hand. 'He has come for the files. Is Jack downstairs?'

'Oh, I'm sorry. He popped out a while back to drop them back in person.' She shot a glance at King, who knew it was because of her outburst.

'Oh, has he?' Baycroft seemed surprised. 'I did say for

him to call me and I would collect them. I don't want the police wasting their time on such matters.'

'It's no trouble,' Hannon said. 'He seemed happy to do it. I think he'll be back shortly. Have you tried calling him?'

'My phone's dead,' King replied. 'No worries. Father, why don't you join me in one of the interview rooms and I'll get DS Townsend to stop by when he's back?'

Baycroft nodded his agreement and as he took a step, his leg seized up, and he stumbled slightly. King caught him by the arm, and despite the man's illness, he was sturdier than he looked beneath his large coat.

'Are you okay?' King asked, her training kicking in. Hannon had also stepped forward.

'Oh, I'm fine.' Baycroft smiled. 'Arthritis. Trust me, ladies, at this age, everything starts going wrong.'

Despite his ailments, Baycroft was an affable man, and Hannon smiled at King.

'Shall I help you to the room?' King offered her arm.

'Perhaps we could go for a walk?' Baycroft asked. 'If I sit any longer, it will only seize up.'

'The Rye's a pleasant walk?' Hannon suggested, and then shuddered as King glared at her. 'I'm sorry, that was insensitive of me.'

Baycroft held up his shaking hand.

'No, no. It is. I've enjoyed it many times. I haven't been able to stomach it since Lauren, but...perhaps if I was able to bless those grounds myself, I could find some closure.'

King looked to Hannon, who looked hopefully back. She was leaving promptly that evening, meaning she clearly had plans and King huffed.

'When did Townsend leave?'

'A while back. Why?'

'Traffic is a nightmare in town. He's probably finding that out the hard way. You get yourself home.' King turned to Baycroft and offered her arm once more. 'Shall we, Father?'

This time, he took her arm, and offered her a gentle smile.

'It would be my pleasure. And please. Gordon is fine.'

'Have fun you two,' Hannon said with a grin, before she strode ahead, and disappeared out of the station. King linked arms with the elderly priest, and the two of them followed, but by the time they'd made it through the door, Hannon was already trying to join the sheer carnage that was unfolding around the 'magic roundabout'. As they'd made their way halfway to the Rye, King remembered she hadn't charged her phone, but as the darker clouds gave way, and a small sliver of sunlight sliced through the clouds before them, she told herself she didn't care.

She wasn't a religious person, but left alone with Father Baycroft meant she could maybe talk through her plight.

Her feelings of failure.

Her reliance on alcohol.

She didn't believe in God, but she did know that a man of Baycroft's age and experience had heard it all, and although he was losing himself to the horrible effects of a disease and the cruel hand of father time, he probably had nuggets of wisdom that could at least help her look at things in a different way.

Maybe help her realise she wasn't a complete failure.

Baycroft clung to her arm for support and as the lake of the Rye came into view, he seized a little, his grief beginning to take control.

With careful steps as they navigated the pathway of the underpass, King guided Baycroft towards the Rye, the two of them connected by the vicious murder that took place there a week ago.

Both of them needed closure, and although King's would only come when the murderer was behind bars, it filled her with a sense of worth that she could bring some to the kind old man.

They stepped through the gate and headed up the circular path towards the lake, and inside King's pocket, her phone was unable to take the most important call Townsend would ever make.

CHAPTER FORTY-NINE

There was nothing worse than feeling useless.

That was always something Townsend had strived to stay away from. Ever since his return from his undercover work, he had felt like the Merseyside Police Service had almost held his hand through his rise to becoming a detective sergeant, and he wasn't ignorant of the fact that it was a make good. Three years spent undercover, which put his and his wife's life in danger, all because his handler had got into bed with a criminal meant they wanted to apologise in a way that would bring the least pressure.

Every case he had worked in Liverpool had left a sour taste in his mouth, as the legitimate fear that he'd be recognised meant he was kept from anything truly important. He chased up leads from the comfort of an office desk and when the opportunity came to step up and step out, he jumped at it.

He was inexperienced compared to every other detective sergeant working in High Wycombe.

But he just didn't want to feel useless.

Now, sitting in grid-locked traffic, that was all he felt.

The pressure of the case had clearly got to DI King,

but her outburst at him wasn't completely without merit. Throughout the week, she'd made it clear to him the importance of chasing the evidence that they *had* gathered, as opposed to hunting the evidence that may not exist. In an ideal world, he knew she wouldn't have had him on the team, but the budgetary restraints imposed upon the SCU meant he had found a home and when the case fell onto their laps, they had no choice but to take it.

They had been thrown a ball, and when he thought about the horrendous misogyny and quite frankly, abhorrent behaviour of King's ex-husband, he understood why she couldn't fail.

But they had.

And Townsend felt like the failure sat mostly at his doorstep.

He glanced up into his rear-view mirror, at the cut that dominated his eyebrow, and hated that it was the only thing they had to show for a week of investigation.

No leads.

No clue.

No chance of finding the killer.

Not now that the responsibility had been given to DCI Lowe, who Townsend knew would relegate him to menial tasks in an attempt to get him to quit.

But there was no quit in Jack Townsend.

Not while there was still air in his lungs.

As he sat in his car with his elbow resting on the door and his head pressed to his hand, he blew out his cheeks with boredom. The murder site at the petrol station had shut down two major roads in and out of town, and combined with the inordinate number of temporary lights that littered the town, it had driven the rush hour traffic to a standstill. Beside him on the passenger seat was the tatty box of files.

Father Baycroft had done the honourable thing in

tracking them down for him, but they were of little use. He didn't expect an underfunded charity home to have exact records, but he had been disappointed in how fruitless the long hours he spent trawling through them had been. But he was a sweet old man, one who had dedicated his life to helping others and now, in the final moments of his own, was still trying to help.

It was something Townsend related to and respected.

After what felt like forever, the traffic began to move and Townsend managed to beat the temporary red light and turn off the main road and up the hill that would take him towards Downley. He passed Benny's road, where he had hunted the man through the wooded backstreets and had a fresh scar for his troubles.

As he ventured on, he steered his way through some narrow country roads, which were heavier with traffic due to the road closures, and once through them, he was racing towards Hughenden Park. The large estate, part of the National Trust, was surrounded by gorgeous greenery and a park that was rammed with children all vying for their space on the apparatus.

Sometimes, his new town was picturesque.

He just wished there wasn't the backdrop of a serial killer behind it.

The inbuilt satnav called for him to take the next right, and as he approached a sign that said 'Hazelmere', he then saw the clinical looking building that was Home Space. There was no signage of any kind, especially as secrecy was their main value. It appeared to be an old 'Bed and Breakfast', which had been bought, and converted by the Church of England into a shelter for the vulnerable. Somewhere along its history, it had become the beacon for victims that the police or social services could rely on, and Townsend stopped at the gate and pressed the intercom.

It crackled.

'Hello?'

'Detective Sergeant Jack Townsend of the Thames Valley Police.' Townsend leant out of his window and held up his police badge.

A sharp buzz signalled their acceptance, and the gate slowly slid to the side, allowing him to pull his car into the car park and reverse park into one of the empty spaces. Once he'd retrieved the box from the passenger seat, he headed towards the door, where a young woman watched with intrigue.

'Detective?' she asked as he approached. He put the box down on the bench beside the door. Next to it was an overflowing ashtray.

'Yes. DS Townsend.' He extended his hand, which she took.

'I'm Marla.' She smiled. No older than thirty, her natural beauty shone through the tiredness that clung to her eyes. 'We weren't expecting anyone.'

'No, and I'm sorry for the intrusion. I'm investigating the murder of Lauren Grainger who used to stay here at Home Space and I was just returning the files that you sent.'

'We sent?' Marla frowned. 'Come on in and talk to Carol. She handles all that.'

Townsend agreed, slightly perturbed by her reaction. He gathered the files and stepped in. The interior was as bland and forgettable as the exterior, which he guessed was by design. The entire purpose of the shelter was to fade into the background, but by removing the homely feel to the building, it would only enhance the notion that any stay was temporary. A few beaten leather chairs sat in the reception area, along with a coffee table covered with outdated magazines. Marla guided him across to the office, where she knocked on the door as she walked in. Two other women looked up from their desks. A young Indian woman and an older woman with thick glasses.

'Carol, this is DS Townsend.' She looked back at Townsend with a smile. 'He says he has your files?'

The confusion on the woman's face didn't bode well.

'Files?' She nodded to the box. 'Is that them?'

'Yes, ma'am,' Townsend replied respectfully. He lowered the box onto her desk as she stood. Carol pulled open the box and lifted a few of them out. Her eyebrows furrowed, Marla stood beside her, arms folded.

'These are not my files,' Carol said without looking up. 'We went digital a few months back, but even then, these don't even match our file template. Where did you get these?'

'Oh, erm, Father Baycroft brought them to us,' Townsend said. He looked at the women, reading the tension in the room. After a few moments, Carol lowered the file back into the box and hesitated slightly.

Something was off.

'I'm sorry, but Father Baycroft hasn't represented Home Space for nearly two years.'

Townsend's eyes widened.

'Excuse me?'

'Our chairman made the decision to remove him from the charity when he became…now how can I put this… slightly radical with our guests.'

'He went a bit nuts.' Marla simplified, drawing a glare from Carol. 'What, it's true?'

'Sorry,' Townsend interrupted. 'Radical how?'

'He felt like the people who came through here needed more than just a safe place to live. He began lecturing them, which soon led to him threatening them with the wrath of god.' Carol said sadly. 'I'm not a very religious person, but these people didn't need that put on them.'

Townsend shook his head in disbelief.

'But we found him as a contact for this charity?'

'Look, dear. We work with what we have and considering that an online presence isn't something we strive for, it's unlikely anyone has updated anything in a long time. I certainly haven't.'

Carol looked around the room, and both Marla and the other woman shook their heads. Townsend took a few steps back, his mind racing.

Then his eyes widened.

'Can you do me a favour?' he asked. 'Can you search for three more names on your database?'

'I'm afraid not without a war…'

'A warrant. Yes, I know,' Townsend interrupted and drew a scowl. 'But this is a matter of life and death.'

His sincerity seemed to land and after a few moments, Carol readjusted her glasses and sat back down at her desk. She opened up the necessary tabs and then Townsend gave her the names.

Natasha Stokes.

Michaela Woods.

Irena Roslova.

Seconds later, Townsend was running as fast as he could to his car with his mobile phone pressed to his ear. He left Baycroft's box of files in the office.

Files that had never belonged to Home Space in the first place.

CHAPTER FIFTY

With the darkening clouds gathering at pace above the Rye, King began to wonder if the walk was such a good idea. It was clearly a thought shared by the rest of the public. Beyond a few dedicated dog walkers in the distance, King and Father Baycroft were completely alone. Even the teenagers, starved for entertainment in the final days of their summer holidays, had vacated the park area, which was an impressive construction of raised platforms and rope bridges. The kiosk had once again decided not to open, and the dozens of white plastic chairs and tables were completely empty.

With careful steps, she guided Baycroft up the incline towards the path that looped around the lake, the old man clutching onto her arm to steady himself. Eventually, they came to a stop.

'This is it,' King said, gesturing towards the pavement by the lake. 'Please, take your time.'

The priest looked crestfallen as they approached, and he let go of King's arm and took a few laboured steps forward towards the pavement where this had all began. Almost a week ago, King and Townsend had stood where

Baycroft was, theorising how the attack could have happened.

How Lauren Grainger's life had been ended.

A sharp strike of regret thundered through King's body. She had been needlessly harsh on Townsend, and without thinking, she withdrew her phone to send him a message. She tutted as she realised that it had died, but Baycroft turned to her.

'Are you okay?' he asked.

'Sorry.' She shook her head and pocketed her phone. 'Never mind.'

'It's a glorious place, this Rye.' Baycroft spoke as he cast his eyes across the lake. The increase of wind sent ripples across the water and a group of swans meandered under the overgrowth of trees. 'Such beauty. Ruined by such violence.'

King took a few steps towards the old man who was lost in his grief.

'I hate to interrupt, but you did say you recognised the name Benny Hughes…' King began, instantly feeling rotten for pressing on the old priest.

'Oh yes, of course.' He offered her a smile. 'Always working.'

King took the compliment as intended.

'It's the least I can do for Lauren. For all those women.'

'Perhaps we can head back and I'll tell you all I know.' Baycroft smiled. 'But first, I would very much like to bless the ground where Lauren was found.'

He turned back to the pavement before them, but King reached out and gently rested her hand on his arm. The breeze picked up again, and she felt a light fleck of rain.

'Sorry, Father. But this wasn't where she was found.'

'Oh?' Baycroft looked confused. 'But I thought—'

'No. I'm sorry, but this is where we believe she was murdered. Her body was found in the woods over there.'

Baycroft followed her pointed finger and then looked at her with watery eyes. King grimaced as the weather began to turn, but the pain in the man's eyes convinced her to offer her arm once again to guide him up the pathway that cut through the trees. As the incline increased, so did Baycroft's struggles, and as he clung to King's arm, she could feel the tremors that ran through his body.

The man was old.

Sick.

Possibly dying?

Who was she to deny him this final comfort for a young lady he had lost?

A cyclist whizzed by, keeping to the designated cycle path, and then the two of them made it to the level surface. The pathway disappeared beyond the trees that loomed overhead, and King guided Baycroft towards the two trees that still had remnants of police tape across them.

'Just through here,' King said. 'But we can stop here if you like?'

'No, no.' Baycroft showed some enthusiasm. 'There's still life in me yet.'

King admired the man's courage, and to help his passage through the woods, she let go of his arms and stepped towards the low-hanging branches. With a little force, she pushed them to the side, clearing the path for the old man to amble through. As he did, he zipped up his coat, protecting him from the ever-increasing drizzle. King scolded herself for not bringing her own jacket.

She released the branches and then joined Baycroft once more, helping him step through the mud and over the protruding roots of the giant trees that now shielded them from the public eye. A few more scraps of police tape could be seen, and the muddy verge of the river had been pummelled by numerous police boots, leaving it uneven. Baycroft clung to King for balance and eventually, they ducked under the final low-hanging branch and emerged into the opening where Lauren Grainger's body had been found.

King could still envisage the horror of it.

The pale shade of her skin.

The gaping knife wounds that punctured her body.

Such evil.

She took a breath and patted Baycroft's hand. The man felt weaker than before.

'This is the place.'

'Thank you, my child.' He groaned. Then, he closed his eyes and began to mumble a prayer. His body was shaking, whether through the cold or the illness, and King took a step away from him to allow him his privacy. As he continued, King turned her focus to the lake itself, looking back across the water to the desolate Rye, which was now being pummelled by the summer shower.

The widespread, open green fields separated the lake from the road, which was locked in a traffic jam. Beyond that, rows of houses.

The entire town.

Stricken with fear and grief after a week of murder.

King could feel her fists clenching with anger at her failure to stop it. Behind her, Father Baycroft was putting his faith in a higher power for justice, and although that was not an option, she wondered if perhaps that same faith could be put in her? Maybe if she had spoken to someone neutral, she'd be able to confront her own demons and feelings of self-doubt?

It was worth a shot.

As she turned, she realised Father Baycroft had stopped his religious ritual, and before she knew what was happening, she felt the full force of the thick branch crash into the side of her skull. The impact split the skin of her eyebrow and she crashed down into the ground, and the world around her spun. She groaned with pain, with her brain still ricocheting off her skull and she rolled onto her back. She looked upwards into the downpour that was penetrating the trees above, and with blurred vision, she could make out Father Baycroft standing over her.

He tossed the branch into the overgrowth beside them with considerable force, as the weakness he had portrayed so convincingly had evaporated from him.

He seemed taller. Broader.

His true self.

King tried to push herself up onto her elbows, but the priest drove a boot into her chest and sent her crashing back down into the mud. Blood was trickling down her face, and she rolled back onto her front and began to pull herself through the mud.

There was nowhere to go.

No one around her.

King gritted her teeth and tried to move faster, but the wooziness of her brain, combined with mud meant her progress was minimal. With her vision clouded by the blow to her head, and the ever-increasing downpour, she thought she could see a figure across the lake, but she couldn't muster the energy to call for help.

Behind her, she could just about hear the squelch of Father Baycroft's footsteps approaching.

She couldn't hear him brandishing the knife.

CHAPTER FIFTY-ONE

It was a pointless task, but Townsend slammed his hand down on the centre of his steering wheel, causing his horn to blast loudly into the street. The traffic was backed up, and unlike the scenes on television, he didn't have a blue light he could slap onto the roof of his car and then dangerously climb up onto the pavement and scream at the pedestrians to move out of his way.

Other horns blasted back, and he thumbed the screen of his phone and lifted it to his ear.

This is Detective Inspector Isabella King. Please leave a message and I'll get back to you.

'Guv. Answer your phone! Now!'

Townsend angrily hung up the call, shifted through his contacts, and then lifted the phone again. It rang four times.

'Come on. Pick up. Pick up.'

The call connected.

'Jack?' Hannon answered quietly. 'What's up?'

'Nic. It's Baycroft!'

'What?' He could hear her shuffling out of a room. 'What the hell are you talking about?'

'The killer. It's Baycroft. All the women – Lauren, Nicola, Michaela, Irena – they were all at Home Space.' He could hear her gasp. 'Baycroft was released from his duties at the shelter a few years back.'

'You're sure?'

'Absolutely. I'm calling the guv, but she's not answering.'

'She said her phone was dead and…oh shit.' Hannon startled.

'What?'

'Baycroft was at the station when I was leaving.'

Townsend froze in his seat. It didn't matter, as he peered through the rain that was soaking his windscreen at the standstill before him.

'Why the hell was he there?'

'He came to pick up the files.' Both pennies dropped at the same time. 'He must know now that you're onto him.'

'I'm stuck in traffic. Call the station, have him arrested.'

'He's with King,' Hannon stammered, her words fraught with worry. 'They were going for a walk to the Rye and…'

'Fuck.' Townsend looked at the satnav on his screen. A mile from the office, which meant roughly a mile to the Rye. 'Call the station. Explain everything. Get them to send whoever they fucking can to the Rye and tell them DI King's life is in danger. If he knows we know, then he's going to take whoever he can down with him.'

'Okay. Okay.' Hannon was clearly fighting her panic. 'What are you going to do?'

Townsend was already throwing open his car door and stepping out into the rain.

'I'm going to get there as fast as I can.'

He could hear Hannon calling after him as he lowered the

phone, disconnected the call, and stuffed it into his pocket. The driver in the car behind him called out, cursing him for making the situation worse, but Townsend ignored him.

He began to run.

His journey back from Home Space had brought him to West Wycombe Road, which snaked all the way from the petrol station where Irena had been murdered, past the turnoff to Sands and all the way down to the town centre. Thankfully, due to the weather, the pavement was empty, and with his heart thumping in his chest and his lungs screaming for air, Townsend raced through the rain. He shot past the petrol station, and a few pubs, and eventually, the Eden Centre loomed on the horizon.

As he approached the town centre, and the myriad of roundabouts and one-way systems, he snaked through the stationary vehicles on the Oxford Road roundabout, drawing a few blasts of the horn from the drivers who disapproved of his recklessness.

He didn't care.

Townsend burst down one of the side streets opposite the Eden Centre, pushing through a group of teenagers who hurled insults in his direction that failed to even register with him.

All he could think about was DI King.

And the killer in her company.

He passed the front doors of the Eden Centre.

He raced past Paradise.

Worried pedestrians stopped and stared as he darted under the underpass, a brief moment of respite from the rain before he emerged back out into the downpour and headed towards the magic roundabout. There was no fear this time, especially as the cars were once again grid locked and without a second thought, he dashed between them, weaving through the crawling traffic and onto the main roundabout, once again drawing a cacophony of horn blasts.

The Rye was in sight.

Townsend pushed through the pain, his lungs screaming for a rest, and as he rounded the final car, he joined the path that led into the Rye itself. The weather had rendered the entire place desolate, and he charged through the tree-top adventure park towards the kiosk that sat on the corner of the lake.

Nothing.

Nobody.

He stopped to catch his breath and turned frantically, casting his gaze across the open fields, but the weather was dulling any view.

He looked across the lake.

Just in time to see DI King try to raise herself from the ground, and for the now domineering Baycroft to drive her back into the mud with the bottom of his boot.

Townsend took off again, thundering up the incline and under the trees, propelled forward by everything that had happened that week.

The deaths of four innocent women.

The crippling imposter syndrome.

The bridges being built with his daughter.

The disparaging comments from DCI Lowe.

The feeling of failure.

And the team that had welcomed him in, and a boss who had stood by his side throughout all of it.

He wasn't ready to give all that up.

Not yet anyway.

Townsend darted past the police tape covered trees, his feet almost slipping in the mud. He steadied himself and then pushed through the final few bushes to the clear verge by the lake, just in time to see Baycroft yank King's head back by her hair, exposing her throat as he drove the knife downwards.

Townsend bounded forward a few more steps and then launched himself through the air, his shoulder crashing into Baycroft who relinquished his grip and tumbled onto the ground. Both men splattered into the mud, as King gasped a sigh of relief.

She turned over onto her side, just in time to see Baycroft stumble to his feet and wildly slash the knife at Townsend, who ducked, drove his shoulder into Baycroft's stomach and then lifted him up by the legs. The old man yelped with fear, and Townsend spiked him down onto the mud, driving the wind from the man's body.

With his jacket and half his face covered in mud, Townsend violently wrenched Baycroft onto his front, pulled his arms backwards, and slapped the cuffs around his wrists.

'Get off me,' Baycroft spat angrily, as he wriggled in the mud. Townsend rocked back onto his knees, trying his hardest to catch his breath. The heavy rainfall now didn't seem so bad, and he let it crash against his mud-slathered face and he turned to DI King who was woozily getting to her feet.

'You okay, guv?' he asked.

King looked at her suit, flicking the mud from her hands with disgust before she looked at him, the blood smeared across her face.

'I am.' She smiled. 'Thank you, Jack.'

'Don't mention it.' He then turned to Baycroft, who had given up his struggle and was now lying on the mud, contemplating his future.

'He's all yours,' King said with a hint of pride in her voice. She offered Townsend a hand up, and once he was standing, his eyes drifted across the lake, where a group of uniformed police officers were charging as fast as they could in their direction.

Townsend smiled.

'Gordon Baycroft, I'm arresting you for the murders of Lauren Grainger, Natasha Stokes, Michaela Woods, and Irena Roslova. You do not have to say anything. But it may harm your defence if you do not mention when questioned something which you later rely on in court. Anything you do say may be given in evidence.' Townsend breathed out a large sigh. 'You got that?'

Baycroft muttered something, but Townsend couldn't hear. Behind him, DI King was already straight back to work, throwing orders out to the uniformed officers who had just arrived and ignoring their concerns for her head wound.

She was relentless.

Townsend glanced down at Baycroft, who was still lying in the mud, and then took a few steps towards the lake. He gazed out over the water, and beyond, his eyes focusing on nothing for too long, as he felt himself absorb the town.

All the fear.

All the horror.

All the heartache for the families who had lost their beloved and not knowing why.

The injustice of the deaths of Lauren Grainger, Nicola Stokes, Michaela Woods, and Irena Roslova.

Townsend closed his eyes, breathed in the damp moisture of the air, and let out another breath.

It was over. It was all over.

CHAPTER FIFTY-TWO

The entire station felt like it came to a standstill as they led Baycroft through the side entrance, his hands pinned to the base of his spine and all three of them caked in mud. DSI Hall appeared in the corridor, his eyes locking onto the unrepented stare of Baycroft as Townsend guided him down to one of the interview rooms. They sat him down in the chair and then left him to stew in his future as they waited for the duty solicitor to arrive.

It was a pointless endeavour.

After a brief stop in their respective bathrooms, both Townsend and King emerged, their clothes still stained with the mud that they'd been able to scrub from their hands and faces. The bandage that was taped to King's forehead was stained with dots of blood. A new duty solicitor arrived, and once they explained the situation, he dryly remarked that it would be pretty one way. They afforded him a brief moment with Baycroft beforehand, but again, it was just to tick the boxes.

They had him.

Before they were about to enter, DCI Lowe suggested

he handle the interview with Baycroft with King, due to Townsend's inexperience.

DSI Hall shut him down.

Without Townsend, DI King would be dead and Baycroft would be long gone.

The endorsement felt good, and Townsend ignored the sinister glare from Lowe and then followed King into the interview room and closed the door behind them.

Baycroft was a man transformed.

Gone was the charming, fragile elder man of God they'd known. In his place sat a man comfortable in his own situation, his eyes now sparkling with intent as the two detectives took their seat opposite him. With his coat removed, Baycroft looked sturdily built.

More than capable.

As King ran through the formalities of the interview for the recording, Townsend studied Baycroft, who bore a hole through King with his eyes.

The tremors were gone.

Were they even there in the first place?

As King wrapped up the introduction, she sat back and regarded the elderly gentleman before her. His clothes were still caked with mud and his thinning, grey hair flopped across his wet forehead.

The solicitor leant forward.

'Before we begin, my client would like the opportunity to freshen up.'

'Denied,' King said curtly, keeping her eyes on Baycroft who met her stare with glee. 'Gordon Baycroft. Did you kill Lauren Grainger, Nata...'

'Yes.'

The answer threw King off her stride, but she continued. 'Natasha—'

'Natasha Stokes. Yes.' Baycroft nodded confidently.

'And Michaela Woods and Irena Roslova. I killed all four of them.'

King clenched her fists and took a breath. The man showed no remorse for the horror of his actions.

'Well, that's all we need,' King said with a nod. Townsend leant forward, his hands clasped and resting on the table.

'Why?' he asked. 'Why did you kill these innocent women?'

'Innocent?' Baycroft scoffed. 'Innocence is something we impose on people or situations. In what world were these women innocent?'

'What were their crimes, then?' Townsend turned his hands over. 'Because as far as we can see, you murdered these women in cold blood.'

'I did what was necessary.' Baycroft held his chin up with pride. 'Do you know what it's like to have a duty, Jack? Not the silly little jobs that this place gives you, or the sense of self-importance you draw from that badge around your neck. I'm talking a *true* sense of duty.'

'Like a calling?' King interrupted with a raised eyebrow.

'Exactly.' Baycroft sat back in his chair. 'I turned sixty-eight years old three weeks ago. That means for just under half a century, I've given my life to serve our lord. Growing up, I saw the hardships of life creep through both my parents. Infidelity. Drinking. The people they became were not the people I wanted to become, and when my first foray into the world of love and companionship ended the same way, I found God at my lowest ebb. That was when I decided to hold him close to me. To spread his good word and to bring as much peace to a rotten world, filled with repugnant people.'

'That's very admirable,' Townsend said dryly. 'I can't

remember the part of the bible where he says to murder innocent women?'

Baycroft smiled through gritted teeth.

'There you go again. Using that word. I'm not going to feed you the usual nonsense of how 'God works in mysterious ways'. There is no mystery. Our lord and saviour created us to be better than the generation before and somewhere along the way, that idea got lost. People began to seek nothing but their own reward, and when they strayed from the path, they sought forgiveness. Can you believe that? They willingly ignored the good lord's word, but then expected a second chance. A third chance. And so on.'

'Right.' Townsend looked bored. 'Again, I don't see what chance you gave these innocent women?'

Baycroft lunged, but the cuffs that strapped his arms behind the chair locked him in place. His eyes were wild and spit drooled from the side of his mouth.

Townsend didn't flinch.

'They were *not* innocent.' Baycroft realised his actions and tried to redirect. 'They all came through Home Space. All four of them. Different times. Different decades. Different reasons. But all of them, at some point in their lives, needed help, and they found it through our lord and saviour. He was there for them. Their situations may not have been their faults, but it was certainly their responsibility to improve them. We helped them. Guided them. Nurtured them. Showed them the path to take to become better people. To become good, honest women who would be better than what they left behind.'

'And they failed?' King said with an eye roll. 'Is that it? They didn't live up to your expectation?'

Baycroft slowly turned his head to King with a look of pure disgust.

'Do you know what it's like knowing that you're going to die?'

'I have some idea.' King spat back. Baycroft grinned.

'Two weeks before my birthday, I was diagnosed with stage four bowel cancer. The doctor effectively started a stop-watch that guaranteed I wouldn't live to see seventy. It's funny, detective, that when someone puts a full stop at the end of your story, you start to consider the path you took through life. Did I do right? Did I help? And when I looked back, I wondered what had happened to all the people who reached out to me for help. All the women and children who came to me in their hour of need, and whom I wrapped God's love around and helped them on their path.' Baycroft's eyes began to water. 'It broke my heart to see how they didn't listen. To see how they threw away their second chances.'

'Don't cry for them,' King said angrily. 'You butchered them.'

'No, I released them.' Baycroft switched again, his teeth bared. 'These women and this so-called innocence that you speak of. They turned their back on it. On me. On God. Lauren. She saw the devastating effects of drugs and the seedy world her mother came from. And what did she do? She became a stripper. Natasha Stokes, divorced due to her own incapability to stay loyal to her husband. Michaela Woods, drug addict. Irena Roslova. Whore. All these women were set on a path of righteousness, and they *chose* to veer from it.'

'So you put them in their place?' Townsend asked, clearly sickened.

'I just did God's work. With my time on this plane dwindling, I took the necessary steps to ensure they made no further mistakes.'

'So why come to me?' Townsend shrugged. 'When I reached out, you could have vanished.'

'You think I didn't have a plan?' Baycroft seemed insulted. 'These four women were not the only targets. There would have been more. Countless others. Sin floods through this town like a tidal wave, yet you both sit here and judge me when I do something about it. What do you do? Do you stop it? I came to you when you called because I knew if I played along as the dutiful old priest, who was shaken by the loss of a young lady, you would look the other way. You even told me the name of a suspect. Benny wasn't it?'

King shuffled uncomfortably on her chair. Baycroft chuckled and continued.

'Wasn't hard to go along with that.'

'And the Parkinsons?' Townsend nodded at Baycroft's hands. 'That was bullshit, too?'

Baycroft answered with a shrug. Easier to hide in plain sight than run a mile.

'But why attack me?' King leant forward. 'Trust me, I'm taking it personally. But I hadn't even met you before today.'

'True. But like I said, the internet can be a cruel place, and when young Jack here kindly went to return my files, I knew it wouldn't take long for the pieces to fall into place. My time was up.'

'So you thought you'd take me down with you, is that it?'

Baycroft shook his head and tutted.

'Oh, dear Detective Inspector. You couldn't be brought down any lower than you have been. Exposed as a drunk. I wanted to kill you, because the women I've killed deserved someone better than you to look out for them. Someone who didn't fail them, and herself, by falling to her own demons. You should be ashamed.'

As ironic as it was for a serial killer to judge her, the words hit King like a fist to the jaw. She took a few moments to compose herself and then straightened in her chair.

'Gordon, you will be charged with all four murders and you *will* spend the rest of your life in prison.'

King stood and headed to the door, terminating the interview as she did. Townsend stood, offering Baycroft one final glance as the former priest smiled at him.

'Good work, Jack.' He smirked. 'The few months I'll spend in prison will be fine, knowing I've done God's work. He will wait for me at the other end of the journey.'

Townsend tried to resist but turned back to Baycroft. The violent, twisted man was locked to his chair. His reign of terror was over, but he still seemed to think he'd won.

'I told you when I met you, Father, that I wasn't a religious man. But your god has lied to you.'

'Oh, really?'

'I went to church when I was a kid. I didn't care much for it, but I always remember *"Whoever sheds the blood of man, by man shall his blood be shed, for God made man in his own image."* Genesis 9:6.' Townsend stared at Baycroft, who seemed lost in his own hypocrisy. 'You won't be rewarded for what you've done. Instead, you will rot until you expire in a prison cell. No God will save you now.'

Townsend turned and headed to the door, leaving Baycroft to sit in his chair and ruminate on the dark, hopeless existence that awaited him.

He'd never know freedom again.

This side of death or the other.

CHAPTER FIFTY-THREE

When the phone call came in, Hannon had feared the worst.

After Townsend had abruptly ended their call earlier that evening, Hannon had frantically tried to get in contact with the station, to warn them of the impending danger that her boss was in.

It had taken too long.

Since then, it had been radio silence, and she'd paced her apartment so much that she was certain she'd need to replace the carpet.

Then the call came in.

Townsend.

'We've got him.' He had said. 'It's over, Nic.'

Hannon felt her heart stutter. It had been the first serious case she'd worked, and the relief and pride of them finally catching the murderer flooded her with emotion. She kept it together long enough to respond.

'King?'

'She's good.' Townsend assured her. 'A little beaten up, but she's tough.'

'Thank god.' Hannon breathed a sigh of relief.

'Great work, Nic,' Townsend said. 'See you tomorrow.'

As she disconnected the call, Shilpa stepped into the room, a towel wrapped around her body and a smaller one wrapped around her hair. She watched the phone drop from Hannon's hands and then her shoulders begin to shake.

'Nic?' Shilpa stepped to her and draped an arm around her shoulder. 'Babe, are you okay?'

Hannon turned to her girlfriend, her eyes red, and her cheeks shiny with tears.

'We caught him,' she said, almost with disbelief. 'We caught him.'

'That's good, right?' Shilpa held her close. 'It means it's over.'

For a few moments, the two of them just stood there, holding each other as the magnitude of the evening fell down around them. For the past week, all Hannon had been subjected to was a rising body count of young women, and a seemingly endless stream of dead ends.

All of it was over.

The brutal slaying of the women.

The constant feeling of failure.

She could be herself again.

Only now, she would be a different version of herself. Now, she would be a Nicola Hannon who belonged as a Detective Constable, who had been a key part in helping to stop a brutal serial killer.

A Nicola Hannon who didn't want to be afraid anymore.

Who *wouldn't* be afraid anymore.

Gently, she eased back from Shilpa and rested her hands on her partner's shoulders and gently kissed her.

'Get dressed.' She suggested. 'We're going for a drive.'

Shilpa stepped back, confused, and seemingly impressed at the clarity in Hannon's voice.

'Babe?'

'We're going to go to my parents'...' Hannon reached out and held Shilpa's hand. 'And I'm going to tell them with so much pride how I'm in love with the most beautiful woman in the world.'

She lifted Shilpa's hand to her mouth and kissed the back of it. Shilpa squeezed it.

'Are you sure? Because the other day, I was just...'

Hannon stepped forward and kissed Shilpa once again.

'I've never been more sure of anything in my life.'

The two women smiled at each other, and Shilpa threw her arms around Hannon once more, holding her as tightly as possible. Then Hannon left her to get changed and sent a text message to her parents to inform them of their impending visit. She had no idea why she'd hidden her sexuality from her parents or from her colleagues at work.

Maybe it was shame?

Maybe it was doubt?

All she knew now was it didn't matter. She wasn't afraid anymore, and as the relief of finally bringing Gordon Baycroft to justice washed through her body, Hannon made a silent promise to herself that she wouldn't be afraid again.

As the door slammed behind her, King walked on autopilot to the fridge in her kitchen. Her clothes were thick with mud, and the front of her skull throbbed like a beating heart. Her brain still felt like it was rattling and now that Gordon Baycroft was locked behind bars, her headache had pushed itself to the front of the queue.

She'd already thrown back a few paracetamol in the car, but now she wanted something else.

Without thinking, she pulled the bottle of wine that had been left in the wake of Irena's death, and she unscrewed the cap.

'What a disgrace.'

'These poor girls deserve better.'

'DI Drunk on the case.'

The messages that DSI Hall had shown her flashed through her mind as she reached for a wine glass, one of the few that weren't stained and left lying in the sink for another day.

King grimaced, and she plonked the glass down on the kitchen counter and then lifted the bottle.

'You couldn't be brought down any lower than you have been. Exposed as a drunk. I wanted to kill you, because the women I've killed deserved someone better than you to look out for them. Someone who didn't fail them, and herself, by falling to her own demons. You should be ashamed.'

The callous words of Gordon Baycroft rung in her ears, and she felt a shiver race down her spine. Despite being a violent and sadistic murderer, the man had held a mirror up to her.

He had spoken the truth.

A truth that cut through her heart and let all the shame bleed out into the rest of her hollow body.

'I need you to take care of yourself, Izzy. Not as your superior, but as a friend. You're not the first detective to hit the bottle. You won't be the last. But you're no good to me, to your team, or to those poor girls and their families if you're not at one hundred percent.'

DSI Hall's words drowned out the voice of the killer, just like the wine would drown out the depression that she knew existed within her. The dread she felt for the day to come, and the anger she clung to for the days gone by.

But there was always a choice.

A choice to be at one hundred percent.

A choice to be the best she could, not just for the

victims of this cruel world, but for the people who relied on her to seek justice when it happened. The families who looked to her for results. Her team who, despite their own incredible tenacity, relied on her for guidance.

King needed to make a choice.

She lifted the bottle and turned from the glass, tipping its contents into the sink. As the thick, scarlet liquid pumped from the glass and splattered the chrome, King took a deep long breath. She had proven to everyone that she could do it.

To DSI Hall.

To her abhorrent ex-husband.

To her team.

And most importantly, to herself.

She was worth more than what she was becoming, and as the final drop hit the sink and she washed it down with the tap, King made a promise to herself then and there, that she wouldn't let the darkness win.

Not anymore.

From now on, the world was going to get the best version of Detective Inspector Isabella King.

It would be a long road, but with a clarity she hadn't felt in the months of her drunken haze, she was more than ready for it.

'Daddy!'

Eve rushed from the front door of the house as Townsend brought the car to a stop on the drive, despite the downpour. Without thinking, he threw open the door and stepped out. She ran a few more steps and then leapt up into his arms and he held her as close to him as he possibly could. The feeling was indescribable, but all he knew was that in that moment, with her petite frame wrapped around his torso, he could have stayed in that moment forever.

'Hey, Pickle,' he said quietly. 'Come on, let's get out of this rain.'

Townsend carried her back up the pathway to the front door, where Mandy was waiting with a huge smile on her face.

'You think I'm hugging you when you're that filthy, you've got another think coming.'

They both chuckled, and as he leant in for a kiss from his wife, Eve threw an arm around her mother's neck and forced her into the embrace.

'Something smells good?' Townsend said, as he lowered Eve to the floor, who vanished in a blur of back into the house.

'I got us a Chinese to celebrate...' Mandy smiled before raising her thumb.

'You got the job? Ah…amazing!' Townsend threw his arms around here again, and she squealed playfully, trying to evade his muddy clothes. 'I'm so proud of you.'

'Thank you. Now…are you going to tell me why you look like you've been dragged across a field?'

Townsend looked down at his clothes, which were soaked through and thick with mud and he didn't care.

None of that mattered.

He looked up at Mandy with relief across his face.

'I caught him, Mandy.' He felt his voice crack slightly, but he kept his composure. 'I caught him.'

Mandy's smile evaporated, and she threw her arms around her husband, burying her face into his cold, wet neck. As she hugged him, he could feel the warmth of her body against his.

His rock.

His everything.

'I'm so proud of you, Jack Townsend.' She eventually

said and then reached up and held his face in her hands. 'I always knew you were cut out for this.'

'Are you guys going to keep snogging?' Eve called from the doorway of the kitchen. 'Because if you are, can you at least give me a baby sister?'

The two parents laughed at the bluntness of their child, and Townsend stripped off his muddy clothes and dumped them in the washing machine, before rushing upstairs to throw on a new T-shirt and some joggers. He could hear his wife explaining to Eve what had happened, and when he emerged at the bottom of the stairs, Eve smiled up at him.

'Did you catch the bad man, Daddy?'

He dropped to a knee and hugged her.

'I did, pickle. I did.'

'Good. I don't like bad men.'

'Me neither. Let's go eat.'

The Townsend family finally sat down at their dining table together and eagerly dished out the delicious takeaway. For five minutes, nobody spoke, as they devoured the spring rolls and chow mein before them, with Eve particularly fond of the packet of prawn crackers that had accompanied the meal. Eventually, Mandy sighed with a smile.

'I'm just so glad it's over.'

'Well…there is just one more thing I have to do tomorrow.'

Mandy looked up from her plate, her eyebrow raised.

'Oh?'

Townsend looked sheepishly to his wife.

'I just need your permission. Just this one time.'

Mandy glared at him across the table. It had been a long time since he'd asked her for it and it wasn't a path she wanted either of them to walk down ever again. Townsend looked at her with hope, and she sighed.

'Just once?'

'Promise.'

'Fine.' She smiled. 'Just make sure whoever it is deserves it.'

Townsend smiled, looked at both his girls, and doubted there was another man alive who was as lucky as he was.

CHAPTER FIFTY-FOUR

The news of Baycroft's arrest had flooded every corner of the news cycle over the remainder of the weekend. It even made the national news, with all eyes focused on the sterling work of the Thames Valley Police for bringing the vicious murderer to justice. Twitter was alive with activity as well, with many nameless accounts supporting the killer, hiding behind their anonymity to spew their vile hatred.

By Monday morning, the High Wycombe Police Station felt like a different place entirely, with the tension gone, and the feeling of duty rippling through the building like its own pulse. It was a little after seven thirty, and sure enough, DCI Marcus Lowe was in the on-site gym, wearing his needlessly expensive gym wear and surrounded once again by his gaggle of followers. It was the usual crowd of young police officers who all saw Lowe as not only a pillar of manhood but also as someone they wanted to aspire to be.

Good looking.

Highly respected detective.

Flash car.

All the things young men aspired to be, and Lowe lapped up the adulation like a thirsty dog kept away from his bowl. He sat on the apron of the run-down boxing ring that was tucked into the corner of the gym itself, his gloves dangling around his neck, and all of them were hanging on his every word.

'I mean, come on. Big boss hands the case over to CID and what happens? Baycroft is behind bars within days.'

Lowe shrugged his impressive shoulders, and a few of the officers nodded eagerly.

'But it said on Bucks Press that it was DS Townsend who made the arrest?' One of the men queried and immediately regretted it. All eyes fell on him, and Lowe chuckled.

'Maybe don't believe everything you read in the papers, son?'

The group started laughing, and the outspoken officer blushed.

The door to the gym flew open, and everyone turned.

DS Jack Townsend walked in.

'Speak of the devil,' Lowe said, and then scrambled to his feet, leaning his back against the ropes. 'Let's give a round of applause to the man of the hour.'

Lowe mockingly clapped his hands together, and his group all chuckled and did likewise. Townsend ignored it completely and walked calmly to one of the weight benches that sat a few feet from the group and placed the gym bag that he had carried on his shoulder down onto the ground. Unlike Lowe, Townsend didn't see the need for expensive gym wear, and as he peeled off his hoody, he revealed a white vest top that clung to his muscular frame. Without a word, he neatly folded it and placed it on the bench, and then took a seat.

Lowe looked at the young officers and frowned.

'What's the matter, Jack? Too much of a big shot to even say hello anymore?'

Lowe's voice carried with it an underlying threat, but still, Townsend didn't even acknowledge him. He unzipped his bag and pulled out a roll of tape, and casually began to wrap it expertly around his wrist, looping it over his thumb and then continued the process for a few more instances. A nervousness now filtered from the group, and Lowe poked his tongue against the inside of his cheek.

'Okay, I see.' The façade dropped. 'As your commanding officer, Jack Townsend, I order you to stand up and leave this gym.'

'I'm not on duty for another half hour,' Townsend replied quietly, not looking up. He ripped the tape and then began to tape the other hand. 'Neither are you.'

All eyes fell on Lowe, who could see his authority being challenged. He grunted, dismissing Townsend's remarks with his hand, and then turned to continue his conversation with the rest of the group.

'Listen, you boys ever want to make it to CID where we play, don't follow that man's example.' Lowe raised his voice to ensure Townsend heard. 'He's just a beat officer playing detective.'

Again, the words had little effect, and Townsend finished the taping and then stood. He rolled his shoulders a few times and stretched out his back, before he dipped his hand back into his bag and pulled out his boxing gloves.

Silence filled the gym.

Even the other staff members who were lost in their own workouts slowed to a stop, and everyone watched as Townsend eased his hands into his gloves for the first time in years. The echoes of his time undercover were what Mandy had worried about, having witnessed him getting beaten to a pulp before her very eyes. That was over eighteen months ago, but she'd been adamant that she didn't want him to willingly step into a violent confrontation again.

It meant he had to stop boxing.

Something he had done for nearly his entire life.

His love for his wife far outweighed his love for the ring, but on the rarest of occasion, he knew that she would grant him permission. Especially if he had a good enough reason.

DCI Marcus Lowe.

Townsend fastened the gloves tightly and then beat them together, and then turned and looked up at Lowe, who looked as if reality had just slapped him in the face. There had been whispers throughout Townsend's first week, about how Lowe had been a bit heavy-handed with some of the young officers. The man was a bully, plain and simple, and as Townsend walked towards the ring, he let Lowe know with one simple look that he hadn't forgotten any of it.

The snide comments.

The idle threats.

The disgusting treatment of DI King.

Townsend stopped a few feet away from Lowe and looked up at him.

'You said anytime, right?' Townsend asked.

Lowe looked around the gym, realising all eyes were on him and were on tenterhooks to see how he would rise to the challenge to his ego. Overcompensating, he jogged a little on the spot and threw a couple of punches.

'It's your funeral, pal.'

The threat didn't land, and Townsend just nodded and then rolled into the ring and began pacing before he found his way to the far corner. Lowe hesitated for a moment, but then seemed to find a second wave of misplaced confidence and stepped in. He stuffed his hands into his gloves, and as he beat them together, Townsend wisely pushed a gumshield into his mouth.

Lowe laughed.

'You'll need that, son.'

Townsend shrugged, and with an excited energy throbbing around the ring, the two men approached each other. Lowe immediately came out swinging, throwing a few nifty jab combinations at Townsend, who weaved expertly out of the way. Lowe swung again, not finding his target, and after Townsend weaved underneath him and out to the other side, he growled with frustration.

'Stop moving and try to hit me you pussy!'

Townsend obliged him.

He rocked Lowe with a left, right combo before drilling him with an uppercut to the ribs. It sent the Detective Chief Inspector stumbling back a little, and Townsend followed up with a right hook that burst through Lowe's feeble block and caught him square on the jaw. Clearly dazed, Lowe stumbled backwards towards the corner, and Townsend relentlessly threw some hard punches to the man's body before an uppercut rocked Lowe's world. He stumbled backwards into the corner, hit the pads, and as he rebounded, Townsend swung a haymaker that shut the man's lights out.

Lowe dropped to the mat.

Out cold.

A collective gasp of shock echoed from the viewers.

Townsend turned and headed back to the ropes, dropped down, and rolled underneath them. Lowe's entourage parted like the Red Sea, and Townsend removed his gum shield.

'Help him.'

Two of the officers did as they were told, quickly

scrambling into the ring to the motionless body of their idol, as the rest watched Townsend stride back to his bag. He removed his gloves, stuffed them back into his bag and then slipped his hoody over his head. Then, as if nothing had happened, he picked up his bag and headed back out of the gym, ready for his day to begin.

CHAPTER FIFTY-FIVE

DI King stood in her makeshift office and peered out through the door at her team. She had been locked in there for over two hours, the phone practically strapped to her ear, but she couldn't help but smile. DC Nicola Hannon was, as always, tapping ferociously on her keyboard, her eyes scanning from screen to screen and only interrupted by the odd reach for a biscuit. Beside her, DS Michelle Swaby was her usual, bubbly self, making her way through the mountain of necessary paperwork that came with the job with nothing but a smile on her face. Now and then, she would break out into a small song, usually a random call back to an advert from yesteryear of a one hit wonder that the world had forgotten about.

On the other side of the compact SCU office, DS Jack Townsend was hunched over his desk, going through their evidence against Gordon Baycroft with the finest of tooth combs.

The man had saved her life.

He'd also proven himself to be a hell of an asset.

It had been the first morning in months that she'd woken without the stench of alcohol clinging to her clothes and the self-loathing that usually accompanied it. So refreshing was the feeling that DI King had pushed herself to go for an early morning run.

She felt like a woman reborn.

And, thanks to the praise that had been showered on her team since Baycroft's arrest, she felt like she finally belonged.

On the other end of the phone, DSI Hall was wrapping up their conversation.

'Now, obviously, it won't be as big as CID's office. But hey, at least you'll be out of the basement, right?' He chuckled.

'Absolutely, Sir. Thank you.'

'You've earnt it, Izzy,' he said warmly. 'You did them girls proud.'

The two of them said their goodbyes and King hung up the phone and stretched the stiffness from her back. Now and then, a small wince of pain shot through her skull, but for the most part, the wound was beginning to heal. Unlike Townsend's, hers wouldn't leave a scar.

Not a physical one, anyway.

She collected her phone, and the emergency powerpack that she now kept on her at all times, and her vape stick, and then stepped out into the main office.

Hannon looked up from her screen.

'Popular today, guv?'

'Well, lots of people have a lot of things to say.' She turned to Townsend. 'Speaking of which, there is a lot of gossip that DCI Lowe had a little boxing match this morning that didn't go too well.'

Townsend spun in his chair, faking his innocence.

'That's a shame.' He smiled. 'I was always told that if you couldn't box, you shouldn't step in the ring.'

King mouthed 'thank you' at Townsend, who gave a gentle salute.

'So, we need to start packing up. The Specialist Crimes Unit is being given an office on the second floor. It's hardly the ritz, but it's big enough for the four of us.'

'Four?' Hannon looked at Swaby, and a smile spread across her face. King joined in.

'That's right. Michelle is joining the team permanently as of today.'

'That's right,' Swaby added. 'So you all get to enjoy my singing *every* day.'

'Oh, fucking great,' Townsend said dryly. All of them chuckled, all thrilled at the addition to the team. King looked up at the board that still dominated the wall, her eyes falling on the four women whose lives had been lost in the past week. 'You okay, guv?'

'I am. Hall just confirmed to me that the FLOs have been in contact with the families over the weekend to let them know what's happened. I've said that if they need anything from us or have any questions, they can call us at anytime.' She tapped the board. 'Lauren Grainger. Natasha Stokes. Michaela Woods. Irena Roslova. All of you, remember these names. Remember what happened to them and remember what we went through to get the answers. All of us had to deal with the pain. Physical or mental.' She looked to Hannon, who seemed uncomfortable. 'But we dealt with it together. Never lose sight of that.'

The whole team exchanged glances, making a silent promise to rely on each other. To be there for each other.

To be a team.

King wiggled her vape stick, indicating she was popping out, but just as she approached the door, Hannon stood up, and let out a deep breath.

'I have something to say.'

All eyes fell on her, and King stepped back in, her hands on her hips.

'Go on.'

'Okay…' Hannon fidgeted uncomfortably. 'I'm…gay.'

The gravity of the announcement wasn't lost on any of the other three. Swaby looked to the other two and then stood up and put her hand on Hannon's shoulder.

'Nic. We know,' she said softly. 'But that took a lot of courage.'

Hannon looked perplexed.

'Wait…you all knew?'

'We are detectives,' King said dryly. 'Pretty good ones, too.'

Hannon shot glances at all three of them.

'Also, nobody cares,' Townsend said with a grin. 'Stop being so selfish.'

Hannon chucked a pen at him, drawing a laugh from King and Swaby. She was clearly taking it in her stride, but even the smile on her face told them all that a weight had been lifted. She lowered herself back onto her chair, adjusted the back support, and couldn't stifle her smile even if she tried. She looked back at King, who offered her a maternal nod.

'Proud of you.'

Hannon's cheeks shone red and King patted Townsend on the shoulder as she turned and left the office for a small break. Swaby and Townsend returned to their paperwork, and Hannon looked at them both.

'I love you guys.'

Townsend didn't turn as he responded.

'Fuck off.' They all laughed. 'Also, we're out of biscuits.'

Panicked, Hannon stood, slipped on her coat, and made her way to the door to correct that situation. As she did, she offered them a coffee, and as she left to run the errands, Townsend sat at his desk and smiled.

His first week as a detective had been like nothing he

could have ever imagined. He'd hunted down a deranged killer, pushed back against those who had doubted his abilities, built bridges with his daughter, and most importantly, finally realised where he truly was.

Behind him, Swaby broke out into a hum of an old song he couldn't recall.

His smile grew bigger.

Inside the Specialist Crimes Unit, he felt like he was home.

GET EXCLUSIVE ROBERT ENRIGHT MATERIAL

Hey there,

I really hope you enjoyed the book and I'd love for you to join my reader group. I send out regular updates, competitions and special offers as well as some cool free stuff. Sound good?

Well, if you do sign up to the reader group I'll send you FREE copies of THE RIGHT REASON and RAINFALL, two thrilling Sam Pope prequel novellas from my best-selling Sam Pope series. (RRP: £1.99/$2.99 each)

You can get your FREE books by signing up at www.robertenright.co.uk

BOOKS BY ROBERT ENRIGHT

For more information about the DS Jack Townsend series and other books by Robert Enright, please visit:

www.robertenright.co.uk

ABOUT THE AUTHOR

Robert lives in Buckinghamshire with his family, writing books and dreaming of getting a dog.

For more information:
www.robertenright.co.uk
robert@robertenright.co.uk

You can also connect with Robert on Social Media:

facebook.com/robenrightauthor
instagram.com/the_independent_author

Cover by The Cover Collection

Edited by Emma Mitchell

Proof Read by Martin Buck

Printed in Great Britain
by Amazon